The Christmas Veto

Also by Keira Andrews

The Christmas Veto

by Keira Andrews

The Christmas Veto
Written and published by Keira Andrews
Cover by Dar Albert
Formatting by BB eBooks

Copyright © 2023 by Keira Andrews
Print Edition

ISBN: 978-1-988260-94-5

This is a work of fiction. Names, characters, businesses, places, events and incidents are either the products of the author's imagination or used in a fictitious manner. No persons, living or dead, were harmed by the writing of this book. Any resemblance to any actual persons, living or dead, or actual events is purely coincidental.

Acknowledgments

Huge thanks to Anita, Leslie, and Leta for their help in bringing Connor and Reid's romance to life.

Chapter One
Reid

Thanksgiving

FINDING A FAKE boyfriend on short notice was proving a challenge.

I glumly gazed around the exclusive upstairs lounge at the Utopia Grand as guests trickled in for my grandmother's annual charity event. Fresh fir boughs lined the cream wainscoting along with wreaths each tastefully decorated with a single red bow. The lights of New York City glowed through floor-to-ceiling windows.

Beside me from our position in the corner practically hiding behind the enormous gold-decorated Christmas tree, Addison nodded to Richard Wolverhampton. Excuse me—Richard Wolverhampton the Third. He was scowling at his phone from one of the cream settees and combing his thin hair forward with his fingers as if that would hide his already-receding hairline.

I nearly spit out my Manhattan and sputtered, "Veto!"

Addison frowned and tucked a dark, glossy curl behind her ear. "Why not? He might agree for the right price. You know he's probably checking the latest bad trade he's made. Rumor has it his parents are cutting him off soon."

"He's a homophobic prick. We both went to Rencliffe, re-member? In tenth grade, he made Edward Linney's life hell. Eddie wasn't even queer, I don't think."

Addison stirred her cranberry holiday mojito with a cinnamon stick. "Maybe Richard's grown as a person."

After a beat, we burst out laughing too loudly, garnering glares from a few of the old society ladies who'd arrived early and now sipped sauvignon blanc while gossiping in whispers. Nostalgia washed over me with memories of our teenage years when Addison and I were perpetually skulking in the corner of these events.

"Do you want me to call my matchmaker auntie in Mumbai? I'm sure she has some hot tips."

"I'm not looking for a *match*. That's what I'm trying to avoid."

"Mm." Addison fingered her silver necklace, the encrusted diamonds gleaming against her brown skin. "Okay, unless you want to rethink one of the Masterson cousins—" She paused for my response.

The fake-boyfriend selection pool was truly grim. "Veto, veto, and veto."

She raised an eyebrow. "You're really channeling Bitsy."

"What? Oh, I guess I am." My grandmother was famous—make that *infamous*—for her one-word dismissal of any ideas she didn't care for. "Look, it has to be believable."

"Fair, but pickings are slim, and everyone will be arriving soon. You need to consider a fake girlfriend instead."

Sighing, I muttered, "I guess so."

"What does it matter? You're bi—as long as you have a significant other for the holidays, your grandmother should lay off her matchmaking scheme. Or, you could remind her you're twenty-nine years old and are a big boy now."

Addison took another sip of her cocktail before adding, "You know, it would be easier just to—hear me out—actually date someone. You've been hooking up with guys on the downlow since Rencliffe. If you're set on finding a man to thwart Bitsy's matchmaking dreams, there must be someone you know who's boyfriend material."

"Definitely no one from high school. Also, I never told you I hooked up with guys back then."

Addison rolled her eyes. "As if I couldn't always sniff out your chaotic bisexual energy."

I had to laugh, affection swelling in my chest. "Did it smell anything like Tom Ford Soleil Brûlant?"

"You wish. Axe Body Spray was more like it."

"Ouch. And I know it would be easier to have a partner for real. But after Gwen, I'm just not in the mood for anything serious."

She sighed. "I hear you. Gwen was a heartbreaker."

"She didn't *break my heart*," I insisted. "I'll give you bruised."

Addison didn't argue, which was why she was my best friend. She simply said, "May I point you back in the direction of telling your grandmother once and for all to butt the eff out?"

"You know my grandmother. Nodding and smiling and agreeing with everything she declares is the only way to go. I'm the oldest. Asher can do whatever he wants. Meanwhile, it's my responsibility to carry on the Cabot family legacy."

Addison dramatically put a hand to her chest, covering the V-neck of her sleek, green cocktail dress. "If only the world could understand the suffering of this rich white man in his custom Armani suit."

I chuckled. "Fair. Though I didn't say I was *suffering*. I just don't want to deal with my grandmother's meddling. If I'd known Cecilia was back from France, I'd have skipped dinner tonight."

"And miss Bitsy's traditional Thanksgiving charity event? You wouldn't dare."

After a burning gulp of my drink, I muttered, "I wish she'd actually do the place up for Thanksgiving. I'm sick of Christmas already, and it's still November."

"Like what, pilgrim hats and paper-mache turkeys? I'm sure

the tables will feature decorative gourds."

"Grandmother does love a decorative gourd."

"Who doesn't? Also, why is she so stuck on marrying you off to Cecilia Weston?"

I snorted. "Money and status, why else? It's her world—we just live in it. And to be clear, her world might as well be Jane Austen's Victorian England."

"Pretty sure Austen was the Regency period."

"Whichever." I desperately gave the lounge another scan. A string quartet played carols, and arriving guests made small talk in clusters. Before I could bite my tongue, I blurted, "I'd rather find a fake boyfriend because Grandmother doesn't believe bisexuality exists."

Addison's plucked eyebrows disappeared under her fashionable bangs. "In you specifically, or in the world at large?"

"Both."

Addison smiled sharply. "Does Bitsy believe in lesbians, or am I your imaginary friend?"

"I think she'd much rather everyone be cis and hetero, but being gay is a binary she can accept. You're also extremely rich."

Addison was part of the Rupani family, who'd made their fortune in India in telecoms. We'd met in an Upper East Side preschool and had an instant affinity for each other based on our shared love for all things SpongeBob.

Addison frowned. "You said your family was cool when you came out this summer."

I shrugged, going for careless and likely missing the mark. "My mom and stepdad and Asher were cool. Aunts and uncles and various cousins. Grandmother's in denial."

She reached for my hand and gave it a squeeze. "I'm sorry."

"It's fine!" I squeezed back before shoving my hand in my pocket.

"Okay, let's find you a man." Addison slurped the rest of the mojito. Her gaze narrowed. "There. Your brother's hot friend. They just walked in."

Confused, I searched the growing crowd. I found Asher, but it took a second to place his companion. "*Connor?* No. Veto. *Veee-to.* He's a kid."

Or he *had* been.

Addison's eyebrows met. "Are we talking about the same guy? White and a bit pasty—doesn't look like he gets a lot of sun. About six feet tall. Dirty blond hair definitely has some product involved in making him look so carelessly sexy. Hot black leather jacket and that tight ass in those Levis?"

Seeing through Addison's eyes, I tilted my head and watched Connor and Asher laugh about something.

Bright, sweet smile that dimples his cheeks.

Huh. When had Connor Lisowski grown up? So *well?* He and Asher were twenty-three now, and I hadn't seen Connor since they were undergrads.

"Ohhh, nice dimples," Addison noted.

Regaining my sanity, I scoffed. "I've known him since he was an angry, pimply teenager." Well, "known" was a strong word. Connor had been Asher's sullen shadow.

"He sure isn't now. I direct you again to exhibit D: *dat ass.* But even if you're not into his wannabe James Dean vibe, it's not like you have to hook up with him. The whole idea is a *fake* boyfriend."

"I know, but…"

"He's less of a risk since no one here knows him. Besides, you're out of vetoes and time, my friend."

On cue, my grandmother strolled into the lounge, chatting with—of course—Abigail Weston and Abigail's only child, Cecilia. It wasn't that I had anything against Cecilia, who was a golden-haired high society ingenue straight out of central casting.

The few times we'd been forced into small talk, she'd been

perfectly pleasant. But I'd just come to terms with being bi, and I wasn't looking for anything but a good time.

As Grandmother surveyed the room as the Terminator might, I practically lunged behind the Christmas tree, narrowly avoiding the fragrant pine needles.

I was well and truly out of options. "*Fine.*"

"You think he'll go for it?"

"I think Asher said he's gay, so maybe? Guess there's only one way to find out. Can you wave them over?"

After a few aborted attempts, Addison grumbled and strode across the lounge, deftly grabbing a champagne flute and skirting a massive poinsettia. She returned with Asher and Connor, and we crowded in the space between the tree and the window.

"What's up?" Asher asked suspiciously. He leaned to the left, peering around the tree. "Ah. Bitsy's back on her bullshit. I'm sorry to inform you that you can't hide here all night. No doubt Gamma's got you sitting with Cecilia so you can bond over turkey and stuffing and get married and have perfect heirs." He gulped from his flute. "You remember Connor, right?"

"We sure do," Addison said, though they'd probably never met. "Actually, Reid's in need of your services, Connor."

His forehead creased. "My…huh?" He scanned up and down my body, which gave me a strange little tingle. "Are you sick or something? I'm only in med school. I'm not a doctor yet."

"Oh, not those services," I said. "Look, time is of the essence, so here goes: I need a boyfriend for the holidays to thwart my matchmaking grandmother. In the new year, she'll go south to the Caymans, and I'll be off the hook until spring."

Connor stared at me. Up close, I could see he had stubble. "You… What?"

Addison said, "You wouldn't have to *really* date. Just come to a few more of these stuffy parties in December. Maybe a few PDAs to sell it."

Connor's brown eyes widened, and I asked, "You're queer too, right? I thought Asher said—" I spotted the flash of alarm in my brother's eyes, but of course it was too late.

Connor jerked his gaze to Asher. "Why the hell would you say that?"

"I didn't!" Asher lifted his palms. "My idiot brother's confused."

"Apologies. I must've gotten you mixed up with someone else." I thought Asher had mentioned it back when he and Connor were in high school, but perhaps I'd misremembered. I tried not to feel defensive. "You don't have to sound so outraged. There's nothing wrong with it."

Connor scoffed. "I know. I have two dads." He drained his champagne.

That rang a faint bell. "Right, right." Connor had been a scholarship kid at Rencliffe when he and Asher met. I vaguely recalled his mother had died, and he'd been classified as "troubled" before settling down. I thought there was something about his stepfather raising him?

It didn't matter—we could only hide behind the Scotch pine for so long.

"Look," I said. "You'd be doing me a huge favor."

Eyes on his empty glass, Connor fiddled with the zipper of his leather jacket, which most certainly did not fit my grandmother's dress code.

Asher added, "There's always free food and booze at these events. It'll be fun." We both wore our dark brown hair short, though his bangs flopped over one eyebrow as he waggled them.

Connor glowered at him. "Why would it be fun pretending to be, um, Reid's—" He motioned at me as if he couldn't bring himself to say the word *boyfriend.*

Asher grinned. "I love my grandmother, but messing with Bitsy's always a good time."

"We've been spotted," Addison hissed.

"I'll make it worth your while," I added.

Connor met my gaze, clearly still dubious. Not to mention *handsome*. Seriously, when had this happened? I didn't remember his voice being this low.

He asked, "How?"

"However you want."

He shifted in his Doc Martens. "You really need help?"

A server in black and white appeared and asked Connor, "Sir, may I take your coat? It will be uncomfortably warm for you at dinner." The guy had likely been dispatched by Grandmother.

Asher said, "Dude, I promise they won't lose it." To the server, he added, "You won't lose it, right?"

"Never," the man replied seriously.

"*Fine*," Connor muttered as he shrugged out of the jacket. The leather squeaked and seemed new.

Under it, he wore a white dress shirt and gray striped tie, which was at least semi-formal. His Levis—which really did hug his long, lean legs—and Doc Martens were less so, but it didn't matter. It wasn't as if my grandmother would approve of him in any outfit.

Besides, she just had to believe we were a couple long enough to back off, and—

"Incoming," Asher whispered, and as the server left with Connor's jacket, we all turned to face Elizabeth "Bitsy" Cabot as she marched toward us, her glossy black pumps striking the marble floor in staccato annoyance.

Her skin was creamy white—never tanned nor too pale—and her hair was decidedly silver rather than gray, styled in a seek bob. She wore a long-sleeved cocktail dress in an orangey-red that was likely called "burnt sienna" or something else appropriately autumnal for Thanksgiving.

"Gamma!" Asher opened his arms wide, and she hugged him,

allowing the childhood nickname that was a relic from the time when Asher couldn't pronounce "Grandmother." Also allowing the hug itself, which was rare, especially in public.

She turned to me, saying, "Reid," and leaned slightly toward me so I could kiss her cheek while our hands briefly met. Her manicured fingers were cool and moisturized.

She gave Addison an air kiss on each cheek and said, "My dear, I'm so glad you're not caught up in that terrible violence in Pakistan."

"Me too," Addison replied with a sweet smile. "I've lived here my whole life, and my family's from Mumbai. India."

"Of course," Grandmother said, already moving on to Connor, who she regarded with the slightest tension at the corners of her red lips. She didn't extend hand nor cheek. "How lovely to see you here with Asher."

Connor's gaze flicked to me. "Uh, actually…"

Was he in? We looked at each other, and after an endless moment of deliberation, he lifted his eyebrows, waiting.

He was in.

Chapter Two

Connor

M Y HEART WAS about to rupture and burst through my ribcage.

Reid. Was. Touching. Me.

His arm was around my shoulders. Any second, the costal cartilage in my chest would go *bam*, and...

Reid was saying something while old lady Cabot stared at me like I was gum she'd peeled off the bottom of her shoe. Not that she'd pick gum off her own shoes—she had staff to do that.

Focus for fuck's sake!

"We've been dating a while now," Reid said. The way his grandmother didn't blink was alarming. I monitored her for signs of a stroke as Reid squeezed my shoulders and said, "It's going great, isn't it, Connor?"

I realized I was standing frozen like a cadaver on an exam table with my arms straight at my sides. "Um, yep." I reached around Reid's toned, firm waist. The right side of my body was at risk of igniting where it pressed against his side. We were both tall, but Reid was a couple of inches above me. He felt big and comforting.

And hot. Did I mention hot?

Back in the day, he'd inspired way too many wet dreams to count. Not that I'd ever, *ever* admitted that to anyone. Seriously, *why* had Asher told Reid I was queer?! No one knew that. Not even my dads, because...

It just wasn't the right time. It was fine—it wasn't like I was seeing anyone. I was a loser virgin, and—

And now, I *was* suddenly seeing someone? Maybe this was the answer to my prayers. Not that I prayed since god was bullshit. If there was actually a god up there who let my mom die, he/she/they could go to hell. If only it existed.

As far as heaven went, touching Reid Cabot qualified. Reid with his thick, dark brown hair, his deep brown eyes, and perfectly even, white smile that made me lightheaded.

Mrs. Cabot still hadn't blinked. "Darling, you didn't breathe a word of this at the board meeting a few days ago."

"Oh, there wasn't an opportunity," Reid said smoothly, still a wall of warmth pressed against my side. "We had so many motions to vote on." He motioned broadly to the buzzing lounge with his free arm. "I'm sure Filling Bellies and Minds will be thrilled with the proceeds from tonight's event."

Reid's friend—Madison? Addison? That was it. *Addison* said, "You've both done such wonderful work on the board. Trans-formed the charity in the best way. I know they're so grateful for your patronage. How many years have you been hosting this Thanksgiving dinner now, Mrs. Cabot? You must be responsible for millions and millions raised for worthy causes over the years."

Mrs. Cabot was forced to answer, smiling tightly at Addison as she talked about tradition and giving back. Meanwhile, Reid and I stood there like an actual couple. It was a good thing I took off my jacket—sweat dampened the back of my neck. My pits would probably reek soon.

Reid casually brushed his fingers back and forth on my upper arm. If I were in a tank top, I'd be able to feel it on my skin… Good thing I was in a dress shirt, because popping a boner wasn't going to make his grandma like me. Not that anything could probably make her like me. Not that it mattered since this was all pretend.

Jesus, was *I* having a stroke?

As Addison and Asher asked Mrs. Cabot more questions she was clearly annoyed to answer, red flashed in my peripheral vision. Good news: It wasn't a stroke symptom. Bad news: It was Olivia in her new cocktail dress approaching on Dylan van Arsdale's arm.

Shiiiiiiit.

I met her gaze and shook my head as much as I could without drawing attention. She was already frowning, staring at me with Reid. Olivia's mind was usually five steps ahead of me as we often joked. Yet she seemed stumped by me and Reid with our arms around each other.

Which was fair since this was absolutely bananas as my dad Seth would have said because he didn't swear.

Olivia's long, dark hair was curled perfectly, and her strapless red dress was a knockout. People often wondered aloud how I could live with her and not be fucking her. The answer was pretty simple.

Apparently, Asher had figured it out, but he was my best friend. Did other people suspect? Did they know somehow? They were sure as shit going to now that I was pretending to be Reid's boyfriend.

I thought back to Asher telling me around the Fourth of July that Reid was bi. He'd acted a bit too casually. We'd been on the roof of my apartment building, which Olivia and I had turned into our secret little patio by wedging gum into the door lock.

Asher and I were up there drinking beer at the little table, sitting in folding chairs and sweating in the thick, humid night air. We listened to sirens and fireworks and watched the displays shining from skyscraper windows. He'd kept his gaze on the view as he'd mentioned that Reid had come out, and my heart had thumped.

I'd waited for him to say something about me, or demand the truth, or at least ask. He hadn't. Hours later, when I'd been almost passed out in bed, I'd jerked off furiously thinking about Reid. Just like I had dozens of times before. *Hundreds.* I'd always had it so bad for him.

Olivia and Dylan were too close now to avoid. Sweat dripped down my spine. Just ten minutes ago, I'd walked into this party looking forward to an open bar and fancy dinner, and now—

I had to say, "Um, hey," to Olivia and Dylan.

"Hey," they replied in unison. Dylan opened his mouth to speak, his forehead furrowed, but Olivia cut him off. "Mrs. Cabot, what a lovely event this is. My mother's sorry she can't be here in person."

Still barely blinking—maybe it was just her thing—Mrs. Cabot gave Olivia and Dylan a smooth smile. "Your mother?"

Her own practiced smile in place, Olivia said, "Angela Barker. One of Filling Bellies and Minds' biggest donors."

"Oh, of course." Mrs. Cabot's smile widened fractionally. "You're her adopted daughter. From China?"

"My sister and I were both adopted from Korea. We're Angela's only children." Olivia was smiling fakely too, and god, rich people were exhausting.

I was used to it after going to Rencliffe and Harvard and tagging along with Asher to these parties, but I should have just gone home for Thanksgiving with Logan and Seth, and my Aunt Jenna, Uncle Jun, and Pop and the kids.

I'd been too stressed by my upcoming finals to make the short trip to Albany. If I were there, right about now we'd be watching football, talking about how stuffed we felt, and having a belching contest while Seth and Jenna complained about how gross we were.

Asher said, "Oh, Gamma, Mom asked if you want to go to the Belvedere dinner since she won't be in town for it."

"Veto, darling. My calendar is full to the brim," Mrs. Cabot said briskly. "I must attend to my duties." Her gaze swept over us all, and if I could read minds hers would probably say, "*Look at this bullshit I have to deal with. Remember when everyone was white and straight and had respectably old money?*"

What she actually said was, "Enjoy the evening. Reid, let's regroup tomorrow, yes?"

It was apparently a rhetorical question since she swept away with head high. She should have considered wearing a cape or cloak to amplify the effect.

We all seemed to exhale in unison. Olivia sipped her champagne and muttered, "Always a pleasure, Bitsy."

"Babe, ignore that old bat," Dylan said, rubbing her arm. He glanced at Asher and Reid. "Uh, sorry. I know she's your grandma, but... How's it going? Asher, you still working for the Allard Group?" He extended his hand, and there was a round of shakes and chat, all while Olivia's piercing gaze bore into me.

She held out her hand to Reid. "I don't think we've met. I'm Olivia Barker-Robertson. Connor's roommate."

"Reid Cabot."

"He's Asher's brother," I said quickly, as if that would answer why Reid and I were still standing close with our arms around each other.

"Uh-huh," Olivia said, nodding. "*And?*"

"Um..." I was really sweating now, the back of my hair damp with it. I was seriously going to reek. "Right, we actually, we're—"

"Dating," Reid finished, giving my temple a kiss. "It's okay. Don't be nervous, *mon amour.*"

"Uh-huh!" was all I could manage, and it was more of a squeak. The warm, slightly wet sensation on my skin from his lips, and the French words—my love?—were too much. Also, why French? Rich people were so weird.

Head tilted, Olivia exclaimed, "What a fascinating development!" She said to Dylan, "Don't you think so?"

Dylan, who wasn't the shiniest coin in the collection plate as my mom used to say, said, "Yeah! Cool. Congrats, guys." He wasn't a homophobe, at least. For a rich white guy who worked for his daddy's company and was extremely privileged, he was okay. He was wild about Olivia, so he had good taste.

"It's wonderful news, "Addison agreed, finishing her drink. I needed another one, stat. The empty glass was damp in my free hand.

To Reid, Olivia said, "Like I mentioned, I'm Connor's roommate." She grimaced dramatically. "New money, which I know is cringe. But I'm sure you know all about me. Since you and Connor are dating."

"I'm sorry about my grandmother," Reid said smoothly. "And yes, it's wonderful to finally meet you."

"Isn't it?" Olivia grinned. "Hey, Asher, what's up?"

"Hey." He gave Olivia a lazy salute. "Oh, I think it's time for dinner."

Reid kept his arm firmly around my shoulders as we filed toward the banquet hall or whatever they called it at the Utopia Grand, one of the fanciest hotels in Manhattan. Reid and I were definitely garnering attention from other guests, and my face was hot with the weight of their stares.

Whispers sliced through the air like knives. My asshole brain imagined: "*See? Being raised by those two men led to this. It's their fault.*"

Which was ridiculous because these people didn't know me or my parents. I was glad for the grounding weight of Reid's arm. I realized I was clutching his waist too tight and relaxed my fingers.

"Sorry," I mumbled, almost dropping my glass while putting it on a tray held by an impassive server.

"It's okay," Reid replied, his breath warm on my cheek. "I've got you."

Operation: No Boners was going to take every ounce of my will power.

"Thanks for doing this," he added in that smooth tenor that went right to my dick as though it was injected in my veins. Was this really happening? My head was spinning, and *Jesus*, he smelled amazing—like a forest. Not just pine trees, but rich and earthy soil.

Did I just think that he smelled like dirt? What was my damage? And since when was I attracted to dirt? Whatever it was, I wanted to lean closer and breathe deeply.

Reid added, "I really owe you one."

The reminder of what I'd be asking from Reid Cabot later in exchange for my fake boyfriend services worked like a bucket of ice water dumped on my head. He'd probably say no, but I had to try. Considering I was completely screwed otherwise, I had nothing to lose.

"Are you sure about this?" Reid murmured in my ear.

Not even a little bit.

One thing was guaranteed: The holidays just got a hell of a lot more interesting.

Chapter Three

Reid

I FINALLY HAD a boyfriend.

Next to me, Connor picked up and put down his dessert spoon. He knew we didn't use *that* spoon until the end, right? That the soup spoon was on the outside?

I needed to get over myself. This wasn't *Pretty Woman*.

"You okay?" I murmured.

"Everyone's staring," he whispered.

I wanted to argue, but it was true. Maybe not *everyone*, but we'd garnered our fair share of attention. Forget the soup—gossip was the favored first course of this crowd. Not to mention the main *and* dessert.

At least Grandmother was seated at a head table with the charity's top executives and not at our round table of eight with Asher, Addison, and a few of the younger Lawrence cousins. Not to mention the conspicuously empty seat designated for my plus-one since Connor was Asher's and Addison had her own invite.

My collar felt tight, and I loosened my tie half an inch, careful not to mess up my Windsor knot. Naturally people were gossiping—I'd known academically it would happen when I'd assessed the risk of this last-minute plan.

As a rule, I wasn't a fan of doing anything last-minute, but the panic of having to play nice with Cecilia Weston had felt far more threatening.

I supposed at the root of this scheme was my hurt and anger at Grandmother's denial of who I'd told her I was. Who I was whether she believed it or not.

Not that I wouldn't date a woman—I had, and I surely would again. But Grandmother needed to see me with a man. Here in front of God, New York society, and the Utopia waitstaff.

"Gamma's laser beams are getting a workout," Asher muttered from Connor's left side as the butternut squash and roasted red pepper soup arrived around our table at the exact same moment with pinpoint accuracy from the servers.

I refused to meet her gaze, smiling broadly as if I didn't have a care in the world. "Good. Let her look." Let her *see*.

"Can you guess what she's thinking?" Connor whispered.

Beside me—leaving the extra seat on her other side—Addison said, "Hon, better to never ask that question."

I smirked. "She's probably thinking, 'If he has to suck cock, can't it be a *wealthy* one?'"

Choking on his spoonful of soup—using the correct spoon, for the record—Connor grabbed his water glass and gulped it down before coughing into his elbow.

"You okay?" I stopped myself before I could thump his back, since that was probably not actually helpful for choking victims. I laid my palm gently between his shoulder blades.

Face pink, he nodded. "Went down the wrong way." A server refilled his water, and Connor drank it with muffled thanks.

Leaning closer, I whispered, "Sorry to make you uncomfortable."

He shook his head. "You're not. Between Olivia and your grandma, I feel like I'm being dissected. With dull instruments."

I chuckled. "I assume you're going to have to tell Olivia the truth."

"Oh, yeah." Connor laughed, the nervous edge softening into fondness. "No way she'll be letting this go. Understandably, since this morning I didn't have a boyfriend. I wasn't even—" He stammered. "Um, well, you know."

"I get it. Do you two go to school together?"

He scooped his spoon back and forth through the rich orange-red soup. "No. We do both go to Columbia, but I'm in med school. One of my dads and my aunt work for Olivia's mom. Olivia wanted out of the dorm, and her mom rented an apartment for us. No way I should be able to afford it, but Angela's really generous. Understatement."

Addison and Asher were doing their part to make conversation with the rest of the table, so Connor and I were able to chat quietly. I asked, "Where are you guys living?"

"It's an apartment at Tenth and Forty-eighth. Five-story walk-up. Not fancy, but obviously *way* nicer than anything I could afford. And I get my own room as opposed to a saggy futon in a studio shared with, like, three people."

"I've heard Angela Barker's quite a character."

Connor's smile took on a soft fondness. Not dimple material, but sweet. "Small, brassy Texan who's like a tornado. She's done so much for me and my dads."

"That's wonderful."

"Yeah. Actually, it's kind of funny." He leaned in closer, his eyes lighting up. His lashes were thick, and there were a few freckles dusted across the tops of his cheeks. "Logan and Seth didn't even know each other when they met Angela, but they pretended to be engaged. For reasons. It probably sounds nuts."

"I couldn't possibly relate." I brushed back his hair and leaned in flirtily for the benefit of Grandmother and the curious onlookers. "I'd never get caught up in something so weird," I whispered in Connor's ear.

He swallowed thickly, Adam's apple bobbing. "Good thing I have experience in this arena."

I laughed. "Carrying on a family tradition."

A dimple appeared briefly in his right cheek. "Apparently. Logan and Seth ended up falling in love for real, though. Different situation."

I leaned back. "Totally." Sure, Connor was adorable, but falling in love? No chance.

After a spoonful of creamy soup with a perfect note of sweetness, I asked, "Logan was originally your mother's partner, right?" Our table mates were still wrapped up in their own conversations, so it felt safe enough ask a few questions of my brand-new boyfriend.

My heart performed a silly little somersault at those two words—"my" and "boyfriend"—in close proximity. I'd had girlfriends, but this was a first. Even if it wasn't true, to be sitting in the Utopia on Thanksgiving in front of everyone with a man gave me a deep thrill.

I really needed to get out more.

"Yeah, they were married," Connor said, circling his spoon through his half-full bowl. "It was really rushed and stupid." He shook his head and started eating his soup again hesitantly, as if he was afraid to spill it.

I finished mine as I tried to remember what Asher had said about Connor's mother. I knew she'd died suddenly and quite young. Some kind of unexpected heart attack, perhaps? Along those lines. Understandable that he didn't want to talk about it.

He did add, "So, Logan was my stepfather, and I guess Seth's my step-stepfather. I only knew Logan a year or so longer, though." He paused. "I guess it's been about ten years since we moved in with Seth."

"And that was part of the…" I waved my hand.

"Yeah." He smirked and whispered, "Operation Fake Boyfriend."

I lifted my wine glass. "Here's to family legacies."

We clinked our glasses and drank. Still watching me, Connor

swallowed. He really had grown up to be quite handsome. I'm not sure I would have recognized him as my little brother's pimply, perpetually scowling friend.

"Asher said your mom's staying in Europe for the holidays?" Connor asked.

"Yes, she's enjoying the sunshine with her new husband. You'll be in Albany with your dads and the rest of the family?"

"Yeah." That fond smile was back. "It's been months. I can't wait to chill out."

"What about your biological father? He's in…Florida, I think?"

Smile vanishing, Connor's shoulders practically hit his ears as he reached for the bread basket, sending a piece of sourdough tumbling onto the white linen.

He said, "Dunno. I mean, yeah, he's in Florida as far as I know. I've never had Christmas down there. He's not—I just have his name. I wish I didn't."

Okay, that was a sore subject. I quickly asked, "How's school?"

Connor's shoulders un-hunched a fraction. "Pretty good. Hard." His cheeks flushed. "I mean, obviously. It's medical school. It's hard."

I chuckled. "I've heard rumors. What drew you to medicine?"

We were interrupted as the servers brought the main course. I couldn't imagine how many turkeys had been sacrificed since we all had white and dark meat on our plates, along with perfectly golden roast potatoes, slightly charred brussels sprouts, and a gourmet twist on green bean casserole that most definitely did not involve a can of Campbell's soup.

I sipped the buttery Chardonnay and nodded my thanks to the server who'd filled my glass.

Connor inhaled deeply, mumbling, "Oh my god, this smells amazing."

Asher grinned. "The Utopia's gravy is the best."

Our table settled into eating, the clink of silverware louder around the room before the din of conversation increased again. Addison, Asher, and the others at our table returned to debating something boring about football. I'd never been much of a sports guy.

After a few bites of the rich, creamy beans, I prompted Connor. "Well? Why med school?"

"I dunno."

"Sure you do. Clearly your grades were high enough, but it's too big of a commitment for that to be the only reason."

He ate a potato and finally mumbled, "I want to help people feel better."

I had to smile. "That's nothing to be embarrassed about. As someone who works for a family business that primarily helps itself, I'm glad there are people like you who want to do some good."

He scoffed. "Sure, but it's the most cliché answer. It's facile. 'I want to help people.' What does that even mean?"

"Hmm. Okay. Well, what *does* it mean? To you?"

Connor fiddled with his fork, eyes lowered. Had he always had those freckles? "I'm not sure. I still need to figure it out."

"That's what school's for, isn't it?"

"I guess. But most of my classmates know exactly which specialty they want to do already. I have ideas, but I'm not *sure*. It was the same at Rencliffe and Harvard. Everyone had a plan, and I was just scraping along."

"I'd hardly call Harvard and Columbia 'scraping along.' But you have the freedom to do anything. Isn't that empowering?" I couldn't stop a surge of envy. "I'm the oldest Cabot son, so I have zero choice. Our dad's dead, so it'll be me taking over the company. The end."

Connor frowned. "I mean, old—uh, your grandmother can't

make you."

My laugh was too bitter. "Oh, you'd be surprised." I shook my head. "But yes, you're right. And I have absolutely nothing to complain about. I couldn't be more privileged if I tried."

"You're in hotels, right? Like this one?" He motioned around us and almost lost his fork before putting it down carefully on the table. "I never really paid attention. Everyone else at Rencliffe except the scholarship kids were loaded one way or another."

"Hotels, yes. The Utopia brand is our biggest."

"Oh, cool. Are they all as fancy?"

"Most, but this is the flagship."

"Must be a good business. Do you like it?"

Had anyone ever asked me that before? I wasn't sure. I refolded my napkin on my lap. "It's fine. The brand's steady. Can't ask for much more."

Connor seemed about to reply but glanced at his phone when it pinged, then rolled his eyes. I couldn't resist being nosy. "What prompted that face?"

"Just Logan telling me not to drink too much if Asher and I go out later. He's always telling me stuff like that. 'Don't drink too much.' 'Stay away from the edge of the subway platform.' 'Don't speed' and 'wear your helmet'—as if I'd go out on my motorcycle without a helmet."

"*Motorcycle?*" My pulse increased just thinking about it. "Isn't that dangerous?"

He groaned softly. "Not you too. Yes, there's higher risk associated with riding a motorcycle, but that risk can be mitigated. I took driving courses. My engine is less than five hundred cc's. I always wear a helmet and safety gear. I drive like everyone else on the road is trying to kill me."

I held up my hands. "Sorry. I can see you've had this conversation before."

"You could say that. And I get it—I do. It's risky. But it can be incredible too." His gaze went distant. "My mom always wanted one. She'd been saving up for years. Then…" After a moment, Connor dropped his head and scooped up a mouthful of beans.

Ah. That helped explain it. Without thinking, I rubbed his shoulder. Connor swallowed and looked at me, and I remembered the angry, scared boy I'd first met years ago.

I couldn't recall where—likely at an alumni day at Rencliffe, or maybe Asher had brought Connor home for a weekend. He'd been a bundle of contradictions then, and apparently that hadn't changed much. He still had jittery, rough edges.

I jumped as Addison cleared her throat loudly enough to wake the dead. I blinked at her, biting back an impatient "*What?*" and going with, "Pardon?" The whole table was watching me and Connor.

"Sorry to interrupt your *tête-à-tête*," Addison said smoothly. "Morgan asked if you're attending the tree lighting next weekend."

I blinked at Morgan Lawrence. "Of course! It's the event of the season." Or, it was a bore and a half, but I was obligated to make an appearance.

Morgan, a banker who sat with his pregnant wife, Louise, nodded to Connor. "I hope we'll see you both?"

Okay, Morgan wasn't so bad. I had to smile at my fake boyfriend being included. Hopefully, one day if I was serious with a guy, it wouldn't be an issue.

"Uh…" Connor looked at me before nodding. "Sounds great. Thanks."

Morgan glanced at the head table—as if afraid Grandmother could hear him—before adding, "Good for you, man. Haven't seen you look happy in a long time."

Before I could respond, the charity president tapped a microphone, and it was time for the back-patting and congratulations. I listened and clapped on cue while chewing over Morgan's comment.

Had I looked *unhappy* before? It wasn't as though I was miserable.

Sure, perhaps I wouldn't describe myself as "happy," but…I could admit that coming out hadn't been quite the liberating, joyous event I'd secretly dreamed of for years. Still. I'd have to work harder.

While I wasn't a gambler, I thought my poker face was better than that.

Chapter Four

Connor

TIME TO TELL Reid. Even though it had tasted like a sweet, spicy cloud, the pumpkin pie soufflé was sitting in my gut like Pop's old bowling ball.

Icy wind whipped on Fifty-ninth Street, and I wished I could do up my jacket. But I'd have to let go of Reid's hand, and his warm fingers were laced with mine, and I tingled all over. I was holding hands with a man. With *Reid*.

Reid Cabot holding my hand would have filled my spank bank to the brim in high school. Hell, Reid Cabot *looking* at me with a nod and distracted, "*Hey*" when I visited Asher's house had been enough. And the few times he'd smiled at me? Epic.

Where were we walking? Central Park unfurled on our right with Columbus Circle ahead. We'd left the hotel at the same time as a lot of other people who'd been at dinner, so I supposed we should keep up the act while we were still in the vicinity.

Damn, I'd have to keep holding Reid Cabot's hand while pretending this was just something we did because we were a couple. What a hardship. Though I did need to address our arrangement.

Couldn't I just enjoy holding his hand for another minute?

Spit it out already.

Instead, I said, "They really need to change that."

Reid's long-legged stride faltered. "Sorry, who should change what?"

"Oh, I guess that only made sense if you could read my mind. Quick, what am I thinking?"

He stopped to peer at me intently as he dramatically put his finger to his temple. A family of tourists eating pretzels brushed by, and I shivered under Reid's gaze. He wore a long charcoal coat that hugged his lean frame. A burgundy scarf hung around his neck. It looked soft. What would his cheek feel like? His face was smooth, but would I feel the hint of stubble?

"You're thinking…" He glanced back toward Fifth Avenue, then ahead of us. "That there must be Italian-Americans to celebrate who weren't colonizers."

"Yes!" It pleased me more than it should have that he'd guessed correctly. We walked on toward Columbus Circle and the tall monument and pedestrian area in the middle with traffic flowing around it. I said, "I read that it was made a landmark so it can't be removed."

"Grandmother was probably on the committee," he muttered before inhaling deeply. "I'm stuffed, but damn those street nuts smell amazing."

I inhaled the honey-salt scent deeply as we passed the cart. "Jesus, they do. You know, I don't think I've ever had them."

Reid gasped. "And you call yourself a New Yorker?"

"Do I? I don't think Albany counts, and I was in Boston for four years. I've only lived in Manhattan a few months."

"It's a state of mind. Wait, am I about to break into Billy Joel?"

"I don't know, are you?" In the distance, "Jingle Bell Rock" echoed from the ice rink in Central Park. "Dunno if you can fight the rising tide of Christmas music."

"Challenge accepted. My dad *loved* Billy Joel." Reid cleared his throat and launched into a song I'd never heard before that was apparently by someone named Billy Joel. Reid had a rich, smooth voice, and the fact that he could sing was sexy AF. Could he speak

French or another language fluently? I was afraid to ask in case I just came on the spot.

"Not bad," I said when he finished the chorus.

"All those years I was forced into the choir at Rencliffe."

"Oh yeah, Asher was too. Lucky for me, I can't carry a tune to save my life."

"Come on." He tugged my hand lightly. "I bet you're better than you think."

"Trust me. I am not." The day I let Reid hear my screeching would be right about never.

He smiled. "Okay, I'll let you off the hook. For the singing—the nuts are non-negotiable. If you're going to be my boyfriend, you have to eat the nuts."

After a pause, we burst out laughing. "That should be your new Grindr bio," I said.

"Maybe I'd have more luck with it."

"Uh… How are *you* not having luck on Grindr?"

Reid scoffed. "So many guys, but… Just call me Goldilocks. You know what it's like."

"I've never seen it!" I said too quickly and too emphatically.

Just call me a liar with a side of cowardly.

"Oh, right!" He waved his free hand. "Sorry. Anyway, you're not missing anything. Which apps do you use? I met my last girlfriend on Love or Bust. It wasn't love, but… Well, maybe I thought it was for a little while, but it was only a summer thing. You should try the app. Once the holidays are over and we're both 'single' again."

"Right. Uh-huh. I will—thanks for the rec."

"Anytime. And tomorrow, we pop your cherry."

My heart lurched into my throat, and I suddenly sounded like a soprano. "What?"

"Street nuts. What other New York institutions haven't you tried?"

I managed to catch my breath. "Probably a lot of things. School's intense."

"There's the food category, and then museums and galleries. Shopping at certain stores. We should make a list."

"Okay." I couldn't hold in my grin. "That would be fun. Are you sure? You've probably done them all already."

"Most. There might be a few obligatory experiences I'm missing. Besides, you're doing me a massive favor."

The little bubble of happiness went splat. "You said you'd do something in return, right? I mean, besides nuts and stuff."

Thanksgiving dinner suddenly threatened to come back up. I hated this so much, but if Reid could help me, Logan and Seth would never have to know how much I'd fucked up.

"Absolutely. Yes, we should talk terms and conditions." He dropped my hand and took his phone from his pocket, suddenly all business. "Happy to put it in writing if you prefer?"

"No, that's okay. Not for my sake, I mean. Unless you want to, which you probably will. Um, you said anything, right?"

Reid chuckled, then gave me an intense look and raised his eyebrow. "Why? What's your price?"

My dick swelled in my jeans like I was a dumb, horny kid. Which I still felt like I was too much of the time. I reminded myself I was in med school. Soon enough, I'd be an actual doctor. An adult. Maybe I'd even find the balls to get over myself and finally get laid.

Okay, that wasn't a helpful train of thought. Reid was waiting, and I had no time to come up with a graceful way to put it.

"Ten grand," I blurted.

Reid's teasing smirk flattened into confusion. "Dollars?"

"Yeah." I kept my chin up. "You've got a lot of money, right?"

"You want me to pay you ten thousand dollars to be my boyfriend for the holidays?"

"No!" My cheeks flushed hot. "*Fake* boyfriend, and I'll pay back all of it. With interest. It would be a loan."

Reid seemed to take this in, his dark gaze assessing me. I willed my dick to behave. He actually stroked his chin. He'd always been clean-shaven since I'd known him, and I'd often wondered what he'd look like with scruff. Not that I was complaining about his amazing face.

Focus.

"Why do you need ten thousand dollars?"

I shifted and crossed my arms, trying to breathe through the flood of shame and rage and pain as I ducked out of the way of a group of teenagers. "Does it matter?"

Reid's thick brows met, and he joined me at the edge of the sidewalk on the park's border. "It does if it's illegal."

"Huh? No way! Nothing like that." At least I wasn't *that* stupid.

Reid was still contemplating me, and despite the humiliation, my hot skin tingled. "Gambling?"

I snorted. "I'd achieve the same outcome from setting my fucking money on fire and watching it burn."

He arched a brow, and I wanted to run my finger over it. "Wise words."

"Seth always says that when Pop wants to go to the casino to play the slots. That's my grandpa. Sort of. Logan's dad." I shook my head, trying to stop rambling. "Anyway, I don't gamble."

"Except on surprise propositions from your best friend's brother."

Some of the tension evaporated, and we shared a smile. There was that tingle again, traveling down my spine.

"Um, right. But seriously, it's not gambling. It's..." The icy-hot shame washed back through me, and I shoved my hands in my jacket pockets. "It's nothing illegal, I promise. It's just..." I struggled to land on the right word. "Embarrassing. I can't cover it, and I can't ask my dads."

He nodded. "Okay. I can transfer it now."

"For real?"

Reid said, "Yeah, no problem," so easily that it was hard not to resent him just a little even as gratitude and sweet, *sweet* relief filled me.

"Thank you. I'll pay you back, I swear. With interest."

"Sure. I know. Interest isn't necessary." He tapped his phone, not really seeming to care if I did or not. But I would—every single red cent, and I'd never, ever be such a moron again. I should have known better. I hated myself for being so gullible.

At least this way, Logan and Seth never had to know. If I asked, they'd give me the money. I knew they would. They'd drain their savings for me, but I'd rather eat glass than disappoint them like that. They'd never really been obligated to do anything for me, yet they'd done *everything*.

Logan had barely been married to my mom before she died, and yet he'd taken me on like I was his. Then Seth had too. No, I had to deal with my stupidity on my own.

"Text me your details," Reid said.

I scrolled my contacts. "I don't think I have you, actually."

"Me either." Reid gave me a wide, gorgeous grin. "Guess we should rectify that, *boyfriend*."

Miraculously, I managed to give him my number without stuttering or forgetting a number as my heart thumped. I should have just AirDropped him.

Boyfriend.

It wasn't real, but that word on those wide, sexy lips was music to my ears.

THE JINGLE OF keys from the hallway made me jump even though I was on the couch waiting with my anatomy textbook open on my lap. Not that I'd read any of it in the darkness. Too bad I couldn't learn the info by osmosis.

The muted TV flickered blue over the long space that included the couch, a small dining table, and the kitchen. Our bedrooms and shared bathroom opened off the living room.

As Olivia entered, she was backlit by the bright hallway. She dropped her keys on the little shelf attached to the wall, a shadow sweeping over her as the door closed.

"Well, if it isn't Reid Cabot's new boyfriend pretending to study."

I didn't bother to insist that I could see fine by the light of the TV since it was an obvious lie. The open textbook was more of a weird security blanket. I tugged at the neck of my ratty old Lake Placid T-shirt and said, "Look, I can explain."

"Oh, you will." She grinned as she kicked off her heels. "This should be good."

"It's not what you think." Olivia and I had hit it off right away, and she was alarmingly good already at calling me on my shit.

She hung her coat in the closet and headed for the bottle of red on the kitchen counter. I closed my eyes, still slouched on the sofa, listening as she poured herself a healthy glass with a familiar *glug-glug*.

She asked, "Why? What do I think?"

I shrugged, keeping my eyes closed and head back. The sofa dipped as she settled on the other end. Then she got up, muttering about her tights before settling again. She poked my arm with her now-bare toe.

"Spill."

I laid out what happened when Asher and I arrived at the event, my eyes still closed even though I couldn't have slept if you'd paid me. Speaking of which, I shifted uneasily and kept *that* part of the arrangement with Reid to myself.

I could have asked Olivia's mom for the money, but it made me queasy to even consider it. Angela was a little…out there, but she'd done a ton for me and the family. I couldn't ask for more from her. Much better to have the deal with Reid. Quid pro quo and all that.

"Dylan said there was a lot of gossip when Reid came out as bi. To be expected from that crowd."

I opened my eyes. "How's Dylan? You looked happy together tonight. Did you talk to him about the text thing?"

Olivia gave me a shrewd look over her wine glass. "Uh-uh. You're not distracting me. Dylan also said Mrs. Cabot told his mom that Reid was 'rebelling' and it was a 'phase,' because she's ridiculous. I mean, he's thirty or something."

"Twenty-nine."

"He's your boyfriend, so you would know."

I closed my textbook and thudded it onto the wooden coffee table. I'd been trying to focus on any other sound than the thumping of my heart, which echoed in my ears as though I had increased intercranial pressure.

"He's obviously *not* my boyfriend. I'll go to a few stuffy holiday events. The end."

Olivia sipped her wine. "You guys looked good together."

I hoped it was too dim for her to spot the blush as my cheeks went hot. "Please," I scoffed.

"You seemed wrapped up with each other at dinner."

"Huh? We were talking. Small talk. That's it."

"Hmm. If you say so." She took another sip of her wine while raising an eyebrow.

I'd grabbed a beer when I got home, and I tipped up the bottle, only getting a few warm drops and remembering belatedly I'd finished it. "Dude, I'm not gay."

"Okay." Olivia ran her finger around the rim of her wine glass, making a low vibration. "I mean, you know it's totally okay if you're gay or bi or…questioning or whatever?"

"Obviously! I have two dads. I mean, kind of. Stepdads."

She frowned. "They are a hundred percent your dads. No qualifiers necessary."

"Yeah. I know."

It had taken years to get used to even thinking of Logan and Seth as my dads. Even longer before I could describe them that way. I'd always called them by their first names and still did.

Actually, I'd probably called Logan "asshole" more than his name the first couple of years. I'd hated him when he and Mom married after he had a serious accident and she was his nurse.

"*Nothing changes if nothing changes,*" Mom had said. That philosophy had led to a few great choices—and some epically bad ones, including the snap marriage to Logan. Then Mom was gone, and—

I inhaled sharply, shoving away those memories. That image I'd never, ever get out of my head.

"Hey." Olivia squeezed my arm gently with her soft hand. "It's okay. Whatever you're feeling, it's okay."

Shaking her off, I strode to the kitchen, the tile there cold under my bare feet. "I'm not *feeling* anything!" I popped the top off another beer and chugged. "Just worried about my exams."

"Okay." She sipped her wine. "Which one's first?"

That was the great thing about Olivia. She could be persistent—similar to her mom even though she'd deny that fiercely—but she knew when to back off. I rejoined her on the couch, and we talked about my exams for a while.

Eventually, Olivia yawned widely. "I'd better get my contacts out. Hey, you want to decorate this weekend? We need to glitter up this joint. I bought a fake mini tree. Speaking of buying things, what are you getting your dads for Christmas? I need to find something for Mom. Want to go shopping?"

"If I have to."

She laughed. "I guess you really aren't gay or you'd be a much better shopping partner." She gave my thigh an affectionate bump with her foot before disappearing into the bathroom.

I swallowed down the flood of nausea with a *gulp*. She'd only been joking. It was a lame stereotype that gay men liked shopping, and I knew Olivia didn't really believe it. She'd been trying to make me feel better since I'd reacted so strongly earlier.

"Fuck me," I muttered. Not that anyone had, which was all on me. I was gay. I could download a dozen apps and find a hookup in Hell's Kitchen in five minutes. "Fuck," I muttered again, finishing the rest of the beer even though it wouldn't settle my nerves.

Most people wouldn't care that I was gay. My dads and the family would accept me. Marrying Logan might have been a massive mistake on Mom's part—boy, had the shiny glow dulled on that relationship quickly—but in the end, he'd been the best change to my life she ever made. Even if it took me years to realize.

My friends would support me too. Olivia, the med school crowd I was still getting to know. Asher apparently already knew? A reminder that made me squirm and leap off the couch to start pacing.

I'd considered saying those two little words—*I'm gay*—a million times. Most people would think it was insane that I had two fathers and was afraid to come out. It probably was, but that didn't change the cold fist of fear that still had a grip on me.

What was I even afraid of? Not being believed—like people would think it couldn't be true that I could have two dads and coincidentally be queer too.

Most of all, I was terrified people would think it *wasn't* a coincidence. That Logan and Seth had turned me gay or some bullshit.

Olivia's phone chimed as she came out of the bathroom, and she muttered, "Good thing I'm still up," before swiping the screen. "Hey, Mom! How's Japan? What time is it? It's late here."

"I know it is, but since when are you hitting the pillow before two a.m.?"

"She has a point," I said.

Olivia rolled her eyes and faced the phone toward me. On screen, Angela called out, "Hiya, sugar! How are your exams going?" She wore a fuchsia suit, and her blonde hair was still almost bigger than she was.

"Good, thanks."

"I was just gabbing with Seth the other day. He and Logan are so proud of you. You'll be a doctor in no time."

That still felt a million years away, but I thanked her. I knew Seth and Logan were proud of me, but it was sad how happy it made me to have it independently confirmed.

Would they still be proud if they knew how stupid I'd been?

My stomach clenched as I nodded and smiled to whatever Angela was saying about the best sushi she'd ever had. It was better for everyone if I dealt with it myself. And I had—Reid was lending me the money, and that would be that.

"Connor, will you please tell my daughter she's being a silly goose?"

I refocused. "Um…"

Olivia sighed. "Mom, I'm not qualified for this board."

"How so?" Angela asked. "This is a charity to help teenagers. You were recently a teenager. They want young people to have a voice instead of a bunch of old fogies like me. And it ties in perfectly with your studies."

I said, "Totally. You want to work in the nonprofit sector. This is an awesome opportunity."

"Stop with the imposer syndrome," Angela said.

Olivia laughed. "*Imposter* syndrome, Mother. And fine, you're right."

Angela whooped. "Connor, you're my witness! Olivia Barker-

Robertson said I'm right."

"Duly noted."

I waved bye to Angela and took my textbook to my room as she and Olivia started bickering about Olivia needing to give her little sister more attention. I flopped onto my bed, not bothering to open the textbook. There was no way I could focus.

Especially not when I'd held hands with Reid Cabot.

It'd been bizarre to hang with Reid without Asher there. Reid had always seemed so grown-up and sophisticated to me. He'd barely paid me any attention before, but now we somehow felt like equals.

I was apparently someone he could pretend to date and people didn't laugh their asses off at the concept. Teenage me was amazed.

And horny.

God, the way he'd had his arm around me. He'd smelled like a forest in the best way, and his suit had been perfectly tailored to his long, lean body. I'd had a million daydreams about what being Reid Cabot's boyfriend would be like.

I'd once seen him kiss a girl at a party Asher and I had only been able to attend because it was Asher's house too and I was spending the weekend. Reid and his college girlfriend were drinking with their friends before heading out to a club.

"Attend" was a strong word. Asher and I had lurked in the background, gulping any booze we could get our hands on from red Solo cups. Even rich kids in Manhattan weren't above Solo cups.

The memory of Reid kissing his girlfriend was vivid yet fuzzy. I only had a vague recollection of her being…girl-shaped. It had been all Reid. His expensive jeans clinging to his ass. The way he'd smiled at her like she was the only one in the room even though hip-hop was blasting and some obnoxious guy was bumping into everyone as he "danced" around the living room.

Reid had whispered to her and kissed her like she was something fragile before enclosing her in his arms. I'd watched from behind a tall potted plant in which someone had left a crushed can of beer, aching for it to be me with Reid.

Now it was.

"As if," I muttered aloud before putting on my noise-canceling headphones to block out Angela's nasal Texas twang that could wake the dead.

Reid would never look at me like he had that girl. This was a temporary arrangement. The only place Reid Cabot would actually be my boyfriend was in my wildest dreams.

Chapter Five

Reid

HOLDING MY BREATH, I strode from my office as quietly as I could while still appearing confident and not as if I were a teenager sneaking out past curfew.

"Reid."

I jolted at the quiet command and painted a pleasant, neutral expression on my face as I turned to Grandmother's glass-fronted office. She was typically only in twice a week given all her social commitments, and I'd avoided her until now.

The door was ajar, and I stepped inside. "I didn't realize you were here today," I lied.

Grandmother peered at me over the top of her sleek reading glasses. "I'm still president of this company."

"Of course. I just know how busy the holiday season is for you."

"Mm. I presume you're leaving early to attend the Lawrences' tree lighting."

I resisted reminding her that six-thirteen p.m. wasn't "early" to leave work. She wasn't going to change after all these years. "Yes."

Her eyes on a stack of paperwork, she asked, "And are you going alone?"

Here we go.

"I'm going with Connor." It had been a week since I'd dropped the bombshell, and I was surprised it had taken this long for Grandmother to address it. "My boyfriend," I added.

Still not looking at me, she said, "Are you sure it's…suitable?"

"Am I sure *what* is suitable?"

Even as I reminded myself I was an adult and there was nothing she could do to prevent me from dating whomever I wanted, my heart raced. I wanted to loosen my tie. It had been so much easier before I'd come out. Safer.

I scoffed at myself for being melodramatic. I was a wealthy, cis white man. I was quite safe even if my grandmother found my bisexuality distasteful and inconvenient. Besides, pretending to date Connor had been my choice.

She faced me squarely now, still sitting behind the oak desk that had been her father's. The rest of the office was modern and monochrome compared to the scuffed wood with drink rings staining the right-hand surface. Whether from coffee or whiskey, we'd never truly know.

"This young man is, well, *young.*"

"Connor's twenty-three. I'm only six years older. He's an adult like Asher."

For a moment, I thought she might actually snort before she said, "Your brother might be nominally an adult, but we both know he's not quite there yet."

"Maybe he would be if he had more responsibility. He could go to the Lawrences' party instead of me."

"Veto. You know how important these events are to maintaining and elevating our position. Which is why I think it's best you attend alone. Cecilia will be there."

"Who?"

She glared. "Cecilia Weston, as you well know. I don't understand why you refuse to take her for dinner. The club has a wonderful holiday menu."

"Because I have a boyfriend."

Grandmother exhaled noisily. "If you insist."

"I do! Connor's my boyfriend. He's smart and sweet and has the cutest dimple when he's happy."

"How can I argue with a dimple?" She raised her hands in surrender before flipping a page from the file on her desk. "I'm sure the Lawrences will be impressed."

Gritting my teeth, I said, "You're welcome to attend instead."

Friday night with Connor would be far better spent starting on the New Yorker activity list I'd made. We could go down to the Meatpacking District and get dinner from one of the vendors at Chelsea Market.

There was a pop-up art exhibit involving household objects crafted out of candy canes. To me, a random modern art pop-up was quintessential New York.

"You know we receive far too many invitations not to divide and conquer. Did you work on the proposal this week?"

I blinked at the abrupt shift of topics. For a foolish, ridiculous moment, I thought she meant my secret project—which was nonsensical since it was *secret*. I automatically answered, "Of course," which was my stock response when my mind had drifted and I wasn't sure what was being discussed.

That happened far more often than I liked to admit.

"This island is an emerging market. We don't want to let Marriott get there before us."

Right. *That* proposal. "Yes, it's all I've been working on. It's not quite ready yet. It'll be next week."

"Mm. All right, darling." She flipped another page, her gaze lowering.

I'd have to work extra hours to get it done, but I would. We'd opened plenty of resorts, and this one wouldn't be much different. She didn't have to know I'd spent the week researching the list of activities for Connor. I was the Senior Vice President under our CEO, who answered to Grandmother yet performed the majority of the practical duties.

Once upon a time, I'd been highly invested in my role and the company. Now, I was damn lucky the CEO was Type A and happy to do most tasks herself.

It was reassuring Grandmother had called me "darling," as pathetic as that was. Even when my father had been alive, Grandmother had been the authority figure I'd most wanted to please for as long as I could remember.

"And you'll arrive early at our holiday breakfast at the community center?"

"As always." It was weeks away, so I wasn't sure why she was asking now.

I attended her Christmas Day event annually. It was sponsored by Utopia and featured hot food as well as baskets of nonperishables and giftwrapped toys. Asher hadn't been since before college, but I supposed I couldn't blame him for not wanting to be up early on Christmas morning for Grandmother's photo ops, no matter how worthy the cause.

I asked, "You'll be ready to dish out the apple-cinnamon oatmeal?"

"With ladle in hand."

"Your annual use of a kitchen utensil."

Grandmother laughed genuinely, her eyes crinkling as she looked up. "Yes, darling. As I've told you since you were a boy, it's better to leaving the cooking to the experts."

I returned her smile. "Remember when Asher and I snuck downstairs at midnight on Christmas Eve to bake cookies for Santa?"

"How could I forget the fire department's visit?" She shook her head ruefully. "The co-op board was not pleased. You were ten. You should have known better."

My smile grew brittle. "Yes, well, I haven't tried baking since."

While I had fond memories of attempting to bake cookies without a recipe with my little brother on a step stool beside me, the aftermath had been decidedly un-festive.

"I have to meet Connor," I said. "See you next week."

She flipped another page so forcefully I heard it rip. "I'll be here over the weekend making sure everything's in order for the general meeting in the new year."

I groaned internally at the implication that I should also be working through the weekend. "Sounds good," I said noncommittally. "Have a lovely evening."

As I pulled the door half-closed, Grandmother murmured, "All this will be yours sooner rather than later."

I turned back warily. "Why do you say that?" Was she sick? She didn't look it—granted she'd had some work done, but she could pass for fifteen years younger than she was.

"Because it's true." She examined me over her glasses. "I won't live forever despite my best efforts."

My stomach tightened. "Are you—"

"I'm perfectly fine. No need to be dramatic. I just want to make sure you remember your priorities." She ran a palm over the oak. "I'd always imagined your father sitting here by now." She swallowed thickly, and for a terrifying moment, I thought she might cry.

I'd never seen her express the emotions she *must* keep buried deep down. Dad had been her only child, and I know she'd loved and mourned him. Now I was the one to shoulder her expectations.

"Grandmother…"

She snapped back to business, flipping another page. "This desk still has plenty of wear in it. You'll look just right sitting here."

All I could think to say was, "Thank you."

"Give my best to the Lawrences."

With that dismissal, I nodded and escaped.

In the elevator, I ordered a ride to the Upper East Side. As I watched the app find a driver, a text from Connor appeared at the top of the screen. I quickly tapped it.

Hey. I'm on my way. Meet you outside? They might not let me in otherwise.

Chuckling, I replied:

You must be wearing the leather jacket again. If you bring the motorcycle, they might mistake you for a gang member. You know, if gangs looked like they did in movies from the fifties.

I watched the three dots appear, flickering as he typed.

You're saying I should leave my switchblade at home? Fine.

In the lobby, the security guard said, "Wow, you look happy for once, Mr. Cabot." He hastily added, "Must be because it's Friday!"

I realized I was grinning. "You got it, Drew. TGIF."

In the car, I went back to the New Yorker list and texted Asher a question. A few minutes later, he replied:

Huh? Why?

Grumbling under my breath, I muttered, "Just answer." What did it matter to him? Before I could respond to my brother, my phone buzzed with an incoming video call. The ride share driver was engrossed in his own conversation through his Bluetooth headset, so I swiped to accept.

Asher's face filled my screen with a frown, his white kitchen cabinets behind him. "Why do you care what Connor likes to do?"

I'd simply asked Asher if Connor would prefer walking the High Line or across the Brooklyn Bridge. I'd received wildly conflicting advice from several friends for my top New Yorker activities, so I was going with my gut.

"Just curious," I said dismissively.

What was the harm in tailoring the list to Connor's preferences? I'd do the same for anyone. Not that the list was part of the deal we'd made, but I'd enjoyed planning the options. I'd found myself looking forward to seeing Connor's reactions to the items on the list and wondering which ones he'd be most excited for…

"That's a really weird thing to be curious about."

"It's nothing. Forget it." Why was he making a big deal out of nothing?

He exhaled with a huff through his nose. "I'm not sure this is such a good idea."

"You were all for it on Thanksgiving." It was too late now. The idea of calling it off made me strangely antsy.

"I thought it might be good for him. Loosen a few of his screws. Why are you asking about the High Line? Gamma sure as hell won't be there. So why would you be taking Connor there? Or across the Brooklyn Bridge, where Gamma *definitely* won't be. The only way she leaves Manhattan is by air."

I really didn't feel like explaining the list to my brother. It wasn't a big deal. The driver laid on the horn at the perfect time, and I shrugged and motioned to my ear as if I hadn't heard the question.

Apparently he didn't feel like repeating it since now he asked, "Is Connor going to the Lawrences' party tonight?"

"Yeah, I'm meeting him there now."

Asher screwed up his face. "I hope people there won't be weird about it. You and him. Not that it's real, but…"

"I'm sure it'll be fine." I fidgeted and readjusted the seatbelt, which threatened to strangle me. "Morgan and his wife seemed very welcoming."

"I guess. Will Gamma be there?"

"No, she has another party. You'd know this if you did your part."

"Hey, I show up to Gamma's events. Well, most. You can handle the rest."

Not that I had a choice. It had always been on me, particularly after our father died, but before then too. I'd dutifully attended the endless events and smiled and made small talk and schmoozed even when I was a kid.

Addison's voice echoed in my mind: "*How will the rich white man ever survive these hardships?*" I was being ridiculous to complain.

Asher blurted, "I don't want Connor to get hurt."

I blinked. "What? Why would he get hurt?"

After hesitating, Asher said, "He's been through a lot. He's finally settled, and now he's in med school. I don't want this to mess him up."

"Why would it mess him up? We have an agreement. An arrangement. It's…business."

Asher made a dubious sound and mumbled something I couldn't make out. I braced myself on the back of the passenger seat as the car swerved around a double-parked delivery van.

"Has Connor mentioned needing money to you?" I asked.

Asher's eyebrows flew up. "No. Why?"

"Nothing," I said dismissively. All right, so this debt wasn't the source of Asher's disquiet. "Hey, did I imagine that you told me Connor's queer? I could have sworn you mentioned it when you guys were at Rencliffe."

"Thanks for spilling that, by the way. Connor's barely answered my texts this week."

"He told me he's studying for a big anatomy exam. I'm sure he's just busy."

"Glad he's talking to *you*."

I shot him a grin. "I'm irresistible."

Asher looked like he was going to say more, but eventually rolled his eyes. "Apparently."

"So… Do you think he really is queer?" It didn't matter, but I'd chewed over the question all week.

"Maybe. I think so." Asher shrugged. "He says no, and he's the one who gets to decide. I dunno. I've been waiting for him to come out for years. I could be wrong."

"Wouldn't be the first time."

He held up his middle finger. "Hilarious."

"What makes you think he's not straight?"

"The way he stared at Greg McBride's ass at Rencliffe, for starters. Not to mention—" Asher broke off and looked away.

"What?"

He seemed to ponder it, about to say something but cutting himself off again. "It's a vibe, I guess. He's always been tightly wound. He's never seemed interested in girls. Which doesn't mean anything. It's little things that added up, I guess. What do I know? I just don't want things to get weird."

"Don't worry about it." Asher was being dramatic. As the car pulled up outside the building, I added, "Gotta go!"

Waiting on the sidewalk under the glow of a streetlight, I added a tip for the driver in the app and peered up and down the dark street. No sign of him, but I was early.

I opened my notes app and surveyed the list, deciding to keep both the High Line and the bridge. There was no reason I had to limit the New Yorker activities to ten.

As Connor rounded the corner in his leather jacket, he saw me and lifted his hand in a wave. I waved back, and as his cheek dimpled, a flare of excitement sparked through me. What would he think of the list?

His cheeks looked flushed with the cold. "Hey. Am I late!" The deepness of his voice still surprised me.

"Right on time. No motorcycle?"

"Nah, I took the subway here. My bike's in Albany. Costs way too much to park it in Manhattan. Can't wait to ride at Christmas."

I shuddered. "I still think it's way too risky."

"You and my dads will get along great." Was he blushing now? He quickly added, "Not that you'll meet them. This isn't—whatever."

"Right." Was it odd that I *did* want to meet Connor's parents? "Ready?" I held out my hand.

For a long moment, Connor only stared at my gloved hand, and I was about to awkwardly retract it when he said, "Right. Boyfriends," and took it with a firm grip. Our leather gloves squeaked.

My stomach flip-flopped.

We made our way past the massive, draped tree in the foyer, and Connor gave his coat to a staff member with very slightly less reluctance than he had at Thanksgiving. He wore dark jeans that hugged his lean hips and a form-fitting sweater.

"Nice," I said, running my hand down his arm. "Cashmere?"

"Uh-huh," he rasped, then cleared this throat. "It was a gift from Angela Barker. Olivia picked it out." He leaned closer. "Speaking of Olivia, I told her the truth." He fidgeted suddenly. "Most of it. Not about the…loan."

"Right. No problem. Everything's taken care of?"

"Yep. You got the payback schedule I sent?"

I smiled. "Yes. But as I said, there's no rush. I'm not worried about it."

Connor jammed his hands in his pockets. "That's nice of you, but I am. I don't like owing anyone."

Morgan approached as we entered the living room, where guests chatted under a high ceiling by beige furniture. The holiday decorations were rich, velvety green and red, and servers with trays of hors d'oeuvres circulated.

As we chatted with Morgan and others, I was aware once again of garnering more attention than usual. Everyone was friendly, and I was relieved as I chewed over what Asher had said. He was protective of his best friend, which was admirable and to be expected.

If Connor really was queer like me, maybe this would be a way for him to… Give it a test drive. Find his sea legs? Whichever metaphor fit the bill.

As I made small talk with Paul and Brittany Matheson, I monitored Connor. He nodded and made the right listening noises but gave off a jittery vibe. I laid my hand on the small of his back.

"Want a break?"

Connor nodded, and I guided him into the adjoining dining room. The table was laden with more finger foods, and we helped ourselves to a few bites. This seemed like a good time to bring up the list. My belly swooped, which was very strange since this wasn't *important*.

If he wasn't into the activities, it was no problem. I'd gotten carried away, but it had been a welcome distraction. Nothing more. Would he even remember we'd talked about it?

I popped a walnut and gouda tartlet into my mouth. "About the nuts…"

Connor swallowed a plump shrimp, dropping the tail into his napkin. "Nuts?"

"The street nuts. Sorry, I wasn't clear. I…" There was a drop of red cocktail sauce at the corner of his mouth, and I couldn't look away. "You've got…"

"Oh!" His tongue darted out just before he wiped with his napkin. "Gone?"

I was still staring at Connor's mouth. "Yes."

"So, what about the nuts? I haven't had any yet."

Right. Focus on nuts. I laughed, since my mind immediately zoomed down all sorts of different avenues.

"That's good," I said. "That you haven't had them. We'll have them together. I mean, if you want to. I thought it would be fun."

The dimple appeared in his cheek. "Totally."

"I made a New Yorker activity list. We talked about it briefly last week."

"Right, yeah." He smiled.

I wrapped my hand around my phone in my pocket. Why did

I feel like I was about to give a presentation to the board at work? Connor was just my little brother's best friend. I'd known him for years—even if he was different now.

"Reid?"

"Yes." I pulled out my phone and opened the notes app. "I've created a list of what I believe are quintessential New Yorker experiences. For me, at least. Because every New Yorker will have their own top ten, and some could be wildly different. And you can veto any of these options for any reason."

"*Okaay.* This sounds weirdly official."

I laughed. "Sorry, 'veto' is Grandmother's favorite word, and it rubbed off on me."

"All right, cool. I accept the terms and conditions."

"Are you sure? I might have sneaky clauses in there."

"I'll exercise my veto power in that case. Besides, I trust you."

The rush of pleasure those three words—*I trust you*—gave me was a surprise. I nodded and gulped my glass of bubbly. We both took a spring roll from a passing server, and I swallowed it too quickly in my eagerness, which made me cough.

"Okay?" Connor asked, leaning closer.

"Yep! No need for first aid." After another sip of my drink, I added, "These are in no particular order, and like I said, you can veto." I hadn't looked at the note on my phone since I'm memorized the list, but now I was questioning my choices.

Connor's brows lowered in a cute little quizzical expression. "I'm sure I'll like them all."

"Of course. It's not a big deal." And wait—*cute?* I needed to slow down on the champagne. I was practically lightheaded. "Number one—but not in any order of importance."

He nodded seriously. "Understood."

"Visit an underground club or bar in the Village. I have one in mind."

His eyes widened, which was also cute. "Oh! That sounds

awesome. I'm down."

Off to an excellent start, but I hesitated. I did look at the list then. Even though I'd said no particular order, it would be better to present the options in an optimal way.

"*Annnd* number two is eat street nuts?" Connor asked.

"Yes. Sorry. I'm not quite satisfied with the list. Why don't we start with those, and I'll keep refining."

Actually, rethinking it now, surprising Connor with the list items as we went would be far more fun. Excitement bubbled up. Gifts were always more fun when you didn't know what was under the tree. Not that I'd had anything under the tree in years. Or a tree, for that matter.

"Sure." That quizzical expression was back, and it was still cute.

What was happening to me?

"Everyone, if we can gather in the foyer for the unveiling?" Morgan called as servers ushered us through.

Though the Lawrences' foyer was massive, it was still crowded with the guests and a ten-person choir in red and gold robes gathered around the base of the tree. The lights were dimmed, and we all *ohhed* and *ahhed* on cue as the curtain draping the dark tree was dropped. Even before the lights were on, it was impressive.

The soprano-led choir launched into "Angels We Have Heard on High" as children hung the final ceremonial ornaments on the tree, using the grand curving staircase to reach the higher branches.

As the song ramped up and the soprano earned her paycheck with a multi-syllable "*Gloria*" that sent chills down my spine, someone flipped an unseen switch.

Even though I knew it was coming—we were standing there in the foyer for a tree-lighting after all—I blinked in surprise as the glittering multi-colored lights blazed to life with a golden star on top. The whole tree seemed to shimmer as if it was alive somehow.

We clapped and exclaimed on cue. I leaned down and whispered to Connor, "They really outdid themselves this year."

He didn't immediately answer, his gazed locked on the tree. "I wish Seth could see it. He loves Christmas. Are we allowed to take a pic?"

"Allowed? The Lawrences would love nothing more than for their tree to trend on social media."

Connor diligently took several pictures of the tree from different angles, then tapped out a message, presumably to Seth.

"You're a good son," I said.

He shook his head dismissively, but bit his lip as if trying to hide a smile. I really wanted to see that dimple again.

The party went on, and I had to make dull small talk when I wanted to hear more about what Connor was studying, even though when I'd asked, he'd demurred and said it was "boring." After doing my duty and schmoozing with everyone I felt Grandmother would prioritize, I managed to corral Connor into one of the hallways off the foyer.

"You ready to go?" I asked in a low voice.

"If you are?"

"Definitely. Let's get our coats and make an early exit."

"Sorry to interrupt," Morgan said as he appeared.

"You're not!" Connor and I exclaimed in perfect guilty unison. Laughing, I asked, "What can I do for you?"

"My mom just wants a picture by the tree. You too, Connor."

"It's okay," Connor quickly said. "I'm not photogenic at all."

I said, "What? That's not true." I'd scrolled back through his Insta once or twice this week, and he had great pics there. Some selfies with his med school friends and a bunch with Asher over the years. It was fascinating to chart his growth from the Rencliffe days as he'd filled out into a man.

There was one photo of Connor straddling his motorcycle in the leather jacket that did make riding it seem more appealing. I still thought it was too risky, but he'd looked so satisfied and in control.

Connor waved us off. "I'll see you after."

I followed Morgan, who was talking about New Year's Eve plans, and looked back to watch Connor tapping at his phone. His pants clung to his long, lean thighs, and I imagined riding behind him on the bike, my legs hugging his hips—

Then the floor somehow disappeared, and there was nothing I could do to fight gravity as I flew.

Chapter Six

Connor

A S SOMETHING HEAVY *crashed* and glass *smashed*, voices rose in alarm. I spun around to find Reid…gone. But Morgan Lawrence, his wife, Louise, and a few other people were staring down with wide eyes. I raced to the top of the three steps leading into the foyer.

Reid sprawled at the bottom on his left side. He laughed tightly. "Who put those stairs there?"

"Oh my god, are you okay?" Morgan exclaimed, still rooted to the spot staring down at Reid.

I crouched at Reid's side before anyone even moved. "It's okay," I said, channeling the confidence my clinical skills professor reminded us was key. *Fake it until you make it.* "Stay very still, okay?"

"I'm fine!" Reid pushed himself up to sitting with his left hand, wincing.

"I'm calling an ambulance," Louise said.

"No!" Reid tried to jump to his feet, but I gripped his shoulder, keeping him sitting. If he hit his head, I didn't want him to stand and pass out.

Reid said, "I just tripped." His cheeks flushed, and he glanced around at the gathering crowd. "I'm clumsy, that's all. Thanks for the concern."

Cataloging his potential injuries, I gently took his right hand, where he'd been holding the shattered wine glass. He'd definitely cut himself, and Louise handed me a cloth napkin I quickly pressed into Reid's palm after making sure there was no glass remaining.

"I'm getting up!" he hissed to me.

I could imagine how embarrassed he was, although of course he had no reason to be. His dark brown eyes implored me, and I relented, holding his right arm as he stood.

"My boyfriend's a doctor," he said loudly. "He'll take good care of me. Thanks for your concern."

Morgan and Louise led us into a small bathroom, and pulled out a first aid kit from under the sink before Reid waved them away with a smile and closed the door.

"*Fuck.*" He leaned back against the door. "Please let no one have caught that on their phone."

Staying close to him in case he got dizzy, I said, "Don't worry. Everyone falls and stuff."

He groaned, closing his eyes. His face was red, and in the bathroom's bright light, I could spot the very faint five o'clock shadow coming in on his chin and cheeks. And on his neck when I leaned a little closer…

Nope. Continue assessment of the patient. Examine his injuries, not his stubble. Or his Adam's apple, or the hollow of his throat.

"I can't believe I just did that," he muttered, eyes still closed.

"What happened? Were you looking at your phone or something?"

He opened his eyes, immediately dropping his gaze to the white tile floor. "Yep. Wasn't looking where I was going."

"Happens to all of us. Now look at me."

He did.

Holy shit, we were standing *really* close in the tiny bathroom. One of those… What did people call them? Powder rooms.

"Um…" Assess the patient! "Are you dizzy?"

"No. Just from humiliation."

"Did you hit your head?"

"No." His mouth pinched. "I'm sure I didn't."

"You don't sound sure."

"No, I'm sure. I didn't hit my head."

"Let me see."

Gently, I took his face in my hands and ran my fingertips over the curves of his head, naming the bones in my head to stay focused on my job and not the softness of his thick hair. I was going to be humiliatingly hard in a second.

"Don't feel any swelling," I murmured.

Not on Reid's skull, anyway.

"I'm telling you I didn't hit my head." His breath was warm on my face.

"Okay." Ugh, my voice came out all fluttery. I dropped my hands. "I'll just do the concussion protocol."

Reid groaned, and the sound did *not* help my efforts to stay professional. "I'm fine! Aside from injuring my pride, I cut my hand. That's it." He pushed away from the door, but I didn't budge.

Which meant that now we were practically kissing we were so close.

Somehow, I managed to speak. "If you didn't hit your head, you'll pass no prob."

"Come on. I should get back out there. Can you put a Band-Aid on my hand?"

"Do I have to go ask if someone *does* have video of it?"

Reid sighed. "I surrender."

We were *so close*. The heat from his body seemed to radiate.

"Are you going to do something?" he asked, his gaze dropping. Not to the floor this time, but I swear to my mouth.

Did *I* hit my head? There was no way Reid Cabot was looking at my mouth like he wanted to kiss it.

No. Way.

I blurted, "What day is it?"

"Friday."

I nodded. "Date?" I could do this. Clinical. Professional.

Reid rattled off the full date, adding, "the new millennium."

"I'm going to say a few words, and I want you to remember them and repeat back to me. Okay?"

Reid put his finger to his temple. "Should I try to read your mind?"

I had to laugh. "Not this time. Okay, here we go."

"Okay, here we go," Reid repeated.

"Not yet."

"Not yet," he said.

"You're giving big older brother energy right now." Somehow it was still sexy but now wasn't the time to examine that. He was the patient, and I was the not-actually-a-doctor-yet. "I'm starting now." As Reid opened his mouth, I pressed my finger to his lips.

A slight puff of warm air met my finger as our eyes met. My mouth went dry. How many fantasies had I had over the years about being this close to Reid?

Fantasies about Reid looking down at me with his eyes dark and intense…

Jesus, maybe his pupils were dilating because of the concussion—which I was supposed to be ruling out!

Dropping my hand, I dictated a little too loudly, "Cat. Horse. Meadow. Bus. Cafeteria."

Reid's lips quirked. "Are the cat and horse friends? Did they take the bus to the cafeteria, or are they still in the meadow?"

I had to laugh again even as I gave him what I hoped was a stern, authoritative expression. "You're being a terrible patient."

"Yes, doctor. Apologies."

I took a deep breath and exhaled. "Can you remember the

words?"

"Cat. Horse. Meadow. Bus. Cafeteria." Reid's voice was low and confident.

"Very good."

"Thank you, doctor."

Lust wasn't just sparking—it was erupting.

This isn't real. He's joking around. Not. Real.

"Anything else?" Reid asked softly, his eyes locked on me.

We were only a few inches apart, and I wanted to lean into the heat of his body... Jesus, Reid could have a concussion, and I was being incredibly unprofessional. I might not have been a doctor yet, but I had to act like it.

"Please name the twelve months backward."

"Ohh. A challenge. December." He paused. "Rebmeced."

It was a struggle to concentrate as it was, and it took me an embarrassing beat to get it. "Very good. You can just recite the twelve months from December back to January."

"Where's the challenge in that?"

By the time Reid finished saying each month itself backward with "Yraunaj," we were laughing.

I said, "Congrats—you passed the standardized assessment of concussion test."

He bowed slightly. "Thank you, doctor."

My pulse fluttered, and I cast around for what to say next, landing on, "Hand!" I cleared my throat. "Um, let me see your hand."

I maneuvered him to sit on the closed toilet seat and bent over his wound in the light of the vanity. In the cramped space, I had to stand around his leg, his knee between mine. With tweezers from the first aid kit, I made sure I hadn't missed any glass slivers before I disinfected the two small cuts on Reid's palm.

"Ouch."

Chuckling, I applied a large Band-Aid, pressing the adhesive to his skin. "All set."

"Aren't you going to kiss it better?"

Boom.

My heart and dick came to life as I met Reid's dark gaze. He was only joking—*obviously* he was joking! A wry smile played on his full lips, and this was the part where I laughed and made some joke or did *anything* except stare at him with all my blood rushing south.

Reid's smile faded. We stared at each other with his injured hand still cradled in mine. I couldn't breathe. I could be in his lap in a heartbeat and—

"Is everything okay?" Morgan asked as he knocked loudly.

I jolted back, almost falling myself and only saved by the wall. "Yep!" I shouted, opening the door.

We left after assuring the hosts Reid didn't need an ambulance, and my mind raced as the car Reid had ordered drove through the park to the west side. Reid groaned, and I snapped to attention.

"Headache?" I asked.

"Yeah." He pinched the bridge of his nose. "I can't believe I did that. Grandmother will not be happy."

"When did this headache start?"

He groaned again. "I passed the concussion test! This is just a schmoozing headache. It's exhausting having to be my best self with so many people. I'm fine. Unless you want to stay over and wake me up every hour to ask me who the president is."

"That's not necessary."

"Right, because I didn't hit my head, and I don't have a concussion. Glad you agree."

"No, because that's been debunked. There's no need to stop a concussed person from sleeping in the vast majority of cases. They need sleep. If you can carry on a conversation, walk without difficulty, and your pupils aren't dilated, sleep is indicated."

"Great. Then I can go to bed and try to forget this."

"Let me see your pupils again."

"Isn't it a little dark?" He laughed. "Okay, why don't you stay at my place tonight? You can check my pupils and put me to bed. I mean, if you'll be worried otherwise."

"Right. Yeah. Okay." What was I doing? This would be torture!

"I have a guest room. All above board. Not that you would think I'd…" He waved his left hand.

"Of course not."

We both laughed awkwardly. Because while I'd always thought Reid was smooth and sophisticated and cool, it turned out he was a little awkward like me. Well, I was a *lot* awkward, but still.

Reid lived in one of those amazing prewar apartment buildings on the Upper West Side. The doorman ushered us in, and there was a concierge as well. I half-expected a guy waiting in the elevator to push the button, but Reid did it himself.

The wallpapered hallway was bright, yet the light was golden and the light fixtures gleaming. Reid's front door led into a small foyer with closet. As I toed off my dress shoes, I gaped at the huge windows in the living room. The ambient light from the city cast a warm glow.

"Wow. This place is amazing," I said. Reid's style seemed a little monotone, but the space was incredible. I couldn't begin to imagine what it cost.

"Thanks." Reid seemed uncomfortable as he motioned to doors on either side of the living room, which held a leather sectional, massive wall-mounted TV, and a full dining table and smooth-edged chairs. "My bedroom's on that side, and the guest room is next to the kitchen."

"Cool. No Christmas tree yet?"

Reid seemed taken aback. It was admittedly a dumb question

since there was clearly no Christmas tree. I could imagine exactly where it would go by the window beyond the dining table. Seth would have a field day decorating in here.

"I've never had one."

"You did as a kid, though. Right?" Asher and I had never spent the holidays together, and thinking about it now, I supposed he hadn't said much about his family traditions.

"Sure." Reid shrugged and flipped on a lamp. "When I was young. By the time I was in high school, we'd outgrown it. We didn't have Christmas morning with presents under the tree—too busy going to events. Grandmother's charity breakfasts."

"Oh." That sounded like torture. "I guess you think it's weird my dads still put up a tree even though I'm not a kid."

"Of course not. I'm sure Christmas at your house is very…cozy. Let me show you the guest room. Oh, you'll need pajamas."

"It's fine. I can just sleep in my underwear."

Reid nodded and cleared his throat but still brought me a Knicks T-shirt after he showed me the brown and beige guest room. It had its own bathroom that was stocked with packages of toothbrushes and everything I could need.

We watched TV for a while, Reid flipping channels until landing on *Scrooged*. We watched the rest of it with the commercials even though we probably could have found it on one of the streaming services.

"How's your headache?" I asked as the credits rolled. I'd been surreptitiously monitoring him, and he seemed fine. He'd relaxed into the couch beside me, and we'd had more wine.

Reid smiled. "Much better. Thank you, doctor."

Shit, the way he said that made me hot all over. "Let me look at your eyes again," I said in a weirdly gravelly voice.

Reid swallowed a sip of red wine, and it stained his lips for a moment. He nodded.

Since Reid had his feet up on the leather ottoman that was also a sort of coffee table, I couldn't stand in front of him. Instead, I just kneeled next to him on the couch with my feet tucked under me. Leaning close, I examined his pupils.

His lashes were thick, and there was one sitting just under his eye. I gently grasped it and held it up on my fingertip the way my mom had years ago. "Your pupils are good. And you get to make a wish."

"A wish," Reid repeated, his eyes locked with mine.

Ugh, he probably thought I was a dumb kid. "I guess you already have everything you want." I started to move, but he grasped my wrist.

"I still get my wish."

Reid closed his eyes, and I was frozen in place, his fingers warm on my skin. Then he opened his eyes and blew a puff of air to send the eyelash flying.

"I guess you can't tell me what you wished for or it-it won't come true," I stammered. God, he was gorgeous. How many times had I daydreamed about being this close to Reid Cabot, and now here I was…

"Those are the rules, doctor."

"Yep!" I bolted back, almost tumbling off the couch as I found my feet. "We should go to bed," I said.

And I said it *out loud*.

I swear, Reid's eyes darkened, his lips parting as his gaze dropped down my body.

Whoa. No. I was clearly imagining it. There was no way Reid would actually be into me. He thought I was straight, and I was an awkward kid he'd known forever. No way in hell.

I jerked a thumb toward the guest room. "'Night! If you feel sick, wake me up, okay?"

"I will." His full lips curved up. "Thanks again, doctor."

I escaped without blowing my load right then and there, so I counted it as a win.

MY PHONE BUZZED around five as I scrolled mindlessly after barely sleeping. I blinked in surprise at Logan's name and jabbed the screen.

"Hello?" I whispered, throwing off the covers in the very soft, very comfortable bed in the guest room. "What's wrong?" I curled my toes into the thick carpet.

"Nothing. What the hell are you doing awake? Don't tell me—you haven't been to bed yet."

He was mostly right since I'd been too wound up to relax, but I said, "Up early studying."

"Whatever floats your boat. I was just going to leave a message."

I rolled my eyes. "You know you could text me."

An engine rumbled, and I figured Logan was in his truck. He said, "And you know I hate all that stuff. Since when do you get up early? You're usually dead to the world with your ringer off until noon."

"I guess I'm growing up. I've had early classes all semester, FYI."

"No shit. I guess you are. Have any exams yet?"

"One. I probably bombed it."

Logan barked out a laugh. "You always say that, and you always do amazing."

I paced on the plush area rug. "I dunno. It's not like I'm the smartest one in the room anymore. I wasn't at Harvard either."

"You're still damn smart. Don't sell yourself short."

I had to smile at how emphatic Logan's tone was. "Yeah. Okay. Seth's all right?"

"He's good. Going Christmas shopping, so you'd better get

your list to him pronto if you want anything. That's what I was calling to say."

Part of me thought I should argue I was too old for that, but I only said, "Okay. Where are you going?"

"Working Saturdays to finish up a job before Christmas. Why are you being so quiet?" He paused. "Got company?"

My heart skipped as I imagined Reid sleeping. On his back, or was he a side or stomach sleeper? Maybe his lips were parted and chest hair sticking up from the low neck of his tank top...

"No!" I protested far too strongly with a strangled laugh. "I mean, yeah. Olivia. Don't want to wake her up."

"Right." Did he sound disappointed? Before I could overthink it, he added, "Oh, I almost forgot. If you and Olivia are free next weekend, Will and Michael invited you to their holiday party. Michael's secretly flying in Will's parents from Scotland, and we're decorating the tree or some shit."

"Awesome. Seth'll love it."

Logan's voice went soft, and I could picture the goofy smile on his face as he said, "Yep."

"And wait, they invited me and...Olivia?" I huffed. "You guys know we're just friends, right? Jesus, you're worse than Angela."

"Nah, it's not that. Will and Michael went to Australia with Angela and her family at Christmas a few years ago, remember? They hung out with Olivia. I'm sure you both have better things to do, but in case you want to come home for the weekend to hang with the lame adults, you're invited."

"Uh, I think we'll pass."

He laughed. "Can't blame ya. You'll be home the weekend before Christmas though, right? For a week at least?"

"*Yes.* But I'm coming back here for New Year's Eve."

"To watch the apple drop?"

"Actual New Yorkers don't go to Times Square on New Year's Eve. That's for tourists."

"Well, la-di-da. So, you're an actual New Yorker now?"

"That remains to be seen." I grinned thinking about Reid's list. "I'm taking an exam on that soon."

"Huh?"

"Nothing. It's a dumb joke."

"Okay, get back to studying for your real exams. You're going to ace them."

I shrugged even though he couldn't see me. "Thanks."

"Hey, one more thing. Have you, uh, heard from Mike?"

The bottom of my stomach dropped, dread crashing through me. I almost asked, "*Who?*" but Michael of Will and Michael always went by his full name.

There was only one Mike we ever talked about, and it had been a long, long time. And "talked about" was an exaggeration.

My lungs constricted, I managed to get out, "No. Why?" It was kind of the truth.

"There was a weird call for you from Florida. The man on the phone gave another name, but I think it was Mike. He's still down there?"

"Dunno. I guess." Before I could stop the stupid words from bursting out, I snapped, "Why? What do you care?"

"I don't." He inhaled audibly, and I could imagine Seth's imaginary voice in Logan's ear telling him not to get mad.

"Okay, whatever." Jesus, why was I acting thirteen again? Logan hated my father, and why shouldn't he?

Why couldn't I?

I forced a deep breath. "Sorry."

"S'okay. I'm glad you haven't talked to him. I know I'm not supposed to say that."

I had to laugh. "It's fine. Anyway, I have to study. Later."

Acid bubbled in my stomach, and I crept into the kitchen to gulp water and poke around in Reid's fridge. Huh. There were actually vegetables and raw meat, like he was going to cook them.

I'd assumed he lived on takeout like me and Asher and Olivia. Like most people I knew.

I opened the cupboards one by one, of course opening every plate, bowl, glass, and mug storage place before finding the food. I should have realized the long cupboard was the pantry, though in my defense, everything in the kitchen including the fridge had identical doors and it was impossible to tell anything apart.

It made me smile that Reid had a bag of goldfish crackers, and I hoped he wouldn't mind if I munched on a few. I wandered to the window in my bare feet and realized the wooden floor was heated. I could see the treetops of Central Park a few avenues over, and lights coming on in other pre-war apartment buildings, including one with actual gargoyles on the roof.

The days were so short in December. The sun wouldn't be up for two hours. I should have probably gone back to bed and tried to sleep, but I stayed by the wide window, sitting sideways on the ledge, eating cheesy goldfish and watching a woman stories below walk a gigantic dog.

The city was so peaceful right now. I wasn't sure I'd ever been up this early to see it when I wasn't rushing to shower and get somewhere. Usually, I rolled out of bed with just enough time to make my first lecture of the day. In undergrad, I'd often missed early classes, but med school was different.

For a moment, I thought I heard something coming from Reid's bedroom. I stayed very still, listening, but there was nothing. I was tempted to peek in on him again, but it would be intrusive. I reminded myself he'd passed all the protocols and needed his sleep.

"So do you," I mumbled to myself, but I stayed on the windowsill. If Reid needed me, I'd be close at hand.

Chapter Seven

Reid

I MAY NOT have had a concussion—I truly didn't hit my head, so definitely not—but the embarrassment was enough to keep my headache lingering.

It was bad enough that my *splat* had been witnessed by so many acquaintances. What was keeping me tossing and turning was that Connor had been there. At least he hadn't seen me go down. I should know since I'd been watching him instead of where I was going.

He'd been at my side before I could really register what had happened. So confident and capable—he'd make an excellent doctor. It was even reassuring to know he was in the guest room on the other side of the apartment.

Good lord, that didn't make any sense. I had a couple of scrapes. I didn't need a doctor—or a med student. There was no reason I should be comforted by Connor staying over.

No reason to look forward to cooking him breakfast or ask him more about how concussion protocols had changed nowadays. Not because I had one, but because I enjoyed listening to him.

It was still early, but after waking before five, my brain refused to quiet. The duvet felt too hot, so I kicked it off and strode naked to the window to crack it open and peek through the blinds.

In the building across from mine, most windows were dark.

Others glowed with the blue light of TVs. Still others had the curtains open and lights on. I smiled to see the old man on the tenth floor sitting at his kitchen table doing what I assumed was his regular crossword.

I'd refused to buy binoculars and be the creepy neighbor, as tempting as it could be when insomnia struck and I found myself in the darkness at the window.

Could anyone see me? I didn't think so since my lights were off, but maybe one of my neighbors was watching, wondering why that naked guy didn't sleep better.

Determined, I stole back under the covers. I'd sleep another hour before getting up to make Connor breakfast. Was there bacon? I could always run out to the bodega if not.

Oh! There was another item for the list: befriending a bodega cat. The cat at my local store was named Bran Muffin, and she always let me pet her.

I rolled to my other side. Then back again. Onto my stomach with one leg pulled up.

"Oh, for…"

With Herculean effort, I resisted grabbing my phone to check the time. Because if there were any notifications, I'd open them. Even if there weren't, I'd be doomscrolling before you could say *blue light doesn't help insomnia.*

Flopping over on my back, I sighed loudly. Addison was right—I needed to get laid. Release the pressure valve. But I obviously wasn't having a booty call with Connor in the guest room.

My mind helpfully filled with images of Connor—his cheek dimpling. His surprised laugh when he let down his guard a fraction. His calm, competent concern when he'd done the concussion tests on me. The way he'd gazed intently, his brown eyes close to mine…

"None of this is real," I repeated in the still of my bedroom.

The swoop of Connor's adorable James Dean hair, the pink of his lips, *dat ass.*

"*Fuck,*" I gritted out, reaching for my cock.

My fully erect cock.

I lunged for the lube in the bedside table. Keeping my lips pressed tight to hold back my moans, I bent my knees and stroked myself. The Band-Aid on my palm added delicious friction even though it was already sliding off.

Honestly, I did try—briefly—to stop thinking about Connor.

It was hopeless.

As I toyed with my nipples with one hand, I thrust up into my fist and imagined Connor was with me.

Kissing me with those pretty pink lips. Those lips stretched around my cock as he sucks me deep. His soft, blond hair under my hand as I caress him and tell him how beautiful he is...

Shit, I was going to come already. My whole body strained as I squeezed the base of my shaft and took a few breaths. I was desperate to give in, but I didn't want this fantasy to be over yet.

Connor spreading his long legs for me. Wide. Vulnerable and eager, looking up at me as I fuck him. Filling his tight ass with my cock, rocking into him as he cries out. Or Connor on his hands and knees taking me, our skin slapping together as we grunt and groan. Connor fucking me hard, his cock so deep in me I think I might break. On my knees sucking him and swallowing his cum. Connor swallowing mine—my cum dripping out of his mouth, splashed on his ruddy skin where I can lick it up and feed it to him in a filthy kiss...

My balls were tight, my nostrils flaring as I choked down my moans. Because Connor *was* here. He was in the guest room, and there were only two doors between us. What would happen if he heard me and thought I was having a seizure or another kind of medical emergency? Would he burst through the unlocked door to my bedroom and find me like this?

Gasping, I spurted everywhere, my vision whiting out as I shook through the orgasm. "*Ohh,*" I whined, milking myself. My legs flopped down to the mattress. My chest heaved.

I hadn't jerked off like that in ages. It was usually a sleepy wakeup in the shower—not this frantic, desperate drive.

Well. I'd let my mind—and cock—get away from me. It was the insomnia. It had been entirely inappropriate, but it was over. Connor would never know. Clearly I was pent up, so I'd swipe right on a few cool profiles online and reset. Connor was probably hooking up left, right, and center.

Never mind that the thought of Connor hooking up with anyone made my blood pressure rise instantly. I unclenched my fists and rocketed off the bed to wash up in the bathroom. I scrubbed my hands, getting out my nail brush for good measure.

It didn't matter since this relationship was *not real*, but... *Was* Connor queer? Asher had initially seemed so certain, though he'd changed his tune. He couldn't know for sure. Connor said he wasn't, which was all that mattered.

I enjoyed the steady hum of the water but switched off the tap with my forearm as I continued scrubbing. Until several months ago, I would have told anyone who'd asked I was straight. I just hadn't been ready to come out as bi.

It didn't help that Grandmother didn't seem to believe me. Or that other people thought bisexuality wasn't quite queer enough.

I'd had sex with men, women, one nonbinary person—I wasn't making it up to be rebellious or edgy. I was genuinely queer.

I was also scrubbing my fingernails raw. Wincing at the line of blood under my index finger, I turned on the tap and rinsed. My heart thudded, and any release from jerking off had evaporated.

Not looking in the mirror, I returned to the bedroom and pulled on my flannel PJ bottoms. I stripped the sheets and remade the bed in the faint light coming through the blinds.

It was still dark outside. Through the cracked window, a distant siren wailed. There was no way I could sleep now, so I shuffled out into the living room and jumped a mile when I saw Connor sitting by the window.

"Sorry." Connor held out his hands and spoke softly even though there was no one else in the apartment to wake up. He was still wearing his dark boxer briefs and my old Knicks tee. His James Dean hair was messy, and I had the absurd urge to smooth it down.

A fresh burst of desire gripped me—swiftly followed by guilt at what I'd just done. He was my little brother's best friend! He was a guest in my home. I should never have let myself get caught up in fantasies.

"Reid?" He was moving toward me. "Do you feel okay?" He'd snapped into doctor mode with that calm, concerned, capable manner.

He could seem so young and unsure at times, but when he was worried about someone's wellbeing, he was immediately reassuring in a way I never would have expected. A way I found incredibly attractive.

I managed to laugh, though it was strangled. "Yes—I'm great. You're up early." Cold sweat prickled my skin. "I didn't wake you, did I?" Wait, I'd just come out of my room. "I was, er, working out."

"In your…PJ bottoms?"

"Yes. It was an ab routine. And squats. Body weight conditioning that doesn't need any equipment."

"Cool. You start early. I've been out here a while." His gaze dropped to my chest. "Are you sure you're okay?"

Did I miss some cum? "Yes! I'm great."

Connor frowned. "You didn't cut yourself anywhere else, did you?"

I had no choice but to look down. I'd scratched my own chest while jerking off—not breaking the skin, but enough to leave red marks. "Oh! No. That's a, er, allergic reaction. Very mild cheese allergy."

"Just cheese? Not all dairy?"

"Only gouda, if you can believe it." Which he surely couldn't because it was a ridiculous lie. I hurried back into my room and tugged on the first T-shirt I pulled out of the drawer.

When I returned to the living room, Connor grinned. "Didn't peg you for a *Phantom of the Opera* fan."

Naturally, *that* was the shirt I grabbed. "Gag gift from last Christmas courtesy of Addison. But I have to admit it's really soft."

"I believe you," he deadpanned. "Totally."

"Look, I'm not cool. It's best that you understand that now."

He scoffed. "Of course you are."

"Please allow me to direct you again to the *Phantom* T-shirt I'm currently wearing. Hey, are you hungry?"

"Yeah. I had some goldfish crackers. Hope that's okay."

"Of course, but I can do better than that. We'll start with coffee, yes?"

He groaned. "*Yes.*"

I ordered my cock to behave and led the way into the kitchen, using the dimmer to keep the lights soft. As I turned on the coffee maker and gathered omelette ingredients—I did indeed have thick-cut bacon—Connor sat at one of the stools on the island.

"It's cool that you cook and everything," he said.

I shrugged. "I'm not a gourmand by any stretch."

"You're cool whether you like it or not. I mean, look at this place. And you practically run a worldwide hotel chain. That's pretty awesome."

As I cracked the eggs into a bowl, I made a noncommittal noise. "Grandmother and the CEO are running things. I mostly do as I'm told."

"You don't like it?"

"It doesn't matter. It's my job." I motioned with the whisk. "I can't complain. I'm extremely fortunate."

"Yeah, but...I assumed you liked it. Asher definitely doesn't have any interest in the family business."

"Don't I know it," I grumbled. "It is what it is. I can't complain," I repeated.

"That's bullshit. Sure you can. I went to Rencliffe with Asher and all the other rich kids. They complained all the time."

I chuckled. "True."

Connor played with the tiny tongs that accompanied the bowl of sugar cubes I'd put out for him. "So, what would you rather be doing?"

"It doesn't matter. I have a great job." I chopped the green onions with quick movements.

"It still matters."

Glancing at Connor, I could see he wasn't going to let it go. He waited patiently, with that calm, concerned aura. "You have a great bedside manner," I said. "Maybe you should be a shrink."

He blinked in surprise. "Me? Thanks. But I want to be more hands-on."

"I meant to ask you what specialty you're considering. You said you had an idea of what to choose."

"I'll tell you when you tell me what you really want to do."

Groaning, I shredded the aged cheddar, grateful I hadn't had gouda in the fridge. "Fine. You're going to laugh."

"I won't," he said, and I could tell he meant it. Sitting in my kitchen as gray light slowly brightened the apartment, the smell of rich coffee filling the peaceful air, it felt safe to tell him.

"You know how we run luxury hotels and resorts?"

"Uh-huh."

"I've been working on a proposal for diversifying the company and building low-cost, sustainable housing. Utilizing solar energy, recycled materials, creating urban green spaces and community hubs." Before Connor could reply, I poured the coffee and said, "I know. It's ridiculous."

Connor took his his mug from me, his forehead creasing. "Dude, we need housing people can actually afford. Why would that be ridiculous?"

"Because I'm the heir to a luxury hotel chain. Look at where I live. What do I know about sustainability or affordable anything?" I paced restlessly to the fridge and opened it blindly before going to the fruit bowl on the counter. I unpeeled a banana and offered Connor half, which he took with a smile.

"Okay, yeah. But I assume you've researched."

"Yes. For the record, none of my ideas are original—many people who know a lot more than me are spearheading similar projects."

"Right. There are only so many ways to reinvent the wheel. But you feel passionate about it?"

My heart was racing. "Yes. I know I should be proud of Utopia, but... I don't care about building more extravagant hotels. We do all this charity work—Grandmother is always fundraising. Which is wonderful! But I want to do more than donate and show up to charity events. I spend my days going through the motions at a company that's chugging along and hasn't innovated in decades. Making a product I don't care about." I took a breath. "I know. Poor little rich boy. Man. Whatever."

Connor said, "No, I get it. Just because you're rich doesn't mean you're not allowed to have feelings. You must be bored as hell."

Relief flooded me. "I *am*."

I'd never had the guts to say any of this out loud, even to Addison. Maybe it was easier with Connor because he wasn't wealthy. Or maybe it was easier with Connor because he just had this straightforward, nonjudgmental bedside manner.

"When I was fresh out of my MBA, I had so many ideas for how we could innovate at Utopia. Grandmother and the board shot down every one. After a while, I stopped trying. There's no way they'd ever invest in this. The company is incredibly profitable. Why change anything?"

"I guess one day you'll be in charge though, right? Then you can do what you want with Utopia."

"I hate the thought of waiting for Grandmother to die, though. Like I'm in a royal family trapped by birth."

Connor smirked. "You need to pull a Prince Harry and run away."

"Tempting."

Connor stirred three cubes of sugar into his coffee. "Couldn't you start your own company?" He laughed. "Not that I know anything about that. Or get a job somewhere else?"

"I can't actually *leave*. I have to take over eventually like you said."

He frowned. "Do you, though?"

For a moment, I was speechless. "Of course. I've been groomed for it my whole life. Especially since my dad died."

"Right." His shoulders hunched a fraction, and I knew he could relate. "You're the heir and not the spare."

I grimaced. "Exactly."

"Okay, so if you don't want to actually leave Utopia—or you don't feel like you can—what would you do if your grandmother didn't... What's that word? Veto?"

"I'd ideally like to start a new division. A pilot project to expand the company. I'd need capital from Utopia to fund the division, but in the long term, it would diversify our income streams and make the company stronger while providing much-needed housing."

"Sounds amazing."

"Except Grandmother doesn't like change. The question is whether I can get enough support from the CEO and board members, and I'm not optimistic. It's foolish to even be wasting my time with this, but I feel like… How many luxury hotels and resorts can we build? There's a huge market for quality affordable housing, and the profit margin is still favorable if not spectacular. Alongside the hotels, we'd still be making plenty."

Connor seemed to ponder that, his hands wrapped around his coffee mug. "Couldn't you ask one of your business buddies to read the proposal? Get some feedback?"

"Sure. If I wasn't a coward."

He didn't laugh. "We all have fears. What's the worst that can happen if you float the idea? It's not like you'll be out on the street, right?"

"No." I flushed. That was the most foolish part—acting as though I didn't have a privileged safety net. "You're right. I haven't because I'm afraid of what they'll say. That it's not feasible. Unrealistic. Laughable."

"Dude, I hope your friends wouldn't laugh at you."

"I'm sure they wouldn't. It's my own insecurity."

Connor shook his head. "It blows my mind that *you'd* be insecure about anything."

"Thank you?"

"Sorry—I didn't mean it as an insult. You've always seemed so together and cool and—" Connor stopped abruptly and gulped his coffee. "Stuff," he added.

I flushed with pleasure although I wasn't exactly sure why. Which was bullshit—I knew exactly why it pleased me that Connor apparently admired me.

"You know, I could ask Angela Barker to look at your proposal," he said.

"Really?" It wasn't a bad idea. She was incredibly successful and smart from what I knew of her.

"Totally. Even if it's not her field, she knows a lot about, well, everything. She's kind of like my wacky aunt even though we're not related. Well, wacky aunt crossed with a business tycoon."

"Really? It wouldn't be too much of an ask?"

"Nah, it's cool. Angela always wants to help."

"I really appreciate it. That would be great if you can approach her." Excitement sang through my veins like a gulp of champagne.

"No prob. Just remember, nothing changes if nothing changes," Connor said.

My chest felt strangely light, and I smiled. "Wise words."

"My mom used to say that." His gaze went distant. "Sometimes, she made huge changes that freaked me out. Like marrying Logan. If she'd lived, that never would have worked out."

I'd turned on the burner under the frying pan, and the bacon sizzled. "I'm sorry you lost her."

Connor stirred his coffee, the spoon clinking on the mug. "It's weird to think about. If she'd—if I'd—" He broke off. "She and Logan were already breaking up, so that would have been that. I'd have lost touch with Logan's sister Jenna and her husband Jun. Their kids. Pop. I would never have met Seth at all. *Logan* probably wouldn't have met him. I wouldn't know Angela Barker or Olivia either. It's trippy to think about how people can come into your life. Or how they might not."

"It's true. Imagine if you hadn't come to the Thanksgiving dinner with Asher. We wouldn't be here together right now."

That thought kicked me in the gut far harder than it had any right to given that dinner had been barely more than a week ago.

Connor met my gaze. "Guess you'd have another fake boyfriend."

That thought made me grimace in distaste. I quickly said, "Or I'd be stuck fending off Cecilia Weston."

"We wouldn't want that."

"To be fair, I doubt Cecilia has any more interest in me than I do in her. But once Grandmother gets an idea in her head…"

"She'll just have to get used to me." He laughed. "I mean, for December." He inhaled deeply. "That smells amazing, by the way."

I took the bread out, and we transitioned into talking about breakfast food as I cooked. "Tapioca pudding has got to be down at the bottom," I said.

"Is that actually a breakfast food?"

"To my dad it was. Not that he cooked a day in his life." I laughed fondly. "He had many strengths, but I doubt he could boil an egg."

"Why did you learn?" Connor sipped his coffee with a cute little satisfied sigh. "You can afford to order in everything."

"I enjoy cooking. Helps me relax. It's something that's just…mine. Low risk."

"You don't cook for other people? Aside from right now, I mean. No fancy dinner parties?"

"I have to attend far too many. Now, have you ever tried black pudding? It's a UK thing."

Connor screwed up his face, and it was cute too. God help me, it really was. He said, "Doesn't sound good."

"You'd be surprised. I—" My phone buzzed, and I frowned at the screen. "It's my grandmother. Not her PA—she's calling me herself."

"Her ears were burning. Shit, does she have your place bugged?"

I laughed weakly at Connor's joke and swiped to answer, "Hello? Are you all right?"

"Good morning, darling. Do you have plans for this evening?" she asked, ignoring my question.

"I do," I said immediately. She wasn't asking out of idle curiosity. "Connor and I are going to a jazz club." I shrugged at him as if I'd just made it up. "Actually, we're just having breakfast together," I added because it would make her uncomfortable. She had to get used to this. Not me and Connor per se, but me and men.

And why not Connor? Why does this arrangement have to stay pretend?

Muffling that internal voice, I smiled as Connor loudly said, "'Morning, Mrs. Cabot!"

Grandmother cleared her throat delicately. "Yes, well. What time is this jazz performance?"

"Seven," I lied.

"Reid, I might be a woman of advanced years, but I do recall through the distant sands of time that live music establishments rarely opened so early."

"It's, uh…"

"I'm not feeling well. I need you to go to dinner with the Seyfrieds. It won't go late, so you'll have plenty of time for your jazz."

Guilt washed over me. "Are you okay?" For her to cancel, it was more than sniffle. She sounded normal, though.

"Upset tummy," she said. "I think the caterer at last night's event will be blacklisted as I'm not the only sufferer."

Yikes. "What about Asher? Doesn't he know the Seyfried son? Whatshisname? Or is it the daughter? Whichever."

She sighed. "Darling, you know what a responsibility these events are. How important they are to the company and our family. Asher's too…inconsistent."

"He's not a kid anymore. He's working at a brokerage."

"Yes, but you're the future of Utopia."

The bacon was about to burn, and I hurriedly transferred it onto a paper towel-lined plate. "What time should Connor and I be there?" I eyed him, and he nodded.

"Darling, I'm sure Connor would be bored stiff. I was attending on my own, so there's only one seat at the table."

I almost growled in frustration. "We're a couple, Grandmother. I'm not going without him." Maybe I could get out of this after all.

But she gave in, and soon I had a text from the Seyfrieds' assistant confirming.

"You don't have to go," I told Connor.

"No, it's cool. I'm sure the food will be good. This was the arrangement, right? Be your boyfriend for these parties until the new year. Speaking of food, can I have a piece of bacon?"

"Of course. You can have everything." I quickly put the bread into the toaster and plated the omelet after separating it into two halves with the spatula.

Connor took a bite of bacon. "Mmm. Perfect."

I sat next to him at the island. "You're sure you don't mind me roping you into extra events?"

"Nope." He seemed about to say something, but then stopped himself. After a gulp of coffee, he added, "Besides, you loaned me the money. The least I owe you is being your date at dinner."

"Is everything...okay with that?" I was dying to know why he'd needed it, but it was an invasion of privacy to ask.

"Yep." He took a big mouthful of eggs and moaned. "Dude, you are such a good cook."

The compliment made me happier than it had any right to, and we went back to debating breakfast foods. Somehow, it didn't feel strange at all to be hanging out in my kitchen with Connor still in his underwear.

Not that I was *looking* at him in his underwear. I strictly kept my gaze up. It had been incredibly inappropriate to get lost in fantasies earlier. It wouldn't happen again. But we were free to hang out and become friends.

I could get used to this, I thought, hoping the holidays went by very, very slowly.

Chapter Eight

Connor

"YOU'RE SURE I shouldn't wear another jacket?" I asked as Reid and I walked from my apartment toward Ninth Avenue. I'd gone home to study for a few hours after we ordered in Chinese food for lunch and watched *Christmas Vacation*, and Reid had insisted on meeting me outside my building and walking together through the park to dinner.

But this isn't a date. This. Is. Not. A. Date.

"A hundred percent," Reid said. "The leather looks good on you."

Even as I reminded myself Reid's compliments didn't mean anything more than him being kind, my heart skipped.

I'd changed into my dressiest pants and another sweater that Reid insisted was fine. My other jacket option was a ratty ski parka, so the black leather did seem the better choice.

We turned uptown, chatting as we walked. Reid seemed to be interested in my explanation of the pathologic processes of inflammation, repair, and neoplasia for my exam.

After seeing him that morning in his *Phantom of the Opera* tee, he was back in his form-fitting designer clothes, including a long tan winter coat and burgundy scarf that brought out the rich depth in his brown eyes.

"Connor?"

"Uh-huh! Sorry, I got distracted by…" I glanced around as we crossed Fifty-seventh Street, remembering our conversation that first night. "Nuts. We should eat some, right?"

That was apparently the right thing to say since Reid's face spread into a grin. "You really want to?"

"Of course. It's on the list, right? How else will I become a real New Yorker?"

The sidewalk thronged with people rushing by as we found a cart. I inhaled the sweet, salty scent deeply. Reid insisted on paying and ordered two bags of the mixed nuts.

We ducked into the doorway of a closed bookstore decorated with a red-bowed wreath strung with fairy lights. The store window display was a mother mouse reading *A Christmas Carol* to little stuffed mice.

As I breathed through a pang of longing, Reid turned to peer into the window. "Cute." He looked to me again. "You okay?"

"Yeah. Just…" I waved my hand. "Never mind. Time for nuts."

"What is it?" He watched me with concern.

"Nothing bad. My mom loved mice. Weird, I know. Not, like, *real* mice."

"Fictional mice only. Wise."

I smiled. "Indeed. When I was little, my father took me to the mall and gave me money to get her a present. I tried to buy a mouse from the pet store to put in her stocking, but the clerk thought that would be a bad idea for both my mom and the poor mouse."

"Your father didn't think it was a bad idea?"

"He was in the bar at the TGI Fridays."

Reid's eyes widened. "How old did you say you were?"

I shrugged. "Too young." Why had I brought up my father? He was the last person I wanted to think about. "So, how about your nuts?" I shook my head. "I mean—you know what I mean."

Instead of laughing at how awkward I was, Reid arched a dark eyebrow. "Well, they're a delicacy. Or so I'm told."

He seemed completely serious and…flirty? My heart thumped.

Then Reid burst out laughing. Not just laughing—he *snorted*.

And it was the sexiest thing ever.

I laughed along, still amazed that smooth, sophisticated Reid Cabot was actually a bit of a dork like me under that polished veneer.

"Okay, we need to focus," Reid said. "Disclaimer. Many New Yorkers would probably disagree with this choice, but for me, eating nuts on the street at Christmas was quintessential New York as a kid. I hated it when we spent the holidays in the Caymans."

"Yeah, that must have been rough," I deadpanned.

Laughing, Reid elbowed me. We were standing close in the alcove, and the multicolored lights stringing the wreath and store window cast a warm, cozy glow over Reid's face. It was the most incredible, amazing torture being this close to him. After shoving my gloves in my pocket, I held the warm bag in my hands.

Reid bumped his bag against mine. "Cheers."

I popped a cluster of cashews and peanuts into my mouth, the honey flavor mixing perfectly with the salt and crunch. "Oh my god," I mumbled. "These are delicious."

They really were, but I'd have lied about it all night to see the way Reid beamed at me. "No veto?" he asked.

"No way. What's next?"

Reid checked the time on his phone. "We might just make it."

"Right now? Don't we have a dinner?"

"It's on the way."

I followed Reid north, and he wouldn't tell me where we were going. Anticipation buzzed through me. We ate the rest of our nuts as we walked and dodged other pedestrians. We were close to the Utopia, where we'd had Thanksgiving dinner and agreed to pretend.

When I'd said yes, I hadn't imagined it would be anything like this. I wasn't sure what I *did* imagine, but it hadn't been this playful vibe. Even though Reid had loaned me ten grand, he hadn't asked about it or nagged me for an explanation even though it would have been a reasonable request.

"Thank you again," I said. "For lending the money. And not grilling me. You're really…cool." I cringed internally. I sounded like a kid with a crush. I *felt* like a kid with a crush.

He smiled. "You're cool too." As we headed into the park, he said, "And if you need help with whatever's going on—whatever you needed the money for—I'll help you."

I was warm all over even though an icy gust of wind whistled through the park. "It's over, but thank you. And I'll make the next payment on Monday. I know the amounts are on the small side right now—"

"Any amount is okay." He gently grasped my shoulder. "I know you're good for it. And now I know where you live."

We laughed, and I was surprised as we bypassed Wollman Rink, which was crowded with skaters, Kelly Clarkson belting about a Christmas tree through the speakers.

"Hmm. Not skating?"

Reid shook his head. "Nope. Not that I'm opposed to it, but for my list, there's another attraction."

"Penguins at the zoo."

"Try again."

"That castle. Belvedere?"

"Nope."

I'd been to Central Park several times, and I racked my brain for what other activities I might have walked past. "There's no way we're renting a row boat on the lake in December."

Reid laughed. "Definitely a summer activity. Actually, I'll add that to the summer list. It's a good one. We can go when falling in won't be as life threatening."

Butterflies *whooshed* through my stomach. We were making summer plans? "What else will be on the summer list?" I tried for casual and probably sounded like I was in cardiac distress.

"Spoiler alert! The rest will be a surprise." He squinted up the path and increased his pace. "They're closing any minute."

I followed his gaze to a sort-of round brick building. Tinny, old-fashioned music echoed, and I realized it was the enclosure for the carousel.

"Oh!" I exclaimed. "I forgot this was here."

"Veto?" Reid asked.

"No way! Let's do it."

"Come on." He took my bare hand with his—we hadn't put on our gloves since we'd been eating the nuts—and we jogged up to the ticket window.

The woman peered at us over the rims of her glasses. "Closing time," she said.

"One more?" Reid asked. "Please? I promised my boyfriend. He's never ridden the carousel before."

"A virgin, huh?" The woman tapped her screen with an exaggerated sigh. "I guess young love deserves one last ride."

As my face flamed, Reid paid for the tickets. A few families rushed up behind us, and soon we were all clambering onto the platform. There were plenty of horses to pick from, and Reid and I climbed a black pair with saddles painted in bright blue, red, and silver.

A woman stood by one of the stationary horses, her young daughter in the saddle squealing in delight as the carousel began to spin. Her enthusiasm was infectious, and I grinned. The classic instrumental carnival music played, and even though it wasn't explicitly Christmassy, it was merry as hell.

"This is awesome!" I said as we spun, my horse bobbing up and down in opposition to Reid's beside me. The carousel gathered surprising speed, and I gripped the pole, the cold wind messing up my hair. I wanted to reach across and hold his hand again, but that would probably be weird.

Reid grinned. "Never too old to ride the Central Park carousel! I haven't done it in years. I've been missing out."

Even if it was childish, it was *fun*. I felt like we were flying. "Makes me miss my bike!"

"*What?* These two things are not similar!"

"They are, I swear. I think you'd be surprised how much you'd enjoy riding a motorcycle."

"Veto." Reid shook his head, laughing. "The wooden horsies are the limit of my risk tolerance."

The ride slowed and eventually came to a stop, and Reid swung his leg over and hopped down, straightening his long woolen coat. We both had long legs, so it should have been just as easy for me to get down gracefully.

"Should" being the operative word.

Because my foot got caught on the stirrup, and I hopped and made a sound that could only be described as a "squeak."

Reid was suddenly behind me, his arms around me and his breath in my ear. "Steady. Hold on."

I tugged my foot, and my leather shoe went flying as I staggered against Reid. I barely moved since he was holding me up so strongly.

"Thanks." I tried to laugh, my head spinning and body tingling. God, he smelled amazing—that earthy pine scent.

My black sock was half off, and I tried in vain to tug it up as Reid deftly pivoted us so he could crouch. At my feet, he held up the leather Oxford and said, "I believe you lost a glass slipper, *mon amour?*"

We laughed, and his fingers tickled my bare ankle as he pulled up my sock and guided my foot back into my shoe.

I shivered, sounding weirdly breathy as I said, "I guess the laces were loose. This is what I get for not wearing my Docs. Trying to be respectable."

Reid looked up with a little smile. "Good thing I was here to lend a hand." He tied my shoe with neat, firm movements that turned me on because I was so *weird*. Or maybe it wasn't the shoe-tying but the whole kneeling-at-my-feet thing.

"To be fair, I wouldn't have been riding the carousel if you weren't here."

"True. But you could have tripped. I'll check the other one too." He retied those laces, then stood. "Who knows what catastrophe has been averted? We're both klutzes, it seems."

"Hmm. Good point." We were standing so close between the wooden horses that the tips of our shoes touched. "I could have—"

"I hate to break up...whatever this is," said the woman from the ticket booth loudly by the gate, wearing her coat and hat with her purse on her shoulder. "But we'd like to go home."

We jerked apart and hurried off the now-empty carousel, apologizing profusely and practically running.

"I can't wait to see what else is on the list!" I exclaimed, and when Reid winked, I came very close to tripping even though my shoelaces were both knotted tightly.

We walked north through the park past trees and posts strung with holiday lights. Flurries of snow danced in the breeze.

"I should bring my dads here to see the lights. The city's amazing at Christmas. Seth would love it, and Logan will do whatever Seth loves. And secretly he'll think it's cool."

Reid glanced around. "Huh. I guess it is beautiful. I don't usually pay attention. Christmas drags on for so long. There are so many events and parties I have to go to." He raised his hands. "I know, I know. Call me Scrooge."

"I get it. After my mom, I didn't think I'd ever care about Christmas again. But Logan and Seth and Aunt Jenna put so much work into it every year. She makes the best turkey. There was one time—" I broke off. "Sorry, this is so boring."

"Not at all," Reid said, but of course he'd say that. He was polite. I wasn't sure exactly what he did in the office, but being polite and looking interested in boring stories was probably his job.

"Anyway—oh, isn't that your friend?"

As we exited the park on Fifth Avenue, a woman across the street waved. It was Madison—no, Addison—and we joined her for the last few blocks.

"Connor, you really are a saint to be coming to this dinner," she said. "It's going to be intensely boring. I can't believe Bitsy bailed. Uptight dinners are her favorite thing ever."

"She must genuinely be sick," Reid said. He nudged my arm. "But seriously, thank you."

"It's okay. We have a deal." I wasn't sure if Addison knew about the money, so I kept my mouth shut.

She said, "Hopefully we can escape early. Want to come over to Paul's? Colette is back from Paris. Should be chill."

Reid shook his head. "Actually, we have plans." He shot me a grin. "An underground jazz club in the Village, assuming Connor has no objections."

"Wait, for real?" Excitement fizzed through me. "I thought you made that up for your grandmother. I'm definitely in."

His grin widened. "You'll love it. And even if you don't, it's a New York experience."

"Great!" Addison smiled at Reid, her head tilted. "So, you two are basically spending the whole weekend together."

Reid laughed. "Well… I suppose so. We didn't plan it this way."

"No, of course not," Addison agreed, still smiling at Reid.

My phone buzzed, and as I glanced at the screen to check the incoming call, I froze.

Dad

Mike had been listed in my contacts as that one word for as

long as I'd had a smartphone. Even though it was a lie—he had never been my *dad*. Logan and Seth were my dads.

But I'd never changed the listing. It would have been weird to list him as, what? Father? Mike? The latter, probably, but when I'd opened my contacts to edit, it had seemed so…final.

God, I was pathetic. Why did I care? I wished so fucking much that I didn't.

"Okay?" Reid asked.

"Uh-huh!" I jammed my phone in my pocket. I wasn't answering. What the fuck could he say at this point? Nothing. I had to grow up and block him, but this wasn't the time or place. I was here for Reid.

We arrived at one of the very fancy apartment buildings with a view of the park, and I felt like if I was separated from Reid and Addison, the doorman would toss me out by the scruff of my neck like I was in an old movie.

The dinner was indeed stuffy and boring, and I nodded and smiled and let Reid do the talking. After dinner, we were ushered into a massive living room dominated by a Christmas tree decorated in silver, white, and gold. Rich people didn't seem to go for the multicolored bulbs or—heaven forbid—anything flashing.

A string quartet played old carols that Seth would know the words to since he'd grown up going to church. Reid and I stood at the edge of the room, ready to slip out.

"Grandmother's best friend is staring at us," Reid murmured. "Don't look."

"Why are you telling me if I'm not supposed to look?" I kept my gaze on the musicians.

Reid chuckled, a warm, low sound that I could listen to all day. "Touché."

"If you mean the old lady at four o'clock, yeah, she apparently thinks we're an exhibit at the zoo."

"That's her. Bunny Epstein."

"Bunny and Bitsy. Good combo."

Reid sipped his wine. I loved the way the red liquid painted his lips for a moment. His tongue was likely stained too…

"Can I kiss you?" he asked under his breath.

As I tried to tear my eyes away from his lips, my brain screamed, *YES!!* Meanwhile, my eloquent mouth spat out, "Huh?"

"Is that crossing a boundary?" He raised a hand. "You're under no obligation. I just know Bunny will be reporting back, and I'm so tired of Grandmother's attitude."

"I get it," I croaked before gulping the rest of my wine. "I'm down."

Reid examined me silently. "Are you sure? I know you said you're straight. I don't want to pressure you or overstep. This isn't a requirement of our arrangement."

"No, you're good." If I believed in spontaneous combustion, I'd be afraid I was about to explode and all that would be left of me would be a pile of ashes in my shoes. "Go for it. It's only a kiss."

"Smile like I said something wonderful."

No acting was necessary since, duh, Reid Cabot just said he wanted to kiss me. Even if it was all pretend, I grinned. Reid smiled back, then leaned down and did it.

He actually kissed me.

His free hand slid around to my lower back, and his lips brushed mine, feather-light and moist. I inhaled his woodsy scent and pressed closer to him as our mouths hovered together. It was sweet and soft, and our lips were open just enough that it wasn't like we were mashing our faces together. I tasted a hint of wine.

It was *everything*.

God, it was almost impossible not to grab him and keep kissing. As we parted, I had to stop myself from touching my lips with my fingertips. *Only a kiss*, I'd told him.

I hadn't mentioned it was my very first.

But Reid didn't need to know that aside from being a virgin, I'd never even kissed anyone during spin the bottle or whatever. Unless he'd figured it out because I had no idea what I was doing. I met his warm, brown eyes and braced for his reaction. It was fine if he laughed, or—

My heart swelled as a tender little smile lifted his extremely kissable lips, and he looked down at me like I was something precious as he brushed his thumb across my bottom lip.

I shivered, and the insane thought popped into my head that I wanted to take his thumb in my mouth and suck it.

As the string quartet launched into "Joy to the World," Reid whispered, "Thanks for playing along," and I managed to nod.

My first kiss was in the books, and the only way it could have been more perfect was if it'd been for real.

Chapter Nine

Connor

THE BUZZER ECHOED through the apartment, and I jerked awake on my bed, knocking a stack of notes onto the floor in a flutter of paper. "Fuck," I muttered as I rubbed my eyes. I could hear Olivia talking to whoever was outside on the old intercom, followed by the long *beeeep* that meant she'd unlocked the lobby door.

I fumbled for my phone to check the time. Where the fuck was my phone? Wait, what day was it? Sunday. Right. It was Sunday morning, and I'd been up studying most of the night until I'd crashed. I reached around the mattress and under the tangled covers.

It had been a week since I'd seen Reid, though he'd texted me encouragement and checked in quite a few times. As I lifted my phone, I fantasized that maybe he'd come over with coffee and bagels to surprise me...

I bolted to my feet as I scanned the texts from Seth. "Wait. What the fuck?" I blurted out loud.

Sure enough, I could hear Olivia welcoming Seth and Logan inside our apartment. They were here? What the hell? I stumbled out into the living room, almost knocking our mini Christmas tree from its perch on the low storage unit under the TV. I caught it, silver tinsel now sticking to my flannel boxers.

"What's wrong?" I demanded.

"Hello to you too." Seth chuckled as he unwound his scarf. "Didn't you get my messages?" His glasses had fogged up, and he waved them through the air before putting them back on. For a second, I thought there were snowflakes in his dark brown hair, but I realized it was just grayer at the temples.

"Just now. I fell asleep." It was somehow almost eleven. Shit. I still had so much studying to do. At least after tomorrow, I could take a break. I still had two exams after, but they were easier. I could definitely go out with Reid a few times.

Thinking of him still made me giddy and fidgety, and I had to focus. What was going on with my dads?

Seth said, "We're picking up a sink for Logan's client, and we thought we'd pop in. Nothing's wrong." He hung his coat in the closet, reaching out a hand for Logan's leather jacket.

But Logan was tense. He unzipped his jacket and didn't say anything, which wasn't completely out of the ordinary, but I recognized the set of his shoulders and the vein sticking out near his temple under his clipped hair. It wasn't as buzzed as it would have been when he was a Marine, but he still went for a no-nonsense style that was very...him.

His pale skin was ruddy, and I wasn't sure if it was from the cold or if he was worked up about something. They were here for a reason. There was a vibe. I tried to think of what I'd done to piss them off but came up blank.

Unless... No. There was no way they could know about the money. I shifted from foot to foot, my stomach lurching. I'd dealt with it, and there was no way Reid would tell them. He didn't even know what the money had been for. Even if he did, he wouldn't.

"Sorry I missed your texts." I shook tinsel off my hand, trying to act normally. "I've been studying all week. My biggest exam is Monday, so this weekend has been intense."

Olivia motioned to my boxers and ratty Harvard tee. "He's

been wearing that all week too. I'm hoping he remembers to shower again one of these days." She checked her watch. "I'm meeting Dylan for brunch, so I'll leave you to it. I hope everything's good in Albany?"

Seth nodded. "Yes. We were at Will and Michael's last night for their holiday party. We decorated the tree, and Will's parents arrived from Scotland. Michael had arranged the surprise."

Olivia grinned. "That's awesome! I'm sorry I couldn't make it. Will and Michael are the cutest. Sounds like a great party."

"It was." Seth smiled, but... Shit. He was tense too. He was way better at hiding it than Logan, but something was definitely up.

After Olivia left, the three of us stood there looking at each other. "What's going on?" I asked.

"Nothing," Seth said. "We were nearby. The place looks great, by the way." He waved a hand at the glittery garlands Olivia and I had hung to go with our tree.

"Thanks. Nothing compared to your tree, but it's nice. Olivia's going home to Texas, and she said you wouldn't believe how many trees and stuff Angela puts up, but you probably would since you know she's big on Christmas." I was rambling while my brain tried to figure out why they were here—and then a terrible thought hit me. "Are you sick?"

Seth and Logan blinked at me and looked taken aback. "Huh?" Logan said.

"Is that why you're here? Is one of you sick or something? And you didn't want to tell me over the phone?" My stomach twisted into an acidy knot as my brain helpfully supplied a list of diseases they might have and I examined them for signs and symptoms.

"No!" Seth held up his hands. "We're not sick. We're fine, and everyone at home's fine."

I eyed them suspiciously. "Even Pop?"

Logan nodded. "My old man's trucking along like usual. I

swear."

"Okay." I exhaled in a rush.

Seth said, "We won't stay long—we know you're studying, and we have to get back to Albany by late afternoon. Jenna's having us over for dinner so she can practice a new scalloped-yet-roasted potato recipe for Christmas. Can't we stop in and say hi?"

"No—yes, of course." I rubbed my face and shuffled to the kitchen. "I need coffee." Okay, if they knew about the money, they'd just yell at me, right? Get it over with? After a moment, I asked, "Um, do you guys want some?" It was weird playing host to my dads.

"Sure," Seth answered. "That would be great. Right?" He gave Logan a look.

"Yeah," Logan said. He went to my bedroom door and peered in. "No one else here?"

"Just me, my textbooks, and my notes." Even though I took notes on my laptop, I printed them out to study to give my eyes a break. "Why? You just saw Olivia leave." I really needed caffeine. "Who else would be here?"

Logan stuffed his hands in his jeans pockets and shrugged.

I got the coffee machine going while Seth talked about the antique sink they'd picked up for one of Logan's clients. They didn't seem mad, and they'd promised they weren't sick, so maybe everything was fine and they really had just stopped in because they were in the city.

"The sink sounds cool," I said, yawning widely. "Sorry. I went out too much last weekend, so this week has been all studying."

"What were you doing last weekend?" Seth asked casually. But maybe *too* casually?

I crossed my arms. "What's going on? You're being weird."

"Because you're not telling the truth!" Logan's nostrils flared. "Why wouldn't you just tell us?"

My heart dropped, and I tasted bile. They *did* know about

how incredibly stupid I'd been. That the debt might fuck up my credit rating for years, and even if I became a doctor, what if I'd screwed myself forever? How had they found out? Fuck, fuck, *fuck*.

Seth raised his hands. "Let's all take a breath. Everything's okay. We're just...puzzled, Connor. We didn't expect to hear it from someone else."

Jesus, had my father told them? No. Why the hell would Mike do that? Panic clawed at me, and I felt like I was back at Rencliffe and the headmaster had hauled my dads into her office to tell them what a fuck-up I was.

But I was supposed to be an adult now. I tried to keep my voice steady. *Fake it until you make it.* "What exactly did you hear?"

"That you're dating Asher's older brother," Seth answered.

I stared at them, playing Seth's words over in my head to make sure I hadn't misheard. "Oh!" I almost laughed in relief. "I..."

But wait—this wasn't great either. Fuck. I wasn't ready for the me-dating-men conversation. Blood rushed in my ears, and I was sweaty and light-headed. I automatically ran though a symptom checklist before trying to focus.

"We're not angry," Seth said.

I scoffed in Logan's direction. "Did you get that memo?"

A reluctant smile tugged his lips, and he snorted. "I'm not *mad*." He blew out a long breath. "I'm worried. I just don't get it. What's going on with this *Reid*? How old is he?"

"Twenty-nine. Look, it's not what you think. But also, I'm twenty-three. I'm not a kid." Sure, I was a virgin who'd never even been kissed before a week ago, but that wasn't the point.

"So, you and Reid Cabot are in a relationship?" Seth asked gently as the coffee machine finished pouring out a mug.

I handed it to Seth before busying myself with another pod.

My face was hot, and I knew I was blushing. "No, we're not," I said truthfully. I didn't want to lie to them. Yes, the money was a lie of omission, but this was different. They were right here in my kitchen.

They'd never asked me much at all about my love life—or lack thereof. Aside from safe sex talks, they'd never pressured me. I'd told them I was too busy with school to date, and they'd always accepted that.

"You're not?" Seth asked. "This was a misunderstanding?"

"Actually, we're following your example," I said, facing them as I flipped the empty coffee pod from hand to hand. "I'm Reid's fake boyfriend for the holidays."

They shared a surprised glance. Logan said, "You're pretending? Does he work for Angela or something?"

I laughed, relaxing a fraction. "No, but his uptight grandmother won't accept that he's bi and keeps trying to fix him up with heiresses like it's the olden days. So, I'm going with him to a few parties as his boyfriend. That's it."

"He's not...taking advantage of you?" Logan asked.

"What? No!" I rolled my eyes. "Oh my god, I'm not twelve!"

"I know, but..." Logan's shoulders finally relaxed. "Okay. Good."

Seth sipped his coffee. "You're carrying on the family legacy."

"That's what I said!" I grinned. "Except you guys really did end up together." And as much as I wanted Reid, it was out of the question.

At least, I thought so? Sure, I'd been obsessing over that kiss all week, and I was dying to see him again to do another item on the New Yorker list. He'd been texting me hints, and he was meeting me at school right after my exam.

Almost like he missed me too.

"Will and Michael went from fake dating to living together," Seth said. "So, you never know. Maybe you and Reid... If you might want that? With Reid, or with another guy." He quickly added, "Or girl. Person. Or not. You don't need to date. Plenty of people don't. It's up to you. We support you in whoever you want to date or not date."

I gripped the empty pod, glad when the next cup finished and I could hand Logan that mug. He and Seth seemed to be waiting for me to say something, doing that patient dad thing they were so good at.

This was it. I could just tell them. I could finally say it. I'd always imagined it would be an eloquent speech I'd prepared for the right moment, but now in my kitchen, exhausted and sleep-sweaty, was this the moment?

My heart pounded. "Um, I've never, like… I don't think…" I tried to find the right words and failed miserably. So much for my perfect speech.

Seth nodded. "Okay. Hey, we never got a hug." He opened his arms, and I gratefully stepped forward.

He murmured, "You know you can tell us anything, right?"

"Everything," Logan said. "Whenever you want."

I hugged him next, and Logan patted my back the way he always did. As I grabbed my coffee, I had to blink my burning eyes hard. I opened the fridge to get the cream, giving myself a minute.

I really could tell them.

Being queer, about the money—everything, like Logan said. But I'd paid the debt. Why upset them for no reason? I couldn't disappoint them now. The thought of it made me queasy again. And shouldn't I wait until I'd actually been with a guy before I came out?

"Con?" Logan's deep voice was tinged with concern.

I splashed the cream into my coffee—and all over the counter. At the sink, I wet the environmental bamboo cloth Olivia had bought and wiped up the mess. Forget the money—that was done and there was no reason to upset them.

But for the rest… I thought of the conversation Olivia and Angela had had. *Imposter syndrome* wasn't something I'd ever thought about applying to myself, but it fit, didn't it?

"Hey." Seth's warm hand clasped my shoulder. "I think you got it."

"Right." I laughed shakily and rinsed the cloth, still not looking at them. I could feel their concern like snow falling all around me in a blanket. "I mean, if I *was* gay—"

Fuck. I'd said it.

I forced myself to turn from the sink and face them. They were both right there waiting like always.

"If you're gay, then that's wonderful," Seth said. His eyes glistened, which was totally going to make me cry too. "We love you just the way you are." Beside him, Logan nodded.

"I *think* so. But I've never…" It was hard to breathe, and I was a hundred percent going to cry. "I am, though. I'm gay."

Then Seth was hugging me again, and Logan had his arms around us, and I wasn't just crying. I was *sobbing*. How had I ever thought even for a second that my dads would react in any other way but this?

"You're okay," Seth whispered. "We've got you."

"And you know it's not your fault, right?"

Seth eased back to look at me, a furrow between his brows, Logan wearing a matching expression. Seth asked, "What do you mean?"

"That I'm not gay because of anything you guys did."

Seth's dark eyebrows shot up, and Logan exclaimed, "Why the hell would we think that?"

"You wouldn't," I quickly said. "I just know how ignorant some people can be."

"I know very well, but those people aren't a concern of ours," Seth said firmly. "They can go to the devil. You hear me?"

Those were strong words from Seth, and I nodded and swiped

at my snotty face. "Okay. So, um, now you know. Man, I didn't expect this to happen today."

"Guess we ambushed you," Logan said. "But when we heard you were dating Asher's brother, we were just confused as hell."

I shook my head. "Who told you?"

As they explained, I blew my nose on a paper towel.

I just came out.

Part of me thought I was going to wake up with my textbook jammed into my hip and find out this was all a dream. But it was real, and even though I was sniffling from crying, I felt like I could breathe more easily. I'd done it, and it hadn't been as scary as I'd imagined.

"Did you know?" I asked. "That I'm queer too?"

They shared one of those looks where they had a whole conversation. Logan shrugged. "It crossed our minds. Jenna said you pinged her gaydar."

The reminder of the rest of the family had me tensing again. "Are you going to tell her? And everyone else?"

"It's up to you," Seth said. "There's no rush."

"Yeah. Okay, cool. Can we just wait a bit?"

Logan nodded. "Whatever you want. You know it took me a while to wrap my thick head around being bi, right?"

"Yeah," I said. "I remember." If it wasn't for falling in love with Seth, I wasn't sure Logan would have had that reckoning.

Logan rubbed his stubbly face. "I'm just glad you're okay and I don't have to kick Reid Cabot's ass."

"Again, I'm twenty-three actual years old," I said, but I had to laugh. "Reid's a perfect gentleman. He's pretty cool, actually."

"Oh?" Seth sipped his coffee. "Glad to hear it. Should we get brunch?"

"When in Manhattan," Logan said. "I think it's the law."

I had a quick shower, still wired with excitement from telling my dads. It wasn't what I'd expected from the morning, but I really did feel relieved.

We managed to snag a table at the Galaxy Diner, my favorite greasy spoon in Hell's Kitchen. I told Logan and Seth about the jazz club Reid had taken me to over bacon and eggs and another coffee.

"It was amazing. They were playing Christmas songs, and the whole place was velvety and cool. We brought our own bottle of vodka, and they gave us glasses and mixer and ice."

Logan's lip curled as he sliced into a massive stack of pancakes. "Couldn't they just get a liquor license and be a regular bar?"

I laughed. "Well, yeah. But then it wouldn't be *underground*. It makes no sense, but it's cool." I didn't mention that it was so crowded we had to sit shoulder-to-shoulder, and that our knees touched under the little round table with a tealight candle on it.

My phone buzzed, and I grinned as I looked at the text from Reid that appeared on the screen. "He just sent me another clue about the next thing we're doing."

"The next thing?" Seth asked before taking a bite of his Western omelet.

"Oh, Reid made a list of genuine New Yorker experiences for me."

"That sounds fun." Seth smiled quizzically. "But I thought you were only pretending to be a couple in front of his grandmother?"

I tore my gaze away from the text, which I was rereading again. "Oh, right. We are! This isn't—this is extra. We're friends, I guess. We met before, but it was years ago." Reid and I were friends now, right? It seemed like it. "Here's the clue for the next activity: 'Don't go low.' Hmm."

Seth loved puzzles. He pondered it. "Obviously, the opposite of low is high."

"He wants to get you high?" Logan tore his attention from the pancakes and glowered.

I rolled my eyes. "You're not even listening. "Hmm. Something high… The High Line! It's this cool elevated park. I've been there once, but I was pretty wasted."

"Do tell," Seth said dryly.

"Hey, I'm old enough to get wasted. It's not like before when Asher and I skimmed off the bottles in the liquor cabinet and make ourselves puke."

Logan laughed as Seth grimaced and said, "Thank goodness." He shook his head. "It's still hard to believe you're old enough to be in medical school, let alone drinking."

I shrugged. "I guess." I started typing out a response to Reid, but then deleted. Should I tell him I'd guessed? I didn't want to ruin his surprise. Although I might have been wrong.

"Earth to Connor." Logan raised an eyebrow. "No phone at the table."

"I know, I know," I mumbled.

"You're old enough for med school, but some things never change," Logan said.

"Well, you'd know way more about being old than I would." I gave him a shit-eating grin.

"All right, you two," Seth said, though he was smiling.

I ate another piece of bacon, and it hit me that I'd come out and everything with my dads was the same. I'd been afraid of telling them for so long, but it was fine. More than fine. It was pretty great. They were still the same dads.

"We're so proud of you," Seth said—like he was reading my mind. How did he do that?

I joked, "Wait until I get my grades, and then we'll see."

Seth chuckled. "You always say that, and you always do wonderfully."

"Seriously, that was one of the first things your mom told me about you," Logan said. "That you're a goddamned genius, and you're full of shit when it comes to predicting your grades."

"I assume you're paraphrasing," Seth said.

I smiled through the pang of affection and pain and longing. "Nah, that sounds like her. Did she ever tell you how she tried to prank me when I got into Rencliffe?" I asked Logan.

"I don't think so."

"I'd been going on for weeks about how I failed the admission test, and I'd never get the scholarship. The day the letter came, I was too nervous to open it, so she did. She kept a totally straight face as she read it, and I was like, Oh my god, I actually blew it. She looked so serious, but when she tried to talk, she couldn't keep it up and started crying and screaming about how I got in."

Logan smiled. "Sounds like Veronica. A total softie."

My throat was suddenly thick, and I croaked, "Yeah," and gulped my coffee.

"She'd be damn proud of you," Logan said gruffly.

I nodded and asked, "Did you, um, see the Knicks game?" before I started crying for the second time that day.

As Logan and I talked basketball and Seth listened patiently, I thought of wearing Reid's Knicks T-shirt when I'd stayed over at his place. One more day of cramming for this exam, and then I'd see him again.

I knew I shouldn't have been so excited. Like I'd told Logan and Seth, I *wasn't* in a relationship with Reid. I'd obsessed over our kiss in every moment I hadn't been studying, but that made sense. It was my first, and it had been with the guy I'd crushed on for years.

It didn't mean anything.

"Connor?" Seth asked. "Are you listening?"

I blinked back to attention. "Sorry. My brain's in overdrive. Studying, and then..." I paused. "I was so nervous to tell you guys. For *years*. Now we're sitting here hardening our arteries like nothing happened."

Logan mumbled through a mouthful, "That's a good thing,

right?"

"Yes." I laughed, and it might have been a bit manic. "It's good. It's the best. You know, Asher had apparently told Reid I was queer. I guess he always knew. I should tell him he was right. He's safe to tell. He won't think anything weird."

"Who's gonna think anything weird?" Logan asked. "And if they do, they can get fucked."

"Right in the ear," Seth added.

Logan and I looked at each other and burst out laughing. Logan slid his arm around Seth's slim shoulders and kissed his cheek. "Those are fighting words from you."

Seth's face reddened. "I'll leave the profanity to you two." He shook his head and smiled. "You can tell Reid too that you came out," he said to me.

"Right. I guess I can." I gulped my coffee and waved to the passing server for a refill. Logan suggested pie and ice cream for dessert, and I agreed even though I was full. I half listened to Seth tell us about Angela's latest expansion of her company.

The nerves returned full force as I thought about telling Reid. It'd only been a couple of weeks since Thanksgiving when I'd forcefully insisted I was straight. He was going to think I was flaky at best and a liar at worst. Or maybe…

I couldn't stop thinking about that kiss. Even if it had been part of the act… Maybe it didn't have to be? I could tell Reid that I wanted him for real.

What was stopping me?

Gee, aside from the fact that he might laugh his ass off at the idea of actually dating? That was too cruel for Reid, actually. He wouldn't laugh, but he'd be unbearably kind in turning me down. That would possibly be worse.

Nothing changes if nothing changes.

My mom's voice echoed in my mind. I'd been in the closet for years, and I'd finally changed that. It had been, like, an hour, but I vibrated with jittery energy and the need to make it more official, if that made any sense. I'd told my dads I didn't want to tell anyone else right away, but it turned out I did?

If I confided in Reid, could something monumental change between us? Or was I just fooling myself?

Only one way to find out.

Chapter Ten

Reid

A S CONNOR LEFT the subway station and strode across the street in his Doc Martens in the fading gray light, I knew I had a serious problem.

The klaxon was blaring. The risk profile was intolerably high. I needed to veto. I had to make my escape before he spotted me on the crowded sidewalk amid the falling snow.

But I didn't move. I only watched him approach, his face lighting up like a proverbial Christmas tree as he spotted me and waved.

I wanted to kiss him again.

It was unacceptable yet undeniable. I'd sleepwalked through meetings all week and thought of little else but how I wanted to kiss Connor again. *More* than kiss him. A frisson of excitement rippled through me at all the things I wanted to do with Connor.

All the things I couldn't do with him since he was only pretending to be my boyfriend.

Only pretending to be queer—although I did wonder about that. I sincerely doubted he was straight, but the only thing that mattered was what Connor thought and felt.

I waved as he approached, and *god*, how had I missed him so much this week? It was ludicrous! He wore his usual ensemble of boots, jeans, and that leather jacket. Snow dusted his head, and his hands were bare. Why didn't he at least have gloves?

"Hey!" I said as we met. Then I was opening my arms, and we were hugging each other, Connor's lean body tight against mine.

Apparently, we hugged now when we saw each other? Connor held onto me tightly, and we only separated because we were blocking the sidewalk and the people rushing past threw elbows.

We laughed awkwardly, and Connor said, "Um, hey." His pale cheeks were pink, and a snowflake melted on his nose.

"How did it go?"

He groaned. "I dunno. I want to say it was a disaster, but Asher and my dads would roll their eyes and tell you I always say that. Which is true."

"I have complete confidence it wasn't a disaster. Sorry I couldn't meet you right after."

"Nah, it made no sense for you to go back uptown after your meeting. Besides, the High Line is right here."

I grinned. "You figured out the next item on the list."

"You gave me a huge clue."

"Or it's that big brain of yours. Still up for it?" I lifted my chin and peered at the heavy white blocking out some of the buildings. "We seem to have picked the first big snowfall of the season to go for a walk."

"I'm game. Didn't you say you had to go to a holiday thing first?"

All other thoughts but Connor had evacuated my mind as soon as I saw him. "Shit, yes." I checked my watch. "It's only a happy hour at a bar, but it's a major client and my grandmother will be there. I have to make an appearance. We'll just have one and duck out."

"It's cool. I could use a drink after that exam." He yawned as we started walking.

"Up late again studying?"

Connor nodded. "I get paranoid that I haven't studied enough, and I'll miss something obvious."

"I thought Asher said at Rencliffe you got straight As."

"Yeah, once I got my shit together. I was almost expelled."

I motioned for us to turn at the next light. "Wow. I didn't realize."

"I wasn't working to my potential." He grimaced. "It was after my mom died, and things were shitty with Logan. Then he got roped into pretending to be Seth's fiancé, and everything turned around. Honestly, I was such an asshole that I'm not sure why Logan didn't drive me out to the woods and leave me there."

I barked out a surprised laugh. "Good thing he didn't. Although maybe you would have been adopted by wolves or something."

"I think you have to be a baby for a Tarzan scenario to work. But anyway, this is medical school. I can't take anything for granted. I'm on a scholarship thanks to my grades, and I need to keep them up."

I squeezed his arm. "I'm sure you did great." Tilting my head, I checked the sign as we approached a bar with its window decorated in pine boughs and gold fairy lights. "Here we are."

"Right. Boyfriend mode activated." He gave me a smile and seemed to almost say something else. Before I could ask what, he slipped his arm around my waist. I settled my arm on his shoulders, letting myself enjoy the feeling of him pressed close. Though "enjoyed" was too mild a word. Reveled was more like it.

As we walked into the welcome wave of heat, I scanned the long room. People spoke in clusters along the bar and at high-top tables creating a din of sound that was accompanied by jazzy Christmas music. I thought I recognized Ella Fitzgerald crooning about Frosty, the debonair snowman.

I spotted Grandmother right away, raising a hand to her and smiling with my other arm firmly around Connor. Her smile in return was thin, and she immediately returned to her conversation with one of the VPs from the client's company, her bejeweled fingers wrapped around a glass of white.

Not wanting to stay long enough to check our coats—and knowing Connor was still leery of losing his jacket—we just slung them over our arms and grabbed two glasses of bubbly from a server. Another had a tray of delicate spring rolls, but Connor declined.

"Not hungry?" I asked as I waved the server away too.

He shrugged and mumbled something. He seemed nervous for some reason, and I stroked my hand up and down his back slowly. I could feel him shiver, and I moved us farther away from the door.

I made small talk with a few VIPs while Connor nodded and smiled when necessary. I kept my hand securely on his lower back.

When we were alone for a moment by the bar, we hung our coats over a stool. I murmured, "Are you sure you're okay? You seem jumpy?"

"Do I?" He seemed alarmed, but laughed it off. "Post-exam nerves, I guess."

I hesitated. "You're sure you're still okay with…this?" Raising an eyebrow, I hoped he'd understand my meaning.

Connor nodded immediately. "Yep. All good." He finished his champagne in a gulp.

"As long as you're sure." Something was off. I spoke quietly. "We can stop. You've already done your part."

His brows met. "It's only the twelfth. I still have a week before I go home. I don't want to stop."

Perhaps this was about the loan? I hadn't pressed him about why he'd needed the money, but could that reason be the source of his nerves? "I don't want to stop either," I said truthfully. "As long as you're sure."

"I'm sure." His eyes glittered, and he opened his mouth to say something before closing it. Then he leaned closer to whisper, "You can kiss me again." He watched me intently before adding,

"If you want to, I mean. For…this."

Was it dishonest to kiss him now? It probably had been last weekend, but I hadn't been able to resist asking. Now Connor was offering, and desire unfurled in my belly. The responsible thing to do would be to refuse and put distance between us. I'd always been responsible. As the elder brother and heir, I'd had to be.

Would it be so bad to be irresponsible for a minute?

The heat from Connor's body felt like a crackling fire, and I inched closer as I cupped his flushed cheek with my hand. His lips parted, and he met me halfway with a press of our mouths. It lasted several thumps of my heart before we eased apart and met each other's eyes.

Then we kissed again.

With more power this time, our heads tilting as our arms slid around each other. I remembered we were in public just before our tongues met. I pulled away with a breathless smile.

"That should do it, *mon amour*," I whispered, and Connor grinned.

We laughed and busied ourselves with fresh glasses of wine. When I glanced around to see if Grandmother was shooting daggers, I jolted in surprise to find Asher in the doorway.

"Hey!" I said far too loudly.

Asher watched us warily. "Hey." Then his expression brightened, and he waved to Grandmother before taking off his wool coat, which was covered in snow. He grimaced and apologized to the server who took it away to the coat cubby.

"What are you doing here?" I asked.

"I'm taking Gamma for our holiday dinner. This is the only night she has free. Well, after this." He slugged Connor's arm. "Hey, man. How did the exam go? I texted you back last night."

"Yeah, sorry," Connor said. "I had to concentrate."

"Cool. You said there was something you had to tell me?" Asher snagged a glass of white from a server. "What's up?"

"Oh, nothing!" Connor flailed, and half his wine sloshed out of the glass onto his sweater. "Whoops. I'll be back in a sec." He squeezed past a few people and disappeared in the direction of the bathroom.

Asher glanced around before jabbing me in the side with his finger and hissing, "What's the deal? Is the thing Connor wants to tell me that you two are fucking?"

I hissed back, "Shh! And no. Don't be ridiculous."

"Dude, I just saw you two kiss like you were about to get busy on the bar in front of Gamma, god, and the staff of whatever company is throwing this shindig."

"If you paid the slightest bit of attention to Utopia, you'd know whose party this is."

Asher boggled. "As if *that's* the important part? Spill it. I was right, wasn't I?" He winced. "No, don't tell me. Connor gets to do that."

"Look, I don't know what he wants to tell you, but we're not having sex." My face burned. This was not the place for this discussion.

"Okay. I believe you." He winked broadly. "Tell Con I'll talk to him tomorrow. I'd better say hi to Gamma."

"Tell her I have to leave early." I shrugged on my coat and grabbed Connor's as he made his way back.

"Tell her yourself!" Asher insisted. "I don't want to get in the middle."

"Too bad." I ushered Connor out the door. I'd shown up and done my duty, and that would have to be good enough for Grandmother.

Naturally, doubt and guilt hit me immediately. Connor and I ducked our heads as a gust of snow swirled around us and we did up our coats.

Would Grandmother be disappointed I hadn't stayed longer? Was I shirking my responsibility to Utopia? Was I endangering the chances of convincing her to invest in my housing project?

"Do you still want to go?" Connor asked. There was already fresh snow in his hair, and his cheeks were flushed and eyes bright.

All my worries melted away. "Absolutely," I said. "Here." I pulled out the beanie from my pocket and smoothed it over his head.

"What about you?" he protested.

"I'll take it back in a bit."

We climbed the stairs up to the park that had been built on an old elevated railway line and snaked through Chelsea. Sirens echoed and horns honked from below as Monday rush hour traffic clogged the streets.

"It's amazing how far away it feels up here," Connor said as we started along the boardwalk, which was covered in a few inches of snow. "I've been meaning to come down, but I never got around to it."

I was glad I'd worn my boots, and I handed Connor one of my gloves. "Did you forget yours?"

After a moment, he took the leather and slipped it on his left hand, putting his right hand in his jacket pocket. "Thanks. Yeah, I'm happy I remembered to wear pants, honestly."

The thought of Connor *sans* pants warmed me, and I laughed as we passed an art nouveau sculpture of a tree slowly being covered in thick, perfect snow. It muffled everything, including our steps. While other people passed by in both directions, the incoming storm seemed to have driven most indoors.

Dried grasses poked up, and thick snow balanced on the husks of dormant flowers. "I've never been up here in winter," I said. "Actually, I haven't been up here in years. That's one of the great things about our list. I take too much in New York for granted, and I need to make an effort to take advantage of what's right on my doorstep."

Connor peered around. Darkness had swiftly fallen along with the snow. "The lights are amazing. We're right in the city, but we're apart from it. In a bubble. Central Park has the same vibe."

"It does," I agreed, watching him watch the skyline. A little smile curved his lips, and I remembered how they'd felt soft yet firm under mine, and how he'd made a tiny sound—a sweet sigh that—

"Buddy!" a man shouted as our shoulders collided. Connor had tugged me aside at the last second, his cold hand gripping mine, or I'd have crashed straight into the guy.

"Watch where the fuck you're going!" the man added before continuing in the other direction.

"Whoops." I tried to laugh it off.

"You okay?" Connor was squeezing my hand and peering up at me with concern that made my heart swell.

"Yep! No concussion, I promise. The only thing injured was my pride. Maybe a shred of dignity. And I might have a bruised shoulder tomorrow. I swear I'm not normally this clumsy."

Only when I'm watching you instead of where I'm walking.

Connor smiled as he let go of my hand to gently prod my shoulder. "You always seemed so cool when I was a kid. So sophisticated."

"Uh-oh. My secret's out. I'm none of the above despite my designer suits." I rotated my shoulder. "It's fine. Really." I took his hand again, our bare skin meeting. "Cold," I said, further proving I was neither cool, sophisticated, suave, or any other synonym.

We stood face to face in the falling snow by the railing, out of the path of the few people hurrying by. Connor threaded our fingers together even though there was no one we knew here to see us and report back to Grandmother.

He blinked up at me, his lips parting as he sucked in a breath and blurted, "I want to tell you something. Ask you something, I guess." The words came out rapid fire.

It took me a moment to process. "All right."

Connor hesitated, biting his lip in the cutest, sexiest way.

I squeezed his fingers gently. "You can tell me."

"What if I'm not straight?"

In my mind, Handel's "Hallelujah Chorus" burst forth. "Then I'd want to kiss you again," I managed to say. "But we should probably talk about—"

With his gloved hand tangling in my hair and pulling down my head, Connor kissed me. He pressed his mouth to mine in a rush, a shudder going through him as we clung to each other, tasting until we had to gasp for air.

His eyes were dark with lust, his lips shiny as he blinked up at me. "Sorry. I interrupted you."

"You're good. This is good." Breathing hard, I held him close, my hand slipping around his lower back. I wanted to push him against the railing or find the closest tree so I could grind our cocks together, but I resisted. Barely.

He was hard against me, and after a glance around—bless Mother Nature for the increasingly heavy, thick snow—I gripped his denim-clad ass and rubbed against him.

Connor gasped softly. "I'm not wrong? You really want to...with me? I know this is supposed to be pretend and everything, but..."

"I want to kiss you all night." I trailed my lips along his jaw to his ear. "I want to do a hell of a lot more than kiss." Connor stiffened, his breath catching. Was that excitement or something else? I lifted my head. "Veto?"

He shook his head, snowflakes catching on his nose and eyelashes. "No veto. Can we kiss again first?"

In response, I captured his mouth, sliding my tongue inside. I waited to see if he tensed again, but he melted against me, moaning. I stroked our tongues together, and Connor made little whimpering sounds. He seemed happy to let me take the lead, so I explored his mouth.

He tasted of champagne, and I could have devoured him—would have if we weren't in danger of being snowed in on the High Line.

Reluctantly, I broke away. "My place. Cab." Connor nodded vigorously.

Our bare hands entwined, we practically ran down the nearest stairs, almost colliding with a parks employee who was shoveling. After apologizing, we made it to the street and groaned in unison at the standstill traffic.

"Subway's faster," I said, and we found the nearest station.

If we'd been in a cab, we could have kissed a bit more. At least hugged and snuggled. On the C train at rush hour? Not so much.

"I missed you this week," I murmured as we held onto the overhead pole, our bodies crushed together thanks to the afore-mentioned rush hour. I ached to be even closer. I wanted him skin on skin.

"Me too," Connor said. His face was flushed, eyes bright, and his hair mussed as he took off my hat and gave it back to me.

Had I *ever* wanted to kiss someone this badly? If I had, I couldn't remember.

"I'm so glad you said yes on Thanksgiving. I never expected this." I laughed. "Understatement of the year."

"Me either." Connor's laugh was giddy. He glanced around, then lowered his voice. "I used to dream about this."

My heart skipped. "About me?"

He nodded.

I leaned close to his ear and whispered, "How did you imagine me?"

Connor's face went beet red as he stammered.

"It's okay," I murmured, resting my hand on his hip under the hem of his leather jacket. "You can show me."

"You make me feel like I'm having a myocardial infarction."

I laughed. "The feeling's mutual. I think."

Connor smiled up at me, and there was that dimple. Why was the subway moving so slowly? We crawled along before picking up speed again. I reminded myself this was still faster than a cab uptown in the snow and traffic.

We squeezed together as passengers pushed past us to exit at Forty-second Street. Even in the crush of people and the stench of someone eating a hot dog with sauerkraut, Connor's shampoo filled my nose. It was clean and simple and perfect for him.

Not that he was *simple*, but…innocent, maybe?"

"What are you thinking about?" he asked suddenly.

"You," I answered truthfully. "And why the damn subway isn't going faster."

Finally, we made it to my stop at Seventy-second. Bare hands grasped, we passed riots of holiday lights amid the falling snow. An old carol—the one about angels singing—played in my lobby. I waved to Gus at the desk and jabbed the close button on the wood-paneled elevator, not able to wait to kiss Connor again.

We gasped and laughed into each other's mouths, kissing messily. I wanted to taste every inch of him, then start again at the beginning. I could have drowned in him, my whole body buzzing with lust and euphoria. He was just so sweet and wonderful, and I wanted to climb into his skin.

"You're gorgeous," I muttered as we stumbled from the elevator still half-entwined—and right into the path of my neighbor. "Mrs. Trent!" I exclaimed, wiping a trail of spit from my mouth with the back of my hand.

With wide eyes, the older woman stared, her mouth agape. Her gaze swept over us, her small black and white sheepadoodle barking at her feet and wagging its tail so hard it was in danger of snapping off.

"Hi, Pepper. Who's a good boy?" I crooned, bending to pet him before tugging Connor forward. "Merry Christmas, Mrs. Trent."

"And to you," she replied, laughter in her voice.

"Oh my god," Connor mumbled. "Is she going to tell everyone in your building?"

I fumbled with my keys, finally getting the deadbolt unlocked. "She's more than welcome to tell them I was sucking face with my gorgeous, sexy-as-fuck boyfriend in the elevator."

Connor smiled, but tension rippled through him, the air going thick as my words registered. Well, one word in particular.

I shut the door behind us. "What I meant was…" That. That had been exactly what I'd meant. Part of me wanted to sweep it under the rug with both hands so I could get back to touching Connor, but I forced myself to stop, think, and address it. "I know you're not really my boyfriend. Not yet? But maybe? If you even want that?"

"Um…" Connor swallowed hard. "I guess we should talk about all that?"

"Yes. It doesn't have to be right now, does it? We can agree that right now, we'd very much like to have sex with each other."

He groaned, stripping off my glove before moving to the zipper of his jacket. "Yep. Sex now. We're on the same page." His fingers twitched.

"Excellent." I abandoned my glove, coat, and boots.

The lights were off and the switch was too far away. I'd left the blinds in the living room open, and golden light from the snowy city cast a warm glow. For the first time, I wished I did have a Christmas tree to make it even cozier.

Since when did I care about coziness? As much as I wanted to rip off Connor's clothes and fuck him until we passed out, I had to stop and take his face in my hands to kiss him softly.

We stood kissing until I blindly took a few steps backward, hoping to hit the couch. I backed into a wall instead, but that would do. Our kisses turned demanding, and I moaned at the sensation of Connor's cold hands on my stomach under my sweater.

Breathing hard, he dropped to his knees and held onto my thighs with tense fingers. Looking up at me under his thick lashes, he asked, "Is this good?"

The sight of Connor kneeling at my feet was *extremely* good, and my cock swelled against the fly of my trousers. "Yes. Did you want something in particular down there?" I teased.

Instead of answering coyly or filthily, Connor looked down. "Um…"

Frowning, I ran my hand over his soft hair, now damp with melting snow. "You don't have to do anything you don't want to," I said.

"I'm tired of being chickenshit." Connor gulped, and if he wasn't out of college, his voice probably would have cracked as he blurted, "I want to suck dick."

"Mine specifically, I hope? Well, to be fair it's the only one in the room. Unless you're *very* flexible."

He blinked, breathing harshly, and I could see him start to fold in on himself, withering in the face of my joking that had clearly missed the mark. I tilted up his chin and gave him what I hoped was a reassuring smile.

"Hey, it's okay. You can do whatever you want. Or we can stop. There's no reason to be nervous."

Connor blinked up at me again, and *wow*, he really was beautiful. Those huge brown eyes were so vulnerable, even as his tone grew forceful. "I don't want to stop. I want you."

He unzipped my pants and freed my cock, peering at it intently and touching the head with his fingers. Shivers tripped down my spine.

"You're cut. I always wondered. I figured because Asher is, you would be too. Sorry, I shouldn't bring up your brother right now."

"It's okay." I traced the shell of his ear.

He licked his lips. "I want you in my mouth."

I nodded, my balls heavy with desire. "I'm all yours."

With a deep breath, Connor practically lunged at my cock, taking me almost to the root before choking. He sucked hard, and his mouth felt amazing wrapped around me—hot and wet and eager.

A little *too* eager—he coughed and gasped for breath, mumbling, "Sorry."

"Hey, hey. Slow down. We have all night."

Shaking his head, he muttered, "Why can't I get anything right?"

"Whoa." I tilted up his chin. "Is this your first time giving head?" It stood to reason since before tonight he'd insisted he was straight. Although I'd certainly sucked a lot of cock before coming out.

Looking anywhere but at me, he nodded, his cheeks flushed. He shrugged—a twitch bordering on violent. He'd dislocate a shoulder if he wasn't careful.

Connor mumbled, "I've never really done anything."

The rhythmic blaring of my mental alarm system erupted. "You mean with another man?"

Another painful-looking shrug. "Not with anyone."

"Nothing at Harvard?"

Head down, he mumbled, "I had to work hard to keep my scholarship. My parents can't afford things like yours can."

Right, but surely in four years at college there'd been a spare moment to hook up? He could have gone to a party once in a while and—

Why was I trying to problem-solve? It didn't matter why Connor hadn't hooked up in college. Nothing else mattered but being here with him now.

"It's okay." I caressed his hair, but he was so tense I wasn't sure if he wanted me to touch him.

"Sorry." He dropped his hands from my legs, and I realized how tightly he'd been squeezing my thighs. "I know this isn't what you signed up for."

This was going all wrong. "Come up here. Please?" He stood with his head low, and I caressed his cheek, encouraging him to meet my eyes, though he didn't. "Don't be sorry. You didn't do anything wrong."

Crossing his arms tightly, Connor bit out, "I know it's pathetic to still be a virgin. It's okay. You can laugh."

Stunned, I blinked. "*No.*" I held his cheek, then pressed my lips to the hot skin. "Baby, I'm not laughing." I kissed his other cheek, his forehead, and the tip of his nose where snowflakes had melted earlier. I stroked his back and sides gently. His eyes swam with unshed tears, and I could barely breathe through the urge to kiss this beautiful boy.

In a *whoosh* of breath, he relaxed into my arms, and I gave a silent prayer of thanks. Now I just had to figure out the right thing to say.

"It's all right," was all I could murmur, my neck damp with his breath where he'd pressed his face into my skin.

Connor swallowed with a *click*. The warmth of his whisper brushed my skin. "I was too chickenshit before," he repeated. "I just want..."

Fuck, I could imagine all too well what he wanted, because it shimmered through my veins. "Tell me," I coaxed, rubbing his hips, which felt intimate without grabbing his ass and being too pushy.

"I'm sick of being afraid."

"Good. There's nothing to be afraid of here. Not with me."

Connor lifted his head. His red face was tear-stained. "I know. After you kissed me at that party, it was like this big mysterious, huge thing was suddenly real." He pressed his hands over my chest, making my nipples tingle through my sweater. "Like we could touch, and even though I'm probably a shit kisser because I have zero practice, it wasn't up on a pedestal anymore. I'm probably not making any sense."

"Are you saying that was your first kiss?"

"Like I told you, I'm pathetic." He couldn't look at me.

I had to kiss him then, capturing his mouth gently but firmly. Connor sighed into me, and we kissed slow and deep. I held him in my arms, and I simultaneously wanted to keep him safe and innocent and protected—while my body hummed with lust and the need to be naked and coming with him.

Breathing through my nose, I imagined the smooth female voice from the latest meditation app I was trying.

"Breathe in Peace. Hold it in your heart center. Don't let it go yet. And now exhale slowly, keeping that peace within you, guiding you even as you breathe out."

Except my cock was still rock hard, my pulse pounded, and sweat dampened my hairline. This was why meditation was BS. Connor moaned into my mouth as our tongues explored.

Once I'd kissed him breathless, if he wanted to get on his knees for me again, I'd push between his swollen lips and teach him how to lick and touch and suck without pushing too far the first time…

It hit me that the best way was to show him. He was hard against me, and I slid my hand against his cock before breaking our kiss and asking, "Is this okay?"

Connor nodded, thrusting against my hand.

"You need to come, don't you?"

He could only whimper in response.

"I've got you, baby. I'm going to take care of you, okay?" I squeezed him before letting go and reversing our positions. Before dropping to my knees, I asked, "Do you want me to suck you?"

"*Fuck.*" He knocked his head against the wall. "Yes."

"Careful. Can't have the doctor getting a concussion." With a wink, I kneeled and slowly opened his jeans. His cock strained against the white fabric of his boxer briefs. Slowly, I kissed him through the cotton, licking at the damp spot where he'd leaked.

"Oh, fuck," he muttered, hands fisted at his sides and body rigid.

"It's okay. You're not going to come yet." I tugged down his jeans and underwear to his knees. His cock sprang out and nearly hit me in the eye, which would have been *real* smooth considering I was supposed to be the expert.

"You can touch me," I said. "Put your hands on my head." I leaned into his fingers. "Like that. Perfect."

I nosed at his groin, wiry hair tickling my nose. Then I nuzzled at his hip while tracing circles on his thighs with my fingers. Light hair dusted his legs, and his muscles quivered. The temptation to touch myself shocked me in its intensity.

I didn't even have him in my mouth yet—I wasn't supposed to be the horny, pent-up one here. I couldn't remember the last time I'd needed to come this badly.

"*Reid.*"

I chuckled. "Did you want something?"

His fingers tightened in my hair. "Please."

Slowly, I licked his balls, then along his thin shaft from the base to the tip, easing down his foreskin. Sitting back on my heels, my own cock still out, I looked up at him while I gave in and stroked myself.

"Can you say it? What you want me to do?"

Connor's dark eyes were locked on me. In the snow's glow, his face was pale and beautiful. "I want you to suck my dick," he whispered.

I bit back a moan, stroking myself harder. "Good boy." I let go of my cock and took hold of his hips, stilling the quaver in his body. Leaning close, I licked at his shiny tip, savoring the bitter drops of precum. "I love how you taste."

He jerked, his cock pulsing. Gazing up at him, I wrapped my

lips around the head and sucked. Not as hard as I wanted to, remembering to go easy.

"Fuck, Reid! I can't believe this is happening." His hands shook on my head. "I dreamed of this so many times."

A thrill raced down my spine, and I pulled off with a slick *pop* to grin up at him. "You really did?"

He nodded. "I had the biggest crush on you."

How had I missed that? It didn't matter—we were here now. I licked at his cock, stroking around the base with my hand. "When you imagined us together, was it like this?" My heart pounded, excitement sparking on my skin.

Connor nodded again. "Like this. Like…doing everything."

Without warning, I sucked him deeply before pulling off. *Everything* sounded amazing to me. "Did you imagine coming in my mouth?"

Gasping, he shuddered, his cock straining by my lips as if desperate to get back inside. "*Yes.*"

"I want to swallow your cum, baby. Will you give it to me?"

At Connor's hoarse assent, I swallowed him again, swirling my tongue around the head of his cock and reaching down to tease his balls. I was ready to blow too, and it only took seconds for Connor to stiffen, his fingers tight in my hair as he spilled in my mouth.

I swallowed convulsively, milking him until I saw stars, my nostrils flaring. He repeated my name like a prayer, staring down at me in wonder as I came with a few strokes, the musk of him lingering on my tongue.

Knowing I was the first to kiss him—let alone suck him off— was an undeniable thrill. Was it tacky for me to get off on being his first? Probably. Did I care?

As I stood and Connor tugged me close for a breathless kiss, his hands still tangled in my hair, the only thing I cared about was giving him more.

Giving him *everything.*

Chapter Eleven
Connor

THAT WAS MY cum I could taste on Reid's tongue. I was practically panting into his mouth, but he kissed me slowly, patiently, so gently. Tears pricked my eyes. He was being so *kind*.

Of course, my asshole brain had to hiss: *He's being nice because you're pitiful.*

I broke free and blurted, "Sorry. I know that was—I'm—" I shook my head. "Sorry."

"Hey, hey." He brushed back my hair and examined my face, which was probably red and blotchy as shit. "Why are you apologizing?"

"Because you're—and I'm—" I rolled my eyes. "You know."

"I don't, actually. You're so damn sexy."

Me. Reid Cabot was saying that to me. After blowing me. *Me.* I tried to think of something to say that wasn't totally cringe. I went with, "You too," which was definitely cringey, but whatever.

He gave me that gleaming red carpet smile. "Hungry? We could order in."

"Okay."

"What do you feel like? Maybe pizza?"

"Okay."

"Or we could do Chinese."

"Okay."

Reid laughed, a low rumble in his chest that made my stomach somersault. "Are you so blissed out you'll agree to anything right now?"

"Yeah." I was grateful to the wall behind me and Reid's big hands rubbing up and down my sides. Jesus, I wanted his hands on my bare skin. We were wearing way too many clothes still.

He laughed again. "How about keto protein bars?"

I smiled. "Okay."

"Day-old tuna sandwiches from a vending machine?"

"Okay."

Reid kissed me, slipping his tongue into my mouth, and another thrill shot through me. He murmured, "Let's order for real. There must be something you're craving."

"Um… Empanada Mama's always good. It's in Hell's Kitchen."

"I don't think I've had it."

"And you call yourself a New Yorker?"

He grinned. "Showing me up. Classic New York move." He kissed me again, then fished his phone from his coat pocket. "Tell me what to order."

It took me a second to recover from the way he'd just kissed me so casually, and how it had felt so normal. How was kissing Reid Cabot *normal?*

"Connor?"

"Right. Uh…" My mind was blank. Jesus, I wasn't a *food* virgin, and I'd ordered from this place a zillion times—I could recommend the best dishes. I was about to ask him for his phone to refresh my memory when I blurted, "Viagra!"

He blinked. "Pardon?"

I had to laugh. "It's a seafood empanada."

"Oh!" Reid tapped his phone. "Okay, got it. Wheat or corn?"

I rattled off suggestions as he tapped and nodded. There. Not a food virgin. Go, me. "And the chicharrónes are amazing."

I pondered whether or not I was still an actual virgin. I mean,

I knew it was a bullshit construct of our society, but it was something I'd built up in my head for so long that it was hard to shake it off.

"Connor?"

"Uh-huh?" I still leaned against the wall with my dick out. I debated whether putting it away would be more awkward than not drawing attention to it. Though Reid didn't seem bothered or anything.

"Dessert? Or are you sweet enough?" He waggled his eyebrows.

How was a guy with custom Armani suits such a *dork*? And how was I? Because that cheesy line made me grin like an idiot. "They've got a coconut dulche de leche cake to die for."

"*Oh.*" He tapped the screen. "Yes. Sold. Okay, order's in."

He stripped off his sweater, and I stared at his bare, hairy chest in the bright snowy glow from outside. *Then* he kicked off his pants and underwear and was naked, so nope, didn't seem like Reid minded that my dick was hanging out.

He took a few steps and extended his hand. "Come on. Let's get comfy."

I took his warm hand even though mine was sweaty and probably gross. "I'm not sure it's possible for you to put on anything more comfortable." I was trying to mimic that cheesy old line people said in movies, but it probably sounded weird.

Reid only smiled as he led me into his bedroom. "Naked is comfy, it's true." He opened a drawer and pulled out flannels and T-shirts. "I'm not a big naked eater, though."

"Good point. That can be…messy."

He let go of my hand to peel off my clothes, undressing me like I was a little kid but in a sweet, cool way and not a weird one. "Want the Knicks again?" He held up the worn tee I'd used before. At my nod, he handed it over.

We were both temporarily naked, and outside of a locker

room, I'd never experienced that. We both looked at each other, not trying to hide it because there was no reason not to look. For a second, I wanted to turn and cover up, but it was also exhilarating. The way Reid's gaze roamed over my skin made me hot all over.

He seemed to like what he saw.

His body was toned and hairy in all the right places. As I bent to pull on boxers, I stared at his dick. It was still wet, and part of that was from *my* mouth. Fuck, I'd loved the feeling of him warm and straining and filling me so completely I'd choked.

Reid was thick, and his balls were bigger than mine. Hairier than mine too, but I could tell he trimmed his pubes. He was rich, so he probably went to a salon or some shit. I was ready to drop to my knees and suck him again as he strolled to the en suite bathroom and ran a washcloth under the tap.

I pulled up the boxers and put on the tee and watched him clean his junk. He knew I was watching—I mean, I was openly staring—and a little smile tugged at his insanely kissable mouth. A mouth I'd kissed. A mouth I'd had my own dick inside. A mouth I was going to kiss again ASAP.

"C'mere."

Mouth dry, I joined him in the bathroom, where he kissed me softly, a finger under my chin. My belly fluttered. If this was a dream, I never wanted to wake up, please and thank you.

We drank beer while we waited for dinner and found the end of *Die Hard* playing. On the couch with our feet up on the coffee table, I leaned into Reid, his arm snug around my shoulders. There was no other word for it—we were cuddling.

The Stella Artois bottle was cold in my hand, and my feet could have used socks, but the rest of me was hot and tingling—and honestly a little crampy from staying still. I could feel the steady rise and fall of Reid's breathing, my arm jammed in between his ribs and mine. I cautiously sipped my beer.

"You can move, you know." Reid squeezed my shoulder.

I stiffened. "Why would I want to move?"

"Because you feel so tense, I'm afraid you're going to snap in half." He chuckled. "It's okay if you're not a cuddler."

"No, I am!" I exhaled forcefully. "I guess I'm not sure if I am? I'm not used to being this close to someone for an extended period of time. Or any time."

"That's fair." He stroked my arm, his fingers dancing over my bare skin beneath the old T-shirt. "Relax. Breathe. Drink your beer. And we can sit apart if it's more comfortable."

"Okay. This is good, though. I like this." Tentatively, I slid my palm over his thigh and rested it there. "At least until the food comes."

"Sounds like a plan."

Once it came, we watched *Home Alone* while we ate. Empanada Mama's was delicious as always. I was pleased that Reid made appreciative moans—moans that also pleased my dick—and praised the food. He had a blob of guacamole in the corner of his mouth, and before I could over-think it—or even think about it at all—I was swiping it away with my thumb.

Plantain chip in hand, Reid's lips curved into a smile, and he sucked my still-hovering thumb into his mouth before releasing it slowly. "Too good to waste," he said with a wink. I made a sound that was a cross between a bleating goat and I don't even know what.

Kevin McAllister had just given the Wet Bandits their seventeenth injury that should have killed them sixteen injuries ago when I realized Reid was asleep. We'd slouched close together after eating, and his hand sat heavy on my thigh with his fingers touching my inner thigh.

His lips had parted, and his breathing was deeper, his eyes moving in REM sleep. His dark, thick eyelashes fanned over his skin, and I wanted to kiss each one. How was he so beautiful and smart and funny and kind—and somehow into *me*?

Was it weird that I almost wanted to call my dads and tell them I'd hooked up? Answer: *Yes*, that was incredibly weird, dude. But after so long in the closet, I wanted to shout it from the rooftops. I'd told my dads I didn't want to broadcast that I was gay yet, but now I wasn't so sure.

Reid mumbled something and shifted, and I held my breath, hoping he'd keep his hand on my thigh. He did, moving it a few inches and sending sparks straight to my balls. Just being touched like that—so intimately—made me want to do cartwheels.

It would probably also be weird to tell Asher since Reid was his brother. Worry tugged at me. Would Asher be cool with us? Not to get ahead of myself or anything.

The loud beep of my phone made me jump, and I cursed as I raced into Reid's bedroom to grab it from my jeans. Reid had shifted and murmured, and hopefully I hadn't wrecked his nap. I answered the call as I processed the name on the screen.

"Can I speak to Connor Lisowski?" a woman asked. "This is CVS calling about the job application you submitted."

"Oh, hi!" I cleared my throat. "Yes. This is Connor."

"It says on your application you're a student?"

"Yes, I'm in med school at Columbia. I just need to make some cash."

She was silent a moment. "You know this position is overnight restocking? It's not in the pharmacy."

"Right, I know. I have classes and studying, so overnight's great."

The woman rattled off more questions, and we made an appointment for an in-person interview that sounded like a formality to make sure I wasn't serial killer material. She said, "One to three shifts a week starting in January works for you?"

"Perfect."

I'd left the bedroom door ajar, and I knew Reid was awake as soon as I tiptoed out into the living room after hanging up. He waved from the couch. "Hey."

"Um, hey. Sorry to wake you. It was a job thing."

"Aren't you a little busy with school for a job?"

I stood halfway between the couch and bedroom, weirdly frozen on the spot. "It's just part time. It's cool. I need to pay you back and stuff."

Reid waved a dismissive hand, something like annoyance flashing over his face. "Don't worry about that. I don't want you burning out. Forget the money."

Whoa. "Um, yeah, I'm not going to forget that I owe you ten grand. No way." I crossed my arms. "Even if we—if we're—no way. I'm paying you back all of it."

He raised his hands. "Okay. Just know you can take as long as you need."

"Yeah. Thanks."

Fuck. Now we were suddenly awkward. I wasn't sure what to do. Rejoin him on the couch for more cuddling? Or was I overstaying my welcome? He didn't seem to want me to leave, but I also shouldn't have taken it for granted he wanted me to stay, right?

"Sorry I fell asleep. Amazing sex followed by beer and great food is a surefire way to knock me out."

I couldn't suppress a grin, the tension releasing. "Was it really amazing?"

"What do you think?" He stood and slowly approached, reminding me of a jungle cat on the prowl. His boxers hung low on his hips, and he peeled off his white tee, letting it drop from his fingers.

"It was amazing. I also don't have a frame of reference for comparison."

He laughed, low and sexy. "So you're saying I might be terrible in bed?"

"Excuse you, I am *not* saying that."

He prowled close and slipped his hands under the Knicks T-shirt, making me shiver, goosebumps spreading over my skin. "How about we go to bed and explore this issue further?" he whispered in my ear before nuzzling my neck.

"Uh-huh. More investigation needed."

Being naked with Reid on his bed, the covers pushed down to our feet, felt incredibly grown-up. Here I was in New York City in bed with my…what? Crush? Hookup? Potential boyfriend?

"This good?" he asked.

"Uh-huh."

We faced each other on our sides and kissed. It only took a minute before we were hard and groping each other. Spit shone on Reid's lips as he broke our kiss with a gasp.

"What do you want to do?"

"I don't know."

He traced my lips with his finger, smiling. "What are you curious about? Anything in particular?"

"Like… Do you do butt stuff?"

"I do." He answered so easily. "Should I elaborate?"

"Yep." My dick throbbed, and I rolled my hips against his looking for friction.

"I've had cocks and dildos inside me. One of my ex-girlfriends loved pegging me with a strap-on."

I swallowed hard. "Wow." Even though I wasn't into girls, that mental image was *hot*. Reid getting fucked? Jesus.

He ran his hand over the swell of his ass. "If you have questions, ask away."

"Did you—were you, like, on your hands and knees for that?"

"Yes. Not just for her. For men too. On my hands and knees. On my back. Riding their cocks. There are all kinds of ways to do it."

My throat was so dry I could only croak. "And you've fucked people in the butt?" We were rubbing our dicks together as we talked, and Reid's fingers were skimming along the crack of my ass.

"I have." His fingers brushed my hole. "Have you experimented here by yourself?"

How was I supposed to make words happen? Ugh, especially *these* words. I managed, "Not really."

"That's okay," he said smoothly, like he meant it.

I cringed anyway. "Aren't you going to ask why not?" I demanded. A mix of embarrassment and weird anger burst up. Not directed at Reid, but myself for being a chickenshit. I felt like a kid, defaulting to defensive aggression in a way I hadn't in a long time.

He stopped his caresses, and I was grateful he didn't remove his hand and roll away from me. He watched me carefully. "You can veto talking if you want. We can—actually, no."

"No?" I was rigid, my heart pounding. I'd fucked this up. The warm weight of his hand on my hip was the only thing anchoring me from breaking into a million brittle pieces.

"We have to talk. I need to know what's going on in there."

"Everything's fine! I'm sorry. Just keep going." I was ready to beg. I was supposed to be an adult. How would I be a doctor if I felt like a stupid kid? Reid was still watching me. Waiting.

I blurted, "I was too scared. To finger myself." Oh my god, how pathetic. "It's okay, you can laugh."

He didn't even smile, his expression calmly serious. "You're safe here. I'm not laughing at you. You can tell me anything."

I had to kiss him for that, sighing with relief as he kissed me back and wrapped me in his strong arms. The temporary spike of anger faded, soothed away by Reid's patient, sweet touches.

When we caught our breath, he said, "Do you want me to show you something?" His rich, deep voice made my toes curl. I nodded desperately. Reid rolled away for a second, and I was already grabbing at him to bring him back.

He laughed then, lube in his hand. "I'm right here, I promise."

"Cold without you," I said, which was partly true.

"Do you want to get under the covers?" He paused. "Turn off the light?"

It was honestly tempting, but I shook my head. "I want to see you."

Reid kissed me hard, his tongue deep in my mouth. We moaned together, and I could have rubbed off against him easily. But no, there was more he was offering, and I wanted every bit of it.

I was on my left side facing him. He coated my right middle finger in lube before urging my hand behind me. "Veto any time. Yes?"

"Yes."

There was no way in hell I was vetoing a single thing.

"You have to push past the rim." He nodded, coaxing me. "That's it."

It was bizarre to be fingering myself in the first place, but especially with Reid watching. But at the same time, it wasn't?

As I tentatively wriggled my middle finger inside, he encouraged me with the confidence I'd always admired when I'd watched him from the corner at teenage parties, crushing on him. Fantasizing, but never imagining in a million years Reid would turn out to be bi and into guys.

Into *me*.

Because he clearly seemed to be, evidenced by the fact that he was watching me finger myself, and his dick was rock hard against my thigh. It burned as I pushed inside deeper, but I liked it. *Loved* it.

"Crook your finger. A little more." He guided me, my right leg hooked over his hip. His hand stole between my legs, and he rubbed my taint, which made me shiver.

"Not sure if you can really reach it from that angle. Can I try?"

he asked.

At my nod, he lubed his own finger and reached between my legs. I moaned as his finger replaced mine, and then he touched what my scientific brain knew was the prostate gland and what my sex brain decided was the greatest piece of flesh in history.

"Fuck!" I almost shouted.

"There you go. Feel that?"

"Jesus, yes, fuck, oh my god! Fuck, I need—" The sensations were almost too much as he touched that perfect spot. I winced.

Immediately, Reid eased out his finger, and I full-on *whined* even though it had been intense.

"It's okay, baby." He urged me onto my back. "You want me to finish you off?"

I nodded eagerly. "You can fuck me."

Reid hesitated as he pushed my legs open, his hands warm on my thighs. "Is it okay if we wait until another night?"

Part of me wanted to whine again and say no. "You want another night with me? Not just now?"

"You bet your tight ass I do." He bent and kissed me, biting at my lip. "I want it all. But right now, I want to suck you again while I finger fuck you."

"Yeah, that sounds pretty good." Understatement of the damn year. I opened my legs all the way, and he pushed up my knees, exposing me.

"You're beautiful," he murmured, his hands roaming over my legs and butt. Crap, I hoped I didn't have any pimples down there.

He leaned down and kissed my ass cheeks. His five o'clock shadow was the perfect amount of rough on my flushed skin.

Especially as he lapped at my balls, licking and sucking as he pushed his finger past my rim again. It burned again to have him inside me, and—

"Oh god! Yes. *Reid.*" The prostate really was a gift I should have been exploring years ago.

My dick leaked, and he didn't even get to suck me again before I came all over myself. I was bent in half, shaking and saying his name. He called me beautiful again and licked the cum off my belly while still stroking inside me. I spurted out a few more drops.

"How do you want me to come?" Reid asked breathlessly, and instead of being awkward, it was incredibly sexy how he kept asking me stuff.

I almost said, "*On me*," but he'd jerked himself to finish earlier. "I want to make you come this time."

He groaned, "Please," and seemed to be waiting for me to decide exactly how.

It wasn't original, but what the hell. "On your back the way you just did it for me?"

Reid eagerly flopped over and opened himself for me, holding his legs. He nodded to the lube, and I squeezed more onto my finger with shaky hands.

It really did help that he'd shown me how to finger myself. I pushed into his hole, and even though the angle was different, the basics were the same. I found the right spot as he cried out. It took some doing to get his dick in my mouth so I could suck him while I rubbed inside him, but he only encouraged me.

"So good, Connor. You're a natural."

That word—*natural*—elated me. I moaned around his shaft, which throbbed in my mouth, bitter drops leaking onto my tongue. Fuck, I loved sucking cock. I knew I wasn't very good at it, but I stretched my lips around him, taking him as far as I could.

"Baby, I'm gonna—" Reid tensed, his hand suddenly on my head as if to urge me off.

No, this time I wanted it all. I wanted Reid to come in my mouth, and I was going to swallow everything—

I choked and sputtered, his jizz dripping down my chin as I

kept going and swallowed as much as I could. His fingers had clenched in my hair, and the tug of pain tightened my empty balls. It was the perfect mix of sensations, especially when Reid loosened his grip and caressed my head.

I didn't want to let go of his cock, but I knew from experience—hey, I had some now!—that it would get oversensitive. I released him from my mouth and eased my finger from inside him as he softened. Breathing hard, we stared at each other, me sitting up between his legs.

"Wow," I said. "Butt stuff is incredible."

Reid grinned. "And there's more where that came from."

More! I grinned back. "With no vetoes in sight."

He pulled me down on top of him for a kiss, and we were sticky and gross, but amazing. It felt right. *Natural.* That word echoed in my head. I'd worried for so long that people wouldn't believe my feelings were real, and maybe some would still be dubious and blame my dads. But there was no way anyone could *influence* me into feeling at home in Reid's arms. This was right.

In the bathroom, we cleaned up, and Reid brushed his teeth before offering me the brush. The thought of sharing anyone else's toothbrush would be gross, but my heart fluttered at the casual way Reid held it out. It felt easy and right as I spit into the sink and he smoothed on moisturizer from a small container that probably cost a ton.

He didn't seem to want me to leave. It would have been a punch in the nuts if he had. But no, he went through what I assumed was his nightly routine and asked questions about school. We were still naked, and the bathroom floor was warm under our feet.

Reid said, "Before you know it, you'll be Dr. Lisowski." He frowned. "What's that face for?"

"Huh?" I looked up from reading the side of the moisturizer.

"When I said 'Dr. Lisowski' you made—there. That face. A

wince crossed with a grimace."

I laughed uneasily. "A grince? A wimace?"

"Yeah. What's that about?"

"Nothing. It just feels like a million years away." I hadn't realized I'd made a face. Twice, apparently.

Leaning his hip on the marble counter, Reid examined me. "I'm going to have to veto that explanation."

"Is that how vetoing works?"

"Irrelevant, and you're changing the subject. Shouldn't hearing 'Dr. Lisowski' excite you?"

I wanted to turn away from his intense gaze. Suddenly, I was very aware of my nakedness. I shrugged and straightened the towel hanging by the sink. "It's not the doctor part. It's my crappy name."

"What's wrong with your name?"

"Nothing technically. It's not the name itself. It's that I got it from my father."

"Ah." Reid smoothed his palm down my back. "I have the impression that's about all he gave you?"

"Yeah, something like that." I hadn't realized how lucky I'd been as a kid when he'd ghosted me for months or sometimes years at a time. Then he'd reappeared in the summer. Now he'd left me with a lot more than his name. Yay, thanks for the crippling debt. At least I'd have this new job. I could handle a couple of midnight shifts.

"You're not close to any of your other family on that side?"

"Nah. Mike burned a lot of bridges."

"That's too bad. You ever think about reaching out to them?"

I blinked. "Actually, no. I haven't thought about them in years. I have my dads, and their whole family. Logan's family. Seth's are terrible. They totally cut him off when they found out he's gay."

I'd picked up scraps of info over the years, and I knew it had hurt Seth deeply. I also knew Logan would have loved to tell them exactly what he thought, which would probably involve a lot of profanity.

"That's terrible," Reid said quietly. He dropped his hand from my back and screwed the lid back on the toothpaste. "I'm lucky my family is accepting."

"Yeah, but you 'grinced' when you said that."

He laughed ruefully. "I'm sure you can guess that's about my grandmother. It's fine. It's not as though she disinherited me."

I slid my arm around his back. "Yeah, but it's like when people talk about tolerance. It's not the same thing at all as acceptance."

Reid blinked down at me before cupping my cheek. "That's exactly what it is. Thank you for putting it into words."

"Um, you're welcome."

He stroked my cheek with his thumb. "Does your family know?"

I smiled, remembering Logan and Seth's visit. "My dads actually just found out. They were awesome about it, obviously. I dunno why I was so nervous about telling them. They believed me right away. That I'm gay."

Reid's eyes tightened at the corners. "Why wouldn't they have believed you?"

"It's stupid." I fidgeted and crossed my arms. "I tied myself up into knots for years for nothing."

"It's okay. It's in the past now." He pressed our lips together before hugging me. "Let's go to bed."

We cuddled naked under the covers with Reid's arm around me, urging me to rest my head on his chest. He brushed his fingers through my hair, making my scalp and neck tingle.

Listening to the steady *thump* of his heart, hair tickling my cheek and the sensation of his nipple against my jaw, how was I not supposed to fall in love?

Chapter Twelve

Connor

"WOW, EITHER YOU crushed that exam or you got laid."

I froze in the middle of unzipping my leather jacket. Asher was grinning up at me from the booth in the back of the pub, dressed in a gray suit for work. I stupidly glanced around to see if anyone had heard and had the ridiculous urge to find a mirror. Did I look different?

Asher's eyebrows shot up. "Holy shit, you did!"

"Shh!" I glanced around again, but the long table of office people laughing over their lunch and doing a noisy gift exchange weren't paying attention. I managed to toss my jacket into the corner of the stained red fabric booth and slide in across from him. "Yeah, exam went great."

He poured me a pint from the pitcher. "*And?*"

"What?" I gulped the cool lager gratefully and realized I hadn't taken off my gloves. Asher was watching me with a shit-eating grin as I stuffed the gloves in my jacket pocket.

We'd never discussed that I was still a virgin. At Rencliffe, I'd gone along with him and the guys in talking about tits and hot chicks, but at a certain point, Asher had stopped asking me about girls when it was just the two of us.

He'd told me all about losing his virginity in way too much detail, but my sex life—or the lack thereof—had become an unspoken topic.

He sipped his beer. "When you walked in, I could tell you'd loosened a few screws."

He'd always teased me about being uptight. "Yeah, like I said. Exam went great." I ran my fingers through the condensation on the glass. Fuck I hoped it had gone great. What if—

"A-ha! There it is. You're worrying about that exam. Something else loosened you up."

"How much beer have you had? You have to go back to work. You're cut off." My cheeks burned, and I took another gulp.

Asher's grin faltered. "You know you can tell me about stuff, right? Like, if you hooked up with someone. Or if you didn't, or whatever."

That old panic flapped its wings, and I was about to scoff and change the subject but stopped. In the now-awkward silence, we stared at each other.

Asher knew. I knew he knew—hell, he'd apparently told Reid in the past that I was queer. Why was this still so hard? It wasn't only because the guy I'd hooked up with was Asher's brother.

Okay. One step at a time. "Um, yeah. I guess I did. Get laid."

Asher lit up like the Christmas tree near our table. "I knew it!" He raised his hand for a high five, which I automatically gave. "Tell me about…them."

"It's um…" Another gulp of beer, my pint already drained. "A guy."

Asher nodded eagerly. "Cool, man. That's awesome."

Affection swelled in me. He was trying so hard to be supportive. He didn't narrow his eyes and look skeptical, or ask *why* I was queer and whether Logan and Seth had made me that way. *Of course* he didn't. And I hadn't really suspected he would. Not Asher. Yet I'd stayed silent with everyone.

"I'm stupid for not telling you years ago," I said. My chest tightened. "I'm gay. Which you know, obviously." My lungs expanded, relief flowing through me. Saying those words was getting easier.

Asher gently kicked my boot with his under the table. "I'm glad you told me now." His concerned expression morphed into a devilish grin. "Now spill. Have you been banging dudes all along?"

I laughed. "Nope. Last night was my first time," I mumbled.

Asher's eyes widened. "Whoa. Bro, you have a lot of catching up to do. I'm almost jealous. Sex has gotten *so* much better over the years. My first time..." He winced—*grinced*, which made me smile to myself. "Oof. We had no clue what we were doing. It was fun, but...short."

"I bet." I nodded to the server as she took our usual food order of burgers and fries.

Asher refilled my glass. "We're older now, though. Did this guy have experience? Judging by how loose your screws were when you walked in, I bet he banged you good."

Oh god. This was the part when I had to tell him that the guy who'd screwed me was his brother. Which he clearly didn't suspect somehow? Before I could say anything, Asher screwed up his face at his phone and typed with his thumbs.

I asked, "What?"

"Reid wants me to go to some charity event for the company this weekend. No way. I have plans."

At the mention of Reid's name, my pulse leapt, my balls tingled, and I fought irritation. Had Asher always been this unfair to his brother? Probably. Even though I'd always crushed on Reid, it had never occurred to me that he'd had unfair pressure piled on him after their dad died. Reid did *so* much for the family.

I sipped my beer. "Can't you just go to one thing for him?"

Asher blinked at me. "What's up with you?"

Okay, I'd done a piss-poor job of keeping my tone casual. "Nothing. It just doesn't seem like a big deal."

"I have plans. This is Reid's thing. I don't work at the company. I do enough of Gamma's events."

I almost blurted that maybe Reid didn't *want* to work at the company but managed to bite my tongue.

"Besides, I thought you were fake dating him and the whole point was to show up at these events on his arm so Gamma would cut the shit with trying to fix him up with whatshername."

"Yeah, but we've done a few already. I'm pretty sure your grandmother believes it."

"Hmm. Yeah, true. She didn't say a word about you two at dinner last night. If she was suspicious, she would have grilled me in a polite, roundabout way that would somehow be more effective than demanding answers."

Why did it make me happy that Mrs. Cabot believed it? Maybe she could accept us? If Reid and I were a real couple—

Nope. Beep, beep, beep. Back that up. One step at a time.

Asher said, "Anyway, back to this guy you hooked up with. Are you seeing him again? Is it going to bug him that you and my brother are acting all lovey-dovey in public? You guys put on a good show."

"Um…"

His jaw dropped. "Holy fuck, dude. Wait, wait, wait. It wasn't an act, was it? I thought maybe, but—no way. You and Reid? *Reid's* the guy you banged last night? Holy *shit*. He is. I can tell by that dopey look on your face. Wow. I guess some teenage dreams do come true."

"What?" I sputtered. "What are you talking about?"

Asher snorted. "Dude. You had a massive boner for my brother all through Rencliffe. And college."

"You knew?" I groaned and dropped my face into my hands. "Tell me you never mentioned it to Reid."

"Duh, obviously not."

Our lunches arrived, and we took turns with the ketchup bottle. Asher dipped his fries in a side of mayo and then ketchup on his plate. On cue, I screwed up my face. "Ew, mayo."

And on cue, Asher put on a super strong French accent. "Peasant, you know nothing of cuisine. If you'd been to Europe as I have, I would have no need to explain."

Then we laughed the way we always, always did, and I wanted to pull Asher to his feet and hug him tightly.

He said, "Man, I had this funny feeling yesterday, but I told myself I was imagining it. On Thanksgiving, I encouraged you to do the whole fake-boyfriends thing because I thought it would be fun for you since you'd always had a crush."

I took the pickle off the side of my plate and put it on Asher's. "Did you think it might help me come out or whatever?"

"Yeah, maybe? It happened so fast. Mostly I just thought it would give you fresh spank-bank material. So, spill. I mean, not about my brother dicking you." He quickly added, "Not because it's gay. If it was anyone else, you could tell me anything."

"It's cool. I get it." Another surge of affection warmed my chest. "I dunno. We've spent a lot of time together the past few weeks."

Asher swallowed a bite of his burger. "Right, going to boring holiday parties."

"Yeah, also Reid came up with a list of quintessential New York things to do."

"What do you mean?" He swiped at a blob of mayo/ketchup on his tie and cursed under his breath.

"Quintessential means—"

"Ha ha, asshole. I got fifteen hundred on my SATs too. Wait, was that why he asked me if you'd like the High Line or the Brooklyn Bridge?"

He'd asked Asher about what I liked? "I guess so." I remembered last night on the High Line in the snow, the city right there but seeming far away, me and Reid in our own world…

Asher laughed. "Dude. You are *swooning* right now. It means—"

"Shut up!" I kicked him, and for a minute, our feet tussled under the scarred wooden table.

We stopped when the server came by to ask how we were doing, both of us trying not to giggle. We hadn't had a foot fight in ages.

"*Anyway*," I said. "We've been doing these other things on the list."

"Like what?"

I told him, finishing with, "I'm not sure what's next. He's been keeping it as a surprise."

"Shit, I had no idea my brother was such a romantic."

My face burned, and I fought a smile. It *was* romantic, wasn't it? "It's fun. Not a big deal."

Asher's smile faded. "Right. Are you guys… Are you still going to see each other after the holidays?"

Yes, or I'll die.

The thought of not seeing Reid again after Christmas knocked the air out of me. I forced a shrug. "Guess we'll see."

"Right," he repeated, worry creasing his brow despite him adding, "just have fun. Get your freak on. Don't stress."

"Totally. No stress. We're just having fun for the holidays. It's a Christmas miracle that I finally came out and got laid."

And fell in love.

Asher lifted his glass. "I'll drink to that."

We clinked, and I ordered myself to stop thinking about being in love. It was only because I'd crushed on Reid for so long that I was being swept away in big emotions. Add in the virgin factor, and of course I felt like I was in love. I needed to keep my head on straight and enjoy my time with Reid. I was heading home in less than a week now.

While the thought of Christmas at home usually filled me with anticipation and counting down the days, now I hoped time would crawl and limp or maybe slip into a nice long coma.

As the bill came, Asher gave the server his card and said, "It's on me."

"But it's my turn."

"Nah, it's Christmas." He glanced away, and I tensed. There was something cagey in that avoidance of my gaze. I'd been at Rencliffe on a scholarship, and Asher had always been generous in buying me stuff. Once I'd gotten summer jobs, I'd insisted we go half and half.

I scowled. "Dude. Spit it out." He'd never been a very good liar.

Asher sighed. "Reid said something about you needing money."

My heart dropped like a rock. For the most part, I'd been successfully compartmentalizing the fact that I owed Reid ten grand. I'd also thought it was our secret, and a stab of hurt knifed through me.

"Did he...tell you?" I asked.

Asher's brows met. "I don't think so? He asked something about it a couple of weeks ago."

"What did he say exactly?"

"Dude, I dunno. I think he asked whether you needed money." He still frowned. "Do you? You know you can ask me, right?"

"I know." I would have had to if not for the deal with Reid. Okay, so Reid hadn't told him. It was fair that he'd asked Asher if he knew anything. I couldn't get mad at him for being curious when I wasn't giving him any hints.

"But do you?" Asher asked.

"No. I'm good. Thanks, though."

"Okay." He checked his phone. "Shit, I have to get back. More spreadsheets to toil over."

"Thoughts and prayers."

He flipped me the finger, and we headed out. As I rode the subway north, I chewed over admitting the truth to Reid. I knew I should just rip off the Band-Aid. But everything was so perfect right now. My ass was a tiny bit tender, and I squeezed my inner muscles, loving the reminder.

I imagined I could still taste him and smell his peppery cologne with the sweet hint of…lily? Lilacs? Jasmine? As if I could identify any floral scents aside from rose. I had no clue.

Sure, when I inhaled now, my nose filled with the gross subway smells of BO, greasy food, and lingering cigarette stench from the guy standing a few inches away as we leaned to the side, bracing for the next station.

But in my head, I could smell Reid and taste his mouth instead of beer and burger. I shivered in anticipation of seeing him again tonight. I still had to study, but the worst exams were over. All I wanted was to be with Reid and touch him. It was like a drug, or what I imagined that kind of craving might be like.

I pushed through the crowd at Times Square, weaving through tourists and scammers and people handing out flyers for comedy shows. It had been the easiest route to get off there and walk a few avenues over to my neighborhood. Hell's Kitchen was still busy with people, but it was always a relief to get past Eighth Avenue and leave most of the tourists behind.

The afternoon was heavy and gray, and the Christmas lights and glittery wreaths and garlands brightened the concrete and brown buildings. Not that I needed the holiday glitz—to me, the sun was beaming down, birds were chirping, and I could have been home in Albany bent over my motorcycle with the wind in my face.

The thought of telling Reid how painfully, pathetically gullible I'd been made me want to puke into the gutter. Everything with Reid was brand new, gleaming and sparkling like a Christmas tree ornament. I couldn't stand thinking of saying those words out loud. The virgin thing had been bad enough, and Reid had been amazing.

Amazing.

My heart swelled to think of how patient and sweet and wonderful he'd been last night. He wouldn't judge me for how stupid I'd been with the money. I was almost positive, reminding myself there were no guarantees in life.

I ducked into Amy's Bread to see if they had any cupcakes left. I wasn't sure if Reid would prefer red velvet or devil's food, so I got both for later, along with a few snickerdoodles.

I'd tell Reid after the holidays. I was going home so soon, and then I wouldn't see him until New Year's. At least, I hoped I would. Anxiety bubbled up, but I tamped it down as I crossed Tenth Ave and neared my place. I was due to take the train home Saturday. That gave me four more days with Reid, and I still had to study and write two exams, and he had to work.

It was barely any time, and I wasn't going to ruin it. I didn't want to talk about money or Mike or any of it. These days were mine and Reid's. I'd finally come out, and all I wanted to do was laugh and kiss and fuck and pull the covers over our heads.

Chapter Thirteen

Reid

"So, you're dicking my best friend."

I blinked up at Asher in the doorway of my glass-fronted office still wearing his coat and woolen hat. "Close the door," I hissed, relieved the hallway seemed empty.

He came in and flopped into my guest chair, crossing his arms.

"Shouldn't you be at work?" I asked.

"It's six."

Jerking, I squinted at the time in the corner of my computer. I'd been researching classic New York restaurants. Sardi's often came up, and I thought a Broadway night with Connor would be great for our list. I was meeting him soon for one last holiday party, this one in the restaurant of a hotel that was our chief rival, which would make Grandmother more brittle than usual.

"Also, what's the deal with dicking my best friend?"

"Shh!" I knew from experience the glass wasn't very thick.

"You're pretending to date him. Why be quiet about it? I guess you *are* dating him now?" Asher glared. "Right?"

"Are you asking my intentions?"

"Yeah. Because you'd better not break Connor's heart."

My own heart skipped. Hurting Connor was the last thing I wanted. *Were* we dating for real now? "It's been five minutes. Take a breath."

Asher sighed. "Okay, but just be careful."

"Always." I closed a few tabs and asked casually, "What did he say about me?"

"Oh no. No, no, *no*." Asher jumped to his feet. "I'm not playing this game. I just dropped by to make sure you're not messing with my boy. You two can figure out your shit without me in the middle. That's a hard veto."

"Message received." I gave him a mock salute.

Asher paused at the door. "I will say that he couldn't go more than five seconds at lunch without looking like he was about to doodle your name in a heart in the margins of the menu." He pointed at me. "And making that same goofy face you're making right now. So don't blow it."

"Hey, does Connor like musicals?"

"I dunno. If you're taking him, he'll like it. Also, aren't you glad I encouraged him to be your fake boyfriend? Addison and I get producer credits on this relationship. Assuming you don't screw it up."

Asher left as quickly as he'd appeared, and I spent another ten minutes searching Broadway ticket sites before hurrying to the Grand Hyperion. Connor wasn't outside, though he'd texted that he'd arrived. Inside, a host took my coat and ushered me toward the restaurant.

Voices murmured, a pianist played "The First Noel," which I'd had to sing in the Rencliffe choir, and servers in black and white passed around elegant hors d'oeuvres. I had no interest in a bacon-wrapped asparagus bite with a walnut-orange confit. Not when I spotted Connor.

He wore a red sweater that hugged his tight, lean body, his skinny black jeans painted on his thighs. I grinned to see he was in his Doc Martens, remembering the shoe incident on the carousel.

God, I wanted to fuck him so badly.

As I crossed the room, nodding and smiling to faceless people who greeted me, my eyes were locked on Connor. It was only after I drew him close for a long kiss, inhaling him gratefully, that I realized he was standing with Addison and Olivia.

I broke my gaze away from Connor's dreamy smile and settled my arm on his shoulders. "Well… Hello, ladies." *Say something else.* "Merry Christmas."

Addison wore a too-delighted smile and a shimmery gold blouse. "And to *you*. God bless us, everyone. I didn't realize you'd joined the Actors Studio." She turned to Olivia and—what was his name? Dylan. Addison said, "Aren't you impressed with this performance?"

Dylan seemed a little puzzled. "Um, sure?"

But Olivia nodded and slow clapped. "This is Oscar-worthy stuff."

Connor hissed, "Shh. No one's supposed to know."

Addison and Olivia looked at each other and laughed. "Don't worry your pretty little head," Addison said. "No one will suspect your relationship is anything but the real deal."

Tense under my arm, Connor met my gaze. I shot Addison a death glare. Even if she and Olivia suspected Connor and I were hooking up, that didn't mean Connor wanted to come out. His face was red, and his knuckles were white on his cocktail glass.

Addison and Olivia's shit-eating grins vanished. Olivia quickly said to Connor, "Hey, how did the exam go? I meant to ask earlier."

But the abrupt change of subject didn't loosen Connor's shoulders. "Good, I think. Maybe."

"You always do amazing," Olivia assured him.

I rubbed his back before realizing that might not be helping. I dropped my arm. On one hand, we were supposed to be publicly a couple, but now that we were *privately* a couple and our friends had clearly figured it out, there was pressure on Connor since he'd only come out to his parents.

My head spun, and I had to jam my hands in my pants pockets to keep from touching Connor, who was now frowning at me. Something caught his gaze beyond me.

"Incoming," he whispered, leaning into my side and slipping his arm around me. I couldn't have stopped myself from doing the same to him even if I tried. The need to touch was irresistible. He felt so good pressed into my side, like he'd always belonged there.

I smiled at Grandmother, who nodded back coolly and veered away from us, going to talk to one of her society ladies instead. On one hand, it was a relief, yet it still stung. Connor must have sensed that and squeezed my waist gently. I kissed his temple, and he smiled up at me softly.

"Wait, are you guys really together?" Dylan asked, Olivia immediately nudging him with her elbow. Hard.

The pianist began "Jingle Bells" as our group looked at each other in silence. Then Connor laughed softly, his shoulders hitching under my arm.

"Yeah," Connor said. "I don't know why I'm being so weird about it. I'm gay, by the way."

"Welcome to the party," Addison said, raising her glass with a wide smile.

Dylan said to Addison, "Wait, you too?"

Olivia groaned softly. "Babe, try to keep up." She beamed at Connor and kissed his cheek. "I'm proud of you," she whispered.

I was too, and I kissed him again. Then one more time. And one more time after that until the girls told us to get a room. We all laughed. From the corner of my eye, I spotted Grandmother watching, a looming specter.

I kissed Connor again, hoping she was getting an eyeful. Hoping it would sink in that I really was bi. Then, before I could stop and assess the risk, I was leading Connor by the hand and stepping in front of Grandmother as she tried to escape.

"Grandmother!" I exclaimed too loudly. "How are you?" I

leaned in and kissed her cheeks. "You remember Connor? My boyfriend?" I was practically shouting, and Grandmother blinked at me.

When I'd introduced them on Thanksgiving, Connor had been a near stranger. No longer the surly kid in the background, but only a business partner. Had that only been less than a month ago? Now, Connor was so much more.

He was rapidly becoming everything.

Squeezing my hand gently, Connor cleared his throat. "Hello, Mrs. Cabot. Lovely to see you again."

She smiled coolly. "Yes. Hello, Mr… What is your surname?"

"Lisowski," Connor replied, and I imagined a ripple of tension in him, remembering what he'd told me about not liking his name because of the association with his biological father.

"Ah," Grandmother said.

We waited for her to say more, but no. Apparently that was all.

He added, "Please just call me Connor."

Grandmother nodded and most certainly did not tell Connor to call her anything but Mrs. Cabot. Frustration and resentment boiled up from a simmer, and it was all I could do not to keep shouting. I wasn't even sure what I'd say. I just wanted to *shout*.

In the silence, Connor asked Grandmother, "What do you have planned for Christmas?"

"My traditional breakfast event for the less fortunate. Reid will be there with me." That sounded like an order.

"Cool," Connor said.

I let go of Connor's hand to rest my palm on the back of his neck. "You should come one year. We serve breakfast to hundreds of people, and there's a Santa and gifts." To Grandmother, I said, "We always need more volunteers, right?"

Her lips briefly arched into an expression that could generously be considered a smile. "Of course."

I fought not to clench my fists. Before, Connor had only been my fake boyfriend, and I'd been frustrated with Grandmother. Connor was so real now, and why couldn't she look past gender to see what a wonderful, kind, funny, fun, loving person he was? Couldn't she see how much I cared about him? It had to be emanating from me like a flashing neon sign.

She made an excuse about needing to talk to someone across the room and was gone before I could formulate my roiling thoughts into words. Likely for the best since I'd have a better chance of success the more articulate I was.

"Okay?" Connor murmured, rubbing my back.

"Let's get out of here. Yes?" I pushed Grandmother out of my mind.

He grinned. "No veto here."

IN THE DOORWAY of my apartment an interminable time later, we stumbled back, laughing and kissing and stripping off our coats.

"Hi," Connor said breathlessly.

"Hi." God, when was the last time I'd felt this giddy?

Possibly never.

"Are you thirsty?" I asked, trying to focus on being a good host instead of just standing there staring at Connor's wet mouth.

"Uh-huh."

Before I could ask what he wanted to drink, Connor was back in my arms, his tongue exploring my mouth. I ran my hands down his back, then up under his sweater to spread my fingers over his bare skin. His hands were cold on my neck and face, but everywhere else was fire.

My phone dinged, and we broke our kiss. Connor bent to take off his boots as I read the message from a ticket broker. I yanked off my own boots and socks and asked, "You're free the night before you leave for another item on the New Yorker list?"

"Yep."

"Okay. But you're going to laugh."

"I won't." Connor straightened and peered at me with such seriousness, his hand moving to rest on my waist. "I promise."

It was just a musical—if he wasn't into it, no problem. It wasn't as though I was a huge theater nerd or anything. Yet I wanted his approval. I wanted it more than I'd wanted anything in a long, long time.

"Reid?" He squeezed my hip gently. "You didn't laugh at me. Why do you think I'll laugh at you?"

I blurted, "You'll be a great doctor."

"Huh?" He laughed, clearly confused.

"You have really good bedside manner."

Connor glanced down at his hand on my hip. "Uh, this isn't appropriate for patients."

I laughed too. "I meant the way you listen. Not *that*. Although I'm not complaining about it."

"No complaints?" Connor stroked over the swell of my ass.

"Nope."

"So, what's your idea?" He gazed at me again with that patient, steady interest, and I led him to the couch. We sat side by side, the leather squeaking as we settled close together.

"How do you feel about singing werewolves? I believe they also rap."

Connor blinked. "Uh… Oh! That new musical everyone's talking about?"

"*Full Moon.* You've heard of it?"

"Yeah, Olivia said it did for werewolves what *Hamilton* did for the dead white men on our money."

"I can get tickets. Unless you want to veto?"

He grinned. "No veto. It sounds bananas. The only show I've seen is when Rencliffe took us to *Hamilton*. This seems like a perfect follow-up."

"If rapping werewolves aren't authentically New York, I don't know what is."

"Totally. Also, are we done talking?" he asked.

"Absolutely."

Connor's lips parted under mine, and I kissed him deeply, sliding my tongue against his as I cupped his face. He made that sweet, glorious little sound—a sigh that might evolve into a moan at any moment. I could have kissed him forever.

With a jolt, I pulled back. Since when I was contemplating *forever*?

Connor's lips were shiny and pink, and I was powerless to resist kissing him again. This time, I took his face in both my hands, deepening the kiss even more. Connor gripped my thigh, leaning into me.

He leaned so far that the next thing I knew, he straddled my lap with a moan that went straight to my cock along with what had to be most of my body's blood supply. We laughed and kissed messily.

Connor was on the same page, and he rocked against me with his erection. He broke the kiss with a gasp and unbuttoned the top few buttons of my shirt after yanking off my tie. Pressing his lips to my neck, he inhaled and murmured, "You make me so hard."

I ran my hands down his back and squeezed his ass. "The feeling is entirely mutual."

"Can we get off?"

"I don't know. Can we?"

Connor lifted his head and stared at me. "Are you seriously bringing annoying big brother energy to our sex life?"

I laughed. "Apologies." *Our sex life.* Those words probably should have sent alarm bells blaring, but instead gave me a thrill I felt deep in my balls. "However can I make it up to you?"

"I want to ride you." His beautiful face flushed red, and he dropped his eyes.

The speed of the answer and his blush made me think this was something that wasn't spur of the moment. "Why is that embarrassing?"

"It's not," he mumbled. His fingers dug into my shoulders as he fidgeted.

"Then why can't you look at me?"

After a big exhalation, Connor met my gaze. I caressed his back in slow, gentle sweeps.

"Tell me, baby," I whispered.

His breath caught, and he bit his lip. "You'll think it's weird."

"I won't." I kept my voice steady and serious, emulating his bedside manner. "I promise." I had a suspicion, and I asked, "Have you fantasized about that?"

He nodded. "It was one of the big ones. When I was younger and I had a raging crush on you."

"Adorable."

He groaned and dropped his forehead onto my shoulder. "I was the most awkward kid ever."

"You're all grown up now, though." I groped his ass, and lust simmered in my veins. "Tell me your fantasies. What were the other big ones?" I rounded my spine and tilted up my hips as I lifted a brow. "Aside from *this*."

A laugh burst of out Connor, and I could feel some of the tension in his body ebbing away. I kissed him softly and nuzzled his nose.

"Do I have to tell you right now?"

I drew back. "Of course not. Do you want to stop?"

He gripped my shoulders as his thighs tightened on my hips. "*No.*"

"Okay. We won't stop. I need to come too. You need to come, baby?"

Connor moaned, rocking against me again. "Yeah."

"You want to ride me? That was the fantasy?"

He nodded. "But we need stuff, and it's all the way in the other room."

We were rutting against each other, in serious danger of spilling in our pants. "God, I know."

I hadn't been this desperate for someone in a long time. I tore at my belt and our flies, and Connor lifted up enough so I could pull our cocks free. We groaned as I grasped our shafts in my hand, using our precum as lube. I was still wearing a suit that had cost way too much to ruin, but I couldn't stop.

"Tell me about riding me," I said.

Panting, Connor gaped at me. "Like…"

"Tell me what you've imagined. Was it like this? Sitting on me?"

"Uh-huh. But naked."

I stroked us, fighting to keep my voice even. It came out hoarse as I asked, "On a couch like this?"

"In bed." Connor licked his lips, his chest rising and falling.

I wanted to tear off his shirt and suck his nipples, but I couldn't have let go of our cocks until we came if armed gunmen had burst in. "You want me inside you?"

He nodded desperately as he rocked with the motion of my hand.

"But you want to have your way with me? Ride me and take me just the way you want?"

Connor nodded again, sweet little sounds of pleasure escaping his throat.

"Do you want me to touch you?"

"*Yes.*"

"Like this?" I jerked us harder. It was rough without lube, but that added to the pleasure. Sweat dampened my temples, and my whole body strained, my bare toes clenched on the floor. "How hard do you think you'll come with my cock buried in your ass and—"

With a cry, Connor shook and shot his load on my shirt, the rest dripping down over my hand. His back arched, his head tipped back, eyes closed as he rode the wave. I licked his throat and tasted his salty sweat, and he tangled his hands in my hair.

"*Fuck*," he whimpered.

I was still aching, but I let go of our shafts to suck my fingers. Connor stared at me with wide, lust-blown eyes. "*Double fuck*," he groaned.

Our eyes locked as I ran my tongue up my index finger, tasting him. Wordlessly, I offered him another finger, and he sucked it into his mouth.

We both moaned.

My balls threatened to explode, and before I could finish myself off with my messy hand, Connor lifted up, pushed my thighs apart, and dropped to his knees. He only had to take my eager, leaking cock into his mouth for a few pulls before I flooded him.

Pulling him back onto my lap, I kissed him, tasting both of us. It was dirty and wonderful, and I whispered, "Next time you ride my cock."

He nodded vigorously, and I made a mental note to find out what Connor's other fantasies were and make every single one of them come true.

We were sticky and needed to clean up, yet we stayed sprawled on the couch. I leaned back, my dick still out and my legs spread. Connor curled beside me with his legs flung over my lap. I could get used to this.

I could *really* get used to this.

My phone buzzed on the coffee table. I said, "I'll pass on an unknown number from Texas, thanks." I was mostly talking to myself.

Connor sat up straight, his legs still draped over my lap. "It could be Angela. She said she was going to look at the proposal this week."

I snatched up the phone and answered. A nasal twang greeted me, "Hiya, sugar. This is Angela Barker."

"Hello, Mrs. Barker." I lifted Connor's legs and started pacing by the windows, juggling the phone while I tucked myself back into my pants. She couldn't see me, but it felt disrespectful.

"I'm not fancy—it's Angela. Now, I'm intrigued as heck by your business plan. You've clearly done your homework. I'm very interested in exploring how BRK can help and wanna discuss it further with y'all."

My mouth was dry. "Oh, it's just me. My grandmother and Utopia aren't involved at the moment."

Angela snorted. "You don't say. I'd be surprised if she was on board for this—even though it makes dynamite business sense. The 'y'all' wasn't literal, don't worry."

"Oh! Right. Okay."

Connor watched avidly from the couch. He'd straightened his clothes and sat up straight.

"I have a few suggestions if you're open to it. I'm waiting for my flight and thought I'd give you a buzz and take your temperature."

"Right. Thank you! I'm hot." *Wait. What?*

"That's what my daughter says."

"No! I meant—" I rubbed my face. Why were words so hard right now? "I'm interested in pursuing this…um…" Thing?

"Just teasin'. All righty, I'll be in touch soon with more."

"Thank you so much. I swear I'm usually more articulate."

"I believe you, sugar. Besides, any friend of Connor's is a friend of mine. He said he went to school with your brother?"

"Yes." I faced Connor, who was smiling. "Recently we've gotten to know each other better."

"Isn't he a doll? Smart as a whip, and he's grown up into such a terrific young man. I'm so proud of him."

Connor rolled his eyes at the praise, which he could clearly hear since Angela's penetrating voice was surely echoing through my apartment. Still, he fidgeted in a way that I suspected meant he was secretly pleased by said praise.

Whoa. How did I know that? But every instinct told me I was right.

I said, "He's actually here now. He says hi."

"Is he? Put him on the horn."

While Connor answered questions that seemed to be about holiday plans and his family, I looked out at the lights of the city. Beyond snow-dusted rooftops, I could see the dark swath of Central Park. The spired roof of the Utopia was just visible to the south. My heart thumped.

It had been months—no, *years* now since I'd first started re-searching and developing my business plan. Honestly, I'd figured Angela Barker would perhaps make perfunctory comments as a favor to Connor.

I hadn't expected this. I hadn't expected anything to actually *happen*. And nothing had happened yet, but it might. I'd never shown Grandmother or the board my idea because I knew they'd never fund it. Not in a million years. *Veto.*

And I'd slink back to my office and continue phoning it in as VP for a company that might be my heritage but didn't excite me or challenge me. Every day was the same, and I knew exactly what to expect.

I looked back at Connor as he hung up with Angela, and my thudding heart felt like it might burst out of my chest.

Connor half smiled. "What?"

He had been entirely unexpected, and I'd never been more excited.

"Nothing," I said. "Thank you for getting me in with Angela."

He joined me at the window. "Of course. It was no problem."

He nodded with his chin. "Is that your hotel over there?"

"It is." I gazed out. "One of many."

"What got you interested in sustainable housing? I don't think you said."

I grimaced. "You're going to laugh."

Connor slid his arm around my waist. "Again, I'm not laughing at you."

"Even though we're having this conversation in my luxury Upper West Side apartment? In view of the luxury hotel my family owns?"

"People with money have the resources to actually get things done. We need more rich people to give a shit beyond charity dinners." He quickly added, "Not that your grandmother doesn't raise a lot of money for good causes."

"It's okay." I put my arm around his shoulders.

How did it feel so *right* with him? Like I could say anything, and he truly wouldn't laugh at me.

I said, "I know what you mean, and you're right. Okay. It was a random YouTube video. The housing crisis, rents out of control, that kind of thing. I fell down a rabbit hole of videos, and I couldn't concentrate at work the next day. Who cares about fancy hotels that serve a fraction of the population when we could build sustainable, affordable housing?"

"I'm still not laughing," Connor said seriously, his arm locked around my waist.

I had to kiss him. There was simply nothing else I could do or say before tasting him again and holding him close. As tempting as it was to take him to bed, his stomach rumbled. We chuckled.

"How about we tick another experience off the list?" I asked. "The best slice of pizza in New York."

"I've had it already—Joe's in the Village."

I mock gasped. "Sacrilege! It's Patsy's on Seventy-fourth. We can walk over."

"Okay, but we need to do a taste test. Patsy's today, Joe's tomorrow." Connor groaned. "But I have to study." He checked his phone. "I should head back to my place."

"After Patsy's. You need brain food. I'm not letting you study on an empty stomach. And we can do Joe's next week if you're busy studying."

He bit his lip. "I won't be here. I'll be in Albany for Christmas."

"Right, of course." I put on a bright smile. "First step: Patsy's. A.k.a. the best pizza in New York."

"We'll see about that. But no way am I vetoing. Too hungry."

We headed out, and I'm not sure which one of us reached for the other's gloved hand first. It was so natural to entwine our fingers as we fell into step together.

I tried not to think about how unbearably lonely it was to think of Christmas next week without Connor.

Chapter Fourteen

Connor

THE NOTE FROM Olivia stuck to the bathroom mirror said:
Spending the night with Dylan. Hope the exam went well!

Yawning, I peeled the sticky paper off the glass and crumpled it into the trash can. It was sweet how Olivia would leave notes like that instead of just texting me. She said her mom had always left notes in the bathroom where they were sure to be seen because "everyone needed to tinkle," to quote Angela.

I pissed—excuse me, *tinkled*—and had a hot shower while I tried to relax and not second guess every answer I'd picked on the multiple choice exam. It was done now, and obsessing wouldn't change my grade.

With a towel around my hips, I wandered past the glittering Christmas tree to the kitchen and stared at the decidedly un-festive contents of the fridge—a head of iceberg lettuce, a carton of eggs, leftover kung pao chicken, and an apple. Along with ketchup, mayo, and a few other condiments.

Sighing, I closed the door and glumly pulled a box of Ritz from the cupboard. It was almost empty, so I polished off the buttery crackers. I missed always having dinner on the table. Logan had become a surprisingly good cook when he wanted to be, and Seth was always trying new recipes.

Would Seth offer a new dessert at Christmas, or go with one of the amazing cakes he'd made before? I should ask him to do the eggnog tres leches again. Or maybe the sticky toffee pudding from his phase of trying British classics after binging *Downton Abbey*.

The pang of homesickness had my eyes prickling. "Get a grip," I mumbled as I tore open the cracker box and squeezed it into the recycling bin under the sink. Sure, I missed home sometimes, but I'd lived away for years now. Why was I so emo and lonely tonight?

Fine, yes. It bummed me out that Reid was busy. Especially since he'd been vague about why, exactly. He had to work late, which I totally understood. When I'd asked what he was working on, he hadn't really answered.

I was leaving in two days. *Fine*, yes, I wasn't blasting off to the moon, and I'd be back on the thirty-first. But didn't he want to spend every second together that we could? Was he getting sick of me already?

I groaned aloud and muttered, "Jesus, way to be a stage-five clinger." I might have had a crush on Reid since high school, but I was a grown-ass man now. I couldn't expect to spend every night together now that we were hooking up.

A thrill shivered through me to even think those words. But they were true! Not just in my horny imagination but real life. I still wasn't sure what Reid saw in me, but he seemed just as into it as I was. God, the way he'd held me so tight and kissed me with that hot little moan…

I ran a hand over my damp chest and played with my nipples. I could go jerk off, which would definitely help in the relaxation department. My exams were over, and the holidays had officially begun. Ho-ho-ho, right? I should treat myself.

Was it weird that I wanted to save it for Reid, though? I laughed out loud. Since when did I have a problem getting it up? It wasn't like I wouldn't be horny for him tomorrow if I got off tonight.

Still, I wanted to wait. I wanted Reid's expensive, sweet-yet-peppery cologne in my nose and his taste on my tongue. I wanted his cock inside me finally and—

I would *definitely* have to jerk off if I kept up this train of thought.

Even more than that, I wanted to make Reid smile and find out how his day went. Talk to him about my exam and my constant worry that I didn't study enough even though I have the textbooks memorized.

Encourage him to quit the job that made him miserable even if it was his family legacy or some shit. I wanted to have dinner and talk about everything. And also nothing. Like, talk about that hilarious new viral vid with the baby and the pug puppy.

The thought of dinner made my stomach growl—and gave me a neon-bright idea as my mom would have said. I breathed through the familiar pang of affection and grief.

I knew she'd be thrilled for me. That if she was alive, she'd accept me and Reid—or me and whichever guy since I couldn't get ahead of myself—wholeheartedly.

The problem was that I was already ahead of myself. I'd revved the engine and zoomed off on my bike with Reid on the back, his arms locked around me, his thighs tight on my hips.

Okay, one step at a time. If Reid was working late, I could make him dinner and invite him over, right? I was done studying, so I didn't care if it was late. We could just eat and go to sleep if he was too tired for sex.

What could I make? Iceberg lettuce wouldn't add much, but I could throw together some kind of omelet with—was there cheese?

With a burst of energy, I opened the fridge and did a victory dance when I found the block of sharp cheddar and wedge of Parmesan in the crisper drawer. Olivia kept fruit and vegetables on the fridge shelves instead of the crisper so we wouldn't forget to eat them. It was occasionally successful.

I hurried to grab my phone from the pocket of my jeans, which I'd left in a ball on the bathroom floor. Shit. How was I supposed to ask him to come over later? Casually? It wasn't a big deal, right? Why was I making a bigger deal out of making him a crappy omelet?

After tapping a quick text—*fine*, I rewrote it seven times—asking if he wanted to come by for a late dinner, I slapped on moisturizer and debated shaving before deciding against it. It would be just my luck to nick myself or worse. An open wound wasn't sexy.

When I opened my bedroom door after checking for a reply again, I jerked to a stop and almost full-on screamed. My phone flew out of my hand and thankfully landed on the bed and not the hardwood floor.

Reid was also on the bed.

On his back, sprawled out, one knee bent, lazily stroking himself. With condoms and lube beside him on the mattress.

Naked. Did I mention naked?

"W—what?" I sputtered, grabbing my towel as it came loose.

"Good evening." With his free hand, he held up his phone. "You know, I *am* free for a late dinner. That sounds perfect, thank you. Should we work up an appetite first? You mentioned wanting to take a ride." He looked down at himself as he slowly stroked himself to full hardness. "Surprise. I thought you deserved a reward after your exam."

My eyes were caught in a loop between Reid's gorgeous face and his gorgeous, flushed cock. It grew as I watched, and all I could do was stand and stare.

"Uh…" After the stress of the exam, I had very few brain cells left.

Suddenly, Reid's easy, sexy vibe vanished. He propped himself on his elbows and asked, "Veto?"

"God, no!" I dropped the towel and practically jumped between his legs. "Merry Christmas to me!"

We bounced on the mattress, and he laughed as he drew me down for a long, dirty kiss with lots of tongue. I kneeled over him, painfully hard already. I could have happily collapsed and humped him, but I had to be patient.

"I thought you'd never open the door," he groaned. "I was about to give up and tell you to get your sweet ass in here."

"Sorry!" I laughed and kissed him again.

"You didn't think it was strange that your door was shut?"

"Nope. It's usually shut because, as you can see, my room is a mess." I motioned to the piles of textbooks and notes and clothes in a heap.

"Olivia did warn me." Reid tugged my head down and sucked hard on the side of my neck. "I don't care," he mumbled against my skin.

Sitting back on my heels, I drank him in. The dark curls of chest hair, his shit-eating grin, the trail of hair leading down to his amazing cock. His toned thighs, long fingers, the jagged scar on his shoulder he'd said was from falling off a jungle gym and landing on a broken bottle. The—

"Connor?"

Blinking, I met his gaze. "Uh-huh?"

"You can touch too, you know. You don't have to only look." He was gentle as he said it. Not making fun of me.

"Right." I'd touched him before, but somehow it was intimidating AF to have Reid in *my* bed. Where I'd only ever jacked off and fantasized. "Teenage me would never, ever believe this was real." I hadn't meant to say it out loud, and my face went hot.

Again, Reid didn't laugh at me. He only smiled and took my hand, placing it on his chest. "To be fair, I'd never have imagined this would happen either. But you're all grown up, and I want you so badly I'm about to beg for you to please touch me."

I caressed his chest, gratified when teasing his nipples earned a moan. Leaning down, I kissed them and sucked, and Reid's big hand rested on my head.

"Mmm-hmm," he murmured. "That feels good."

I experimented with more touches and kisses, and Reid encouraged me. It was still nerve racking to be the one in charge. He was sweet and patient as I fumbled around, and I ran through different scenarios in my head.

Should I just grab a condom and climb on his dick? That was what we'd talked about, and we were both hard. But it felt like he wanted more first. Like he was offering himself to me even though I didn't have a clue what the fuck I was doing.

"Hey." He lifted my face and rubbed my temple slowly with his thumb. "Why are you so tense? Are you sure you don't want to veto?"

"I'm so sure. I just—" I hesitated, and Reid nodded, silently urging me to spit it out. "I don't know what to do."

His eyebrows shot up. "I beg to differ. That was you who climbed on my lap the other night and turned me on so much I almost came in my pants, yes?"

"Yes, but…" I shrugged, looking away.

"It's okay. Do you want a suggestion?"

I nodded.

Reid leaned up on his elbow as he urged my face down. His lips brushed my ears. "Before you ride me, will you fuck my mouth, baby?"

I honest-to-shit *gasped*, and all I could do was nod and crawl up his body. He tossed the pillow away and opened his mouth for me—for *me!*—and it was wet and tight and incredible.

Reid ran his hands up and down my thighs and around my hips as he took my cock as far as he could. Having him under me like that made me hot all over, and with a surge of confidence, I found a rhythm. That he trusted me to do this when I was on top of him, pinning him down, had my head spinning in the best way.

He slurped and groaned, and I don't even know what sounds I was making. My room was filled with heat and body noises, and it was everything I could have imagined from my dirty dreams.

Almost.

I pulled out and squeezed the base of my dick, forcing back the orgasm that I didn't want yet. I awkwardly backed away from Reid's face until I was straddling his waist. His lips were red and glossy, and he grinned as he reached for a condom.

"Ready, cowboy?" he asked.

Was I *ever*.

After lubing myself with shaking fingers, I took Reid inside me inch by inch as he kept hold of my hips. Not pushing or directing me—only there with me every step.

"You're so big," I gasped before bursting out laughing. "I sound like a porno."

He laughed too. "As long as it feels good, that's all that matters. I'd apologize for my *clearly* above-average cock, but… Sorry not sorry."

Jesus, he did feel big. I wouldn't have stopped for a nuclear bomb, though. Not a chance. I took a deep breath and fully seated myself. My breath stuttered. I'd never felt so *full*. Everywhere, not only in my ass.

My chest was tight as if my heart had swelled. I tried to swallow past the knot in my throat. After all the years of being too chickenshit, I was *doing it*. I had a dick inside me.

"Baby?" Reid brushed his thumb over my cheek, and I realized a tear had slipped out. "Does it hurt?"

"No. Yes. A little. It's not—" I forced a long, deep breath. "I was starting to think I'd never get the nerve to do this. And now I'm doing it. With you." I blinked away more tears, a wild laugh bubbling up. "You really are big. Feels amazing." I squeezed around him experimentally.

Reid groaned. "If this was a porno, I'd say, 'You're so tight,' and tell you that you're going to make me come. For the record, even though this isn't a porno, you are so tight and you're going to make me come so fucking hard."

We laughed again, and I wiped away the lingering tears before squeezing around him again. It was tender inside, but the pain was part of the pleasure. I slowly rose up a few inches and then back down, experimenting with the sensations. The feeling of fullness made my head spin.

There was so much going on at once. Reid's cock inside me, stretching me. Our skin sweaty everywhere we touched. Reid rubbing my thighs and hips, more heat with each stroke of his commanding hands.

"That's it," he murmured. "You feel amazing, baby."

Reid couldn't seem to stop touching me. He ran his hands hungrily everywhere he could reach, telling me how good I was doing. I arched my back as I started to really ride him, finding a steady cadence and rubbing my prostate in a way that made my dick pulse with precum.

My thighs trembled as I worked myself on Reid's cock, and I couldn't believe he'd been waiting naked in my bed to surprise me while I'd been showering and moping with crackers.

"Thank you," I said, or gasped or moaned or some other sound I couldn't name.

"No thanks necessary." He inhaled sharply and bit his lip, his fingers tightening on my thighs. Sweat glistened on his forehead. "I was about to say I could do this all day, but that would be a lie since I'm going to come soon." His breath hitched. "Very, very soon."

His cock was curved, and I rolled my hips to find the perfect angle, leaning on his chest. "Me too," was all I could manage.

"Can I touch you?"

"*Please*," I groaned, and as Reid took my dick in his slick hand, it only took a moment before I stuttered and shot all over him.

I clamped down on his cock, jerking and seeing stars as pleasure crashed through me. Reid clutched my hips and thrust up, gasping and moaning my name.

My name.

Reid Cabot was coming inside me with only a thin layer of latex between us. I slumped over him, and we shook and mumbled nonsense as Reid wrapped his arms around me. Our skin was sticky like we'd just run five miles.

"Okay?" Reid eased me onto the mattress beside him.

"Uh…" How was I supposed to form words right now?

"Judging by your dopey smile, I'll take that as a yes." Chuckling, Reid ran a damp cloth—he really had been prepared—over my junk and then gently wiped it between my ass cheeks. "Sore?" He prodded tentatively.

"I'm good." My ass was tender, but I tried to hide it.

"I saw that. That was a grince."

I laughed. "Just a little. I mean it—I'm good. Great."

"Marvelous? Splendid?"

"One might even say spectacular."

"Sublime?" Reid offered.

"Mmm. Wondrous."

We smiled through sweet little kisses. We were both such nerds sometimes, and somehow it made Reid even hotter.

"I feel like I just took an epic ride on my bike for hours. Sore muscles, but exhilarated."

"Riding me is far safer than that motorcycle." He nuzzled my cheek before rolling away.

"No, stay here." I reached for him as he tucked the covers around me.

"I'll be right back. Need to get rid of the condom." He glanced down at his chest. "And scrub your load out of my chest hair."

"We should have a shower together. I've always wondered what that would be like."

He cocked an eyebrow. "Did you fantasize about it? You and me under the water? *Soaping* each other?" He said it slowly, suggestively.

"Yeah. Pretty much every time I jerked off in the shower in high school." Maybe I should have been embarrassed to admit that, but the words flowed so easily.

A slow grin lifted Reid's gorgeous mouth. "I'll keep that in mind."

As much as I wanted to get in the shower with him now, my limbs were heavy, and I couldn't stifle a yawn. Reid kissed me and straightened the pillow under my head before ducking out. He was back in a minute.

Snuggled under the covers, I ran my fingers through his damp chest hair. "I wish you didn't have to stay here for Christmas," I said, too sleepy to stop myself.

He sighed heavily in the darkness. "Me too. But I can't miss Grandmother's Christmas fundraiser. She's annoyed enough with me—I can't risk really making her angry."

"Why not?" Screw her. I knew that was easier said than done, though. I'd never even cut my father out of my life, and I should have years ago.

Reid tensed. "Asher and I are all she has. Our dad was her only child. I've disappointed her enough already."

"By being bi?" Frustration and anger broke through my sleepy haze. "That's so unfair. And it's *her* problem. Not yours."

"I know," he whispered. He could go from confident and in control to vulnerable so quickly.

"Risks aren't always bad." I kissed his neck softly. "Sometimes, taking a leap ends up being the most incredible decision." To lighten the mood, I added, "One might say astonishing. Remarkable. Heart-stopping." I punctuated the words with little kisses to his cheek, neck, and shoulder.

"Breathtaking?"

"Mmm, definitely." I leaned up and pressed our lips together. We sighed into the kiss before settling again, this time Reid spooning me and nuzzling the back of my neck. I yawned and said, "I was going to cook you a terrible omelet, but I'm too tired."

His warm breath tickled my skin as he chuckled. "Let's order. Empanada Mama again? I'm hooked."

"Sure." I was pleased he'd liked it so much. "Hold on, my phone's somewhere under here."

"I've got it." The warmth of his body shifted as he picked up his own phone.

"No, you ordered the other night." I sat up and rooted around in the covers. I'd be lucky if we hadn't crushed it.

Reid was already tapping. "Don't worry. I've got it."

Something bristled in me. "No. This is my place, so I pay. You paid at your place. I already owe you enough."

He sighed noisily. "Let's just write it off. Forget about it. I have money."

"*Ten grand?* No." I wanted to grab the phone away, but I choked down that impulse. Through gritted teeth, I asked, "Reid, will you please stop ordering?"

He opened his mouth as if to argue before closing it and putting down his phone on the side table. "Sorry."

"Thank you." I'd gone from drowsy to zipping with anger, and I took a deep breath. "I'm not hand-waving ten thousand dollars. I'm paying back that money."

"Okay." He nodded. "I get it. I just hate to think of you working nights at CVS when I have more money than I could ever need."

"Give it to charity."

"I do! Believe me, I do."

I did believe him. "Okay, but I'm not a charity case. I was an idiot, and I have to pay off that debt, and I will."

"What happened?" he asked softly.

Ugh, that was the last thing I wanted to talk about in the afterglow of my first time being fucked. To be fair, I'd brought it up, but no. That had to wait.

"I don't want to talk about it right now." I rubbed my face. "Can we just go back to happy cuddling, please?"

He reached for my hand, and I squeezed his fingers. He said, "Absolutely. Let's find your phone."

It was wedged between the mattress and the bottom of the headboard, but unharmed. I tapped out our order and said, "I pay at my place. You can pay at yours. Deal?"

"Deal. Now we have some cuddling to do before the food arrives." He lifted the covers and we got comfy again. Tracing the shell of my ear with his fingers, Reid asked, "Still feeling marvelous?"

I snuggled against him, letting myself relax. "Yep. Stupendous, even."

"Mmm. Phenomenal."

I thought of another word: *fantastical.* Although that could mean quirky or odd or bizarre, it was definitely wild that I was in Reid Cabot's arms.

And it was *real* between us. We were in my bed. This wasn't fake. No matter what happened, Reid wanted me tonight. I ordered myself not to think about the possible outcomes for our relationship in the long run, or about the money I owed him.

Those conversations would come. I'd be going home for Christmas without him too soon. Whatever tomorrow and tomorrow and the days after that brought, tonight was ours.

Chapter Fifteen

Connor

"**H**OW'S YOUR FAKE boyfriend?" Seth asked as we buckled into his SUV. "I suppose your task is complete? I think you said it was only leading up to Christmas."

The question hit me harder than I expected. For a second, I thought I might burst into tears, which would have totally freaked out Seth.

"Uh, yeah. It was all good. Totally fine." Geez, why was every muscle in my body clenched? Reid and I hadn't broken up or anything. We hadn't talked about that at all.

"Are you sure?" Seth braked for a yellow light. "I know Logan was being quite…overprotective, but Asher's brother is an honorable man, isn't he?"

"A hundred percent! Yeah, he's great." I'd almost said "wonderful," and now I was in danger of gushing. I fought to even my tone, but my boot tapped restlessly. "He's a cool guy. I'm glad I could help him out."

All true.

There was nothing stopping me from telling Seth that Reid and I had hooked up for real—minus the details, because no, I actually did not want to discuss getting busy with my dads.

But it was still so new and…delicate. I had to find out where Reid and I stood in the new year before I told my family. That was reasonable, wasn't it?

"Okay. Are you sure your exams went all right? Are you feeling a bit dysregulated?"

I laughed softly. "Haven't heard that word in a long time."

Back when I was a teenager and Logan and I were still fighting too much—even though we were better than when Seth met us—Seth had read a bunch of psychology books to try and find coping strategies. He'd calmly mediate while I snarled and swore.

I said, "It's weird to think about how angry I was back then. How…on the brink. I don't know how you guys put up with my mood swings. And yes, my exams went well. I hope. I guess I'll find out in January."

"Okay, you sound remarkably calm about that." He checked his blind spot and exited onto the highway, and we passed malls and a blur of outlet stores.

"Super regulated over here."

Seth squeezed my arm. "Glad to hear it. Now that your pre-tend relationship is over, are you thinking about dating?"

"Sure, I guess." My foot jiggled again, and I shifted in my heated seat.

"I'm sure you know all about which apps are popular these days, and how to be careful."

I groaned. "*Yes.* Stop right there, I'm begging you."

"All right." He chuckled.

"And you guys haven't told Jenna and everyone, right? I do not want to spend Christmas with people trying to hook me up with so-and-so's cousin or coworker because they know one other queer person."

"We haven't said a word. Though you know that whenever you're ready, the rest of the family will be delighted. To say nothing of Angela."

I had to laugh. "She does love to roll out the rainbow carpet."

I almost told him about Angela helping Reid, but I wanted to keep the Reid talk to a minimum. Also, nothing might come of it.

I really hoped it would, though. Reid needed to take a risk instead of being buried under family obligations, even if those obligations involved being rich.

I scrolled through Seth's playlists, grinning as I found the *Full Moon* soundtrack. "I saw this last night! It was awesome."

"How did you get tickets? It's been impossible. Since when are you interested in musicals?"

"I am gay now," I joked. "I think it's in the job description."

"Har, har."

Reid and I had laughed and clapped and had an amazing night on Broadway. He'd scored incredible seats—I didn't want to think about how much they'd cost—and we'd had dinner at the Italian restaurant with all the caricatures of famous people on the walls.

I said, "I got lucky with the lottery. Besides, I'm a New Yorker. I have to see the hot new Broadway show."

"In your job description," Seth agreed. "Tell me all about it!"

I did, without giving away any spoilers he might not have known just by listening to the soundtrack. As he talked about his favorite song, my mind wandered to Reid. We'd had a few drinks, and sitting in the fifth row with Reid's knee pressed against mine, I'd felt loose and happy and…

In love.

That was an issue for another time, and I refocused on Seth, agreeing with him about the song's crescendo. Reid and I had had our own crescendo back at his place at the end of the night, with me riding him again with more confidence.

There were so many positions I wanted to try, and I already missed Reid more than I thought would be possible.

Obviously, I missed my mom a huge amount. But this longing was entirely different. Electric and immediate, an ache of anticipation. I was home for a week, and it seemed like an *eternity*.

The afternoon was darkening already, and I watched the Christmas lights twinkle to life as we headed into Aunt Jenna's neighborhood of small, neat houses with little yards.

Jenna and Jun's place was ablaze with gold lights along the gutters and around the windows. I couldn't wait to see our house—Seth and Logan always went all out.

The driveway was full of cars, so Seth parked his SUV on the street. I asked, "Is Jenna having a party, or is it just us?"

"A party, but there won't be too many people."

Inside, there was a flurry of greetings. Logan gave me his patented back-slapping hug. Jenna pulled me close, smelling of Victoria's Secret vanilla perfume, and predictably said I was taller, which I was not. Jun waved from the kitchen and asked Jenna if the dipping sauce was supposed to be boiling.

It was not.

The other guests were Seth and Jenna's friends from work—Will and his partner, Michael, and Matt and his fiancée, Becky. Will's parents were visiting from Scotland, and I shook hands with them and immediately forgot their names. They went to the kitchen, insisting on helping with the food.

Matt had always seemed fun to me as a kid with his shaggy blond hair and jokey attitude, but now as he asked me casually, "Anyone come home with you for Christmas?" alarm bells rang.

Too many avid expressions waited for my answer. "Nope," I said. "Just me."

Becky said, "My cousin saw you at a dinner in New York with Reid Cabot."

I appreciated that she didn't beat around the bush at least. "Oh yeah, we're friends. I went to school with his little brother."

Maybe it would be easier to just come out and tell everyone the truth. Call for attention and announce that I was gay and fucking Reid and wasn't taking questions at this time. But I tensed, my heart thumping. No. Not yet.

"Leave the lad alone," Will chided in his extremely sexy Scottish accent. He had dark stubble and blue eyes, and I hoped it wasn't disloyal to Reid to admit that Will was hot.

Will only had eyes for Michael, who was blond and cute and currently shaking his head at Matt. Michael said, "You two are shameless."

"Who, us?" Matt put a hand to his chest. "I'm mortally wounded by your accuracy."

I should have taken the out and gone over to Seth and Logan, who were probably talking about me too. Instead, I couldn't resist asking Will and Michael, "Is it true you guys pretended to be a couple before you got together?"

They shared a sweet smile that would have made me so jealous in the past, and Michael slipped his arm around Will's waist. Michael said, "Yep. I'd been in love with him for years, and he had no idea. Then we ended up pretending to be boyfriends because… Well, it sounds ludicrous."

"Situation normal around these parts," Matt said. "We love a caper. Just look at Connor's dads."

"Yeah, it worked out pretty well," I agreed. I smiled at Will and Michael. "Glad it did for you too."

"Best thing that ever happened to me," Will said before kissing Michael's cheek. "Of course, I had to remove my head from my arse first."

If Reid and I ended up together, we'd be three for three on fake couples becoming real.

Don't get ahead of yourself!

Still, it was hard not to daydream….

Jenna and Jun's sons, Ian and Noah, were playing a video game in the lounge, where Logan and Jenna's father, Pop, sat in his chair in corduroy pants and a green sweater, his swollen feet up and clad in extra-large slippers.

Cross-legged on the carpet, the kids tore their attention away from the screen for a second to call, "Hey!" and I waved back as they jabbed their controllers.

In the past, I'd have been right there with them, but I realized I didn't even recognize the game they were playing. Jesus, I was getting old. Or maybe just insanely busy.

Tell me you're in med school without telling me you're in med school.

The Christmas tree across from Pop's chair beside the TV glowed with gold lights and shiny silver tinsel. The ornaments were a mix of school macaroni projects and sparkling balls and teardrops from the store. Wrapped presents spilled out around the base.

"Hey, Pop." I squeezed his hand and perched on the arm of the couch. Pretty much everyone called him "Pop," so I did too.

He grunted and squeezed back, his gaze on the screen even though I wasn't sure he understood the fast-moving game. The edema from his congestive heart failure had worsened, and I bit back the urge to ask him about his prescriptions and investigate whether they needed to be tweaked.

"How are you feeling?" I asked, shifting my fingers to his wrist for his resting heart rate.

Pop shook me off. "Acting like a doc already. I'm fine, boy." He wheezed softly as he breathed, and his white hair had gone even more wispy. He wasn't frail, though. That grit remained.

I had to laugh. "Okay. Glad to hear it." I leaned over, trying to get a look at his legs. "Are you wearing your compression stockings?"

His response was a grumble that I recognized as a no, and I knew it was a subject he'd argued with Aunt Jenna and Logan about. I said, "You know it'll help even if it's a pain getting them on and off."

He grunted. "How're you doing? Knockin' 'em dead at school? Breaking girls' hearts?"

I let the stockings go—for the moment. "Trying not to kill anyone. It's a bad look for med students. And nah. No girls. No hearts breaking." I hoped mine wouldn't be shattering soon.

"Boys, then."

Pop still stared at the TV. Ian and Noah shouted over each other, the game making a ton of noises from beeping to explosions. I had to take a deep breath and blow it out, sawdust in my mouth as I stared at Pop. How did he know?

"Um… Yeah, actually," I said. "There's one in particular." I wasn't sure why I was spilling this when I'd only reaffirmed minutes ago that I wasn't ready to come out to everyone tonight.

This had been so easy, though—no announcement necessary. Another one down.

"That's good. Wanna grab me another beer?"

Part of me wanted to advise him on the risks of alcohol at his age with his conditions, but I only squeezed his arm and said, "Sure, Pop."

Returning from the lively chaos in the kitchen, where Jenna and Jun bickered over mini quiches and bao buns filled with crispy pork belly, I flopped on the couch beside Pop's recliner. We both drank Pabst from the bottle and watched the boys play their game.

As a teenager, I'd spent countless hours on this end of the couch near Pop, watching football, NASCAR, game shows, and even soap operas. We'd rarely spoken, but the silence had been a comforting warm blanket while I'd still been finding my feet and navigating my prickly relationship with Logan. Silence had suited me just fine.

Occasionally, over a commercial, he'd said things like: "*My boy can be a dumbass, but he'd give you the shirt off his back.*" Or "*It's okay to miss your momma. But she won't mind a bit if you're happy. She's happy in heaven.*" Then he wouldn't say anything for hours.

While I didn't believe in heaven, I remember being amazed Pop had known that as I'd settled into the family, my guilt for being happy had worsened. He had a way of saying things that resonated more than what my therapist had said, even if the messages were the same.

I realized I didn't know how the conversation had gone when Logan had told Pop he was bi and in a relationship with Seth. Maybe something like this?

"Thanks," I said, my throat thick.

"For what?"

"You know."

He grunted, and I smiled to myself. Pop had always made his words count.

As THE VIDEO call made a low beeping, I lunged for my phone beside me on the mattress, sending Hercules, my dads' tabby cat, leaping off the bottom of the mattress where he'd been curled by my feet.

I sat up and swiped. Reid's face appeared on screen, and we said, "Hey!" in perfect unison. We were both shirtless.

"I miss you," I blurted before I could hope to gather a tiny shred of chill. My calm, cool, and collected well was bone dry. Reid had gone with me to Penn to catch the train that morning— it had only been hours.

But he didn't laugh at me. He only said, "Me too," and normally, I'd have gone through a checklist to make sure my erratic heart rate wasn't a symptom of a bigger issue.

Also, the fact that he'd gotten up early with me still made my heart skip. I'd insisted I could just order a ride and go myself since there was no point in him going with me when he'd just have to get a car back uptown. Penn Station was a mess of people and smells and *ugh*, but Reid had held my hand right to the crowded train platform.

"Are you in your room from when you were a kid?" he asked.

"Teenager, yeah."

"What's that behind you? And why are you grinning?"

"Because it's a poster of Ricky Tortuga. Yes, the race car driver. I went through a NASCAR phase, okay?"

Reid laughed. "And Ricky was the object of your affections?"

"Oh, yeah. Along with you."

He smirked. "I was in esteemed company."

"Indeed. Teenage me would die to know I'd one day be in this bed talking to you."

"Well, we could do more than talk." He gave me a suggestive smile.

I honest-to-god *squeaked.* "Like, phone sex? I can't! My dads are right down the hall."

"Mmm. You might get caught." His voice was still low and seductive.

"You're supposed to be risk-averse!" I hissed. "Veto!"

"All right, all right. We'll save phone sex for another time."

"It's not that I'm opposed to the idea in general, for the record. I don't want you to think I'm a prude."

"You've had your finger in my ass and my cock in your mouth. Not to mention *my* cock in *your* ass. 'Prude' is not a word that springs to mind."

Heat washed through me, my dick twitching in the old boxers I wore to bed. "You're not making this easier."

Reid raised a hand. "Apologies. I surrender."

"Besides, Hercules is in here. I can't do *that* with the cat watching." I turned my phone and cooed to Hercules. "Say hi to Reid."

Hercules only scratched at the door, so I got up to let him out. "He'll probably want back inside in, like, two minutes."

"Sounds about right for a cat. So, you haven't redecorated since high school? Let me see the rest. I only got a flash."

I groaned. "It's way too embarrassing."

Reid quirked an eyebrow, and I wanted to reach through the screen and lick it. Was licking eyebrows normal?

He said, "I'm waiting."

Sighing noisily, I turned my phone and panned it around my small room. The jeans and hoodie I'd worn today were thrown over the desk chair. The desktop was cluttered with old notebooks and Harvard textbooks that didn't fit on my overstuffed bookcase. Also an old deodorant stick, a pile of expired bus passes, and I didn't even know what.

"It's messy, I know." He'd seen my room in New York, so that surely wasn't a surprise. The more embarrassing part was the poster of a Victoria's Secret model with angel wings from one of those fashion shows. "My attempt to be straight," I said.

Reid chuckled. "Adorable." He squinted. "What's that paint-ing over the dresser?"

"I don't know, actually." The framed print was so familiar to me that I almost didn't notice it. I focused on the golden strokes of wheat in a field and low-hanging clouds tinged with the orange glow of sunrise—or sunset? Unclear. "My mom got it at a garage sale when I was little. We moved a lot, but this print always came with us."

"It's beautiful."

"Thanks." I cleared my throat, which had become uncomfort-ably thick.

"You must miss her," Reid said quietly.

I climbed back into bed and curled on my side under the blankets, holding my phone and leaning it on the end of my pillow to keep my face in frame. He was in bed, and he did the same. I could almost imagine we were together, our knees bumping and feet sliding together.

"I do," I said. "It never goes away. It changes shapes, but it's still there. You know what I mean?"

Reid nodded and leaned his head on his hand. "I miss my dad, but it's not the same as it was initially."

"If he was still here, do you think you'd be stuck working at Utopia?" As soon as the question escaped my mouth, I regretted it. "I'm sorry. That's a dick question."

"It's okay. Probably. Or maybe I'd be working somewhere else before ending up at Utopia eventually to keep it in the family. It's my legacy, et cetera, et cetera."

"But not Asher's."

"It's ridiculous, I know. If this was the olden days in England, I'd inherit the title, and he'd get scraps. I'd love for him to take the title now, but he doesn't want it." Reid shrugged, his bare shoulder appearing into frame briefly. "Did you always want to be a doctor? I don't think we've talked about this."

My gut clenched, and my gaze flicked to my mom's painting. "When I was little, I wanted to be—"

"Wait, let me guess. A race car driver?"

"Nope. And I never considered it during my NASCAR phase either."

"Hmm." Reid tapped his chin exaggeratedly. There was a tiny divot in his chin—not a cleft, but a minuscule scar. I wanted to lick that, too. He asked, "Pilot?"

"No!" I shuddered. "Flying's scary."

"What? But you ride a *motorcycle*!"

"Only in good conditions, and I'm in control. It's different."

Reid scoffed. "You know the statistics on plane crashes versus motorcycles have to favor air travel by a massive margin. The risk of flying is incredibly low. It does increase depending on the airline—there are certain airlines in various countries that I'd never use since their safety regulations aren't up to par. But overall, it's the safest way to travel by a landslide."

"I know intellectually that this is all true," I conceded.

"Okay, okay, lecture over. I get it. Hmm. Did you want to be a firefighter? Cop?" He kept guessing as I shook my head.

"Teacher? Astronaut—no, too risky." He tapped his chin again. "Musician?"

"Yes!" I was pleased he'd guessed. "A percussionist. My mom took me to the symphony once because she said I had to get 'cultured.' I loved the drums and especially the cymbals."

"Sounds about right for a kid."

I laughed. "I think she regretted it immediately but wanted to support my dreams."

"When did you start dreaming of medicine?"

I knew he was going to ask that, and I'd tried to prepare myself to answer steadily without reliving it. Huge fail, as usual. I tensed, the vision of her bare feet with pink-painted toenails filling my head. They'd been the first thing I'd seen when I opened her bedroom door.

My voice was hoarse. "When my mom died."

Reid's eyes widened. "Was it… Was she ill?"

"You don't know the story? Asher never told you?"

"I don't think so. I'm sorry—you don't have to talk about it."

Strangely, I wanted to. Even as I fought for breath, I wanted to tell Reid. I wanted to download my memories into his brain and climb into his skin and have him know *everything*.

I swallowed thickly. "My mom died of a brain aneurysm. It happened in the night, and I found her in the morning when it was too late."

Reid sucked in a breath. "Oh, baby. I'm so sorry."

Shit. My eyes burned, and I blinked rapidly. I'd told this story multiple times and had managed to keep it together, but the tenderness in Reid's deep brown eyes was undoing me. Rigid, I breathed through my nose.

He murmured, "You can cry."

I'm sure he wasn't the first person to tell me that—Logan and Seth surely had—but it was different somehow. Reid had been *inside* me. And even if that didn't mean much to other people, it meant a ton to me. I'd never felt as naked as I did with Reid—even though I was wearing my boxers at the moment.

So, I did. I cried.

I didn't try to stop the tears, my face wet and blotchy as I sniffed loudly. I told him about finding her on the floor, gray and waxy, and knowing she was dead deep down. Calling 911 and doing CPR, her ribs cracking even though I only had bony, weak arms.

I swiped my hand over my nose. "I wondered if I could have saved her if I'd been there when she collapsed. The doctors said it wouldn't have made a difference, but I still thought about it constantly. I decided if I couldn't help her, I'd help other people." I shrugged. "That's the story."

Reid blew out a long breath, his eyes gleaming. "Thank you for telling me."

"It's not a secret or anything." Still, this time when I told it, I didn't feel the residual anger I usually did. I'd never be at peace with losing her, but the rage that had taken over my life really was in the past.

"No, but I can see it takes a lot out of you. I wish I could kiss you right now."

"Me too."

"I'm so glad you came to that Thanksgiving dinner."

My heart skipped. "Me too," I repeated. I wanted to tell him I was falling in love—that I'd fallen already, and I was still falling and falling. Would he catch me?

"Guess it's time for bed," Reid said. "Get some sleep."

"Yeah." It was jumping the gun for love declarations, so I went with, "I wish you were here." I hesitated. "I mean—obviously that would be weird, right? It's too soon to meet my parents. And I know you have to be in New York for Christmas. Anyway, I meant to ask if you're coming to Asher's party on New Year's Eve? That's when I'm coming back. I know you wouldn't normally go.

You have your own friends and stuff."

I was babbling, and I forced myself to stop. I'd wanted to ask him before I left, but everything had been so perfect that I hadn't wanted to think about the future in case he said no. Even if it was only a week and a bit away. At Penn, we'd only said we'd see each other soon.

Reid smiled. "I wouldn't miss it."

I let my grin say it all.

Chapter Sixteen

Reid

HAD MY APARTMENT always been so...plain? Boring? Why didn't I have holiday decorations? Sipping coffee in my bathrobe, I wandered into the living room. It was still dark—one of those winter mornings where it could have been the middle of the night instead of seven.

I should have gone to the gym, but I'd hit snooze. Three times. Or five. I hadn't slept, though. I'd been up half the night, tossing and turning and wishing Connor was beside me.

In the light from the kitchen, I imagined a tree by the window gleaming with a rainbow of colors and sparkling decorations. Presents piled underneath with big bows on top.

I snorted. Presents for who? Connor was in Albany. I'd never exchanged gifts with my family as an adult. The fun parts of Christmas were for kids, and all we were left with was social and business and charitable obligations. And the hard truth was that the charity work was intrinsically tied to Utopia and our reputation. It was all business.

If Connor were here, how would he decorate? He and Olivia had fun garlands and a wonky little tree that reminded me of Charlie Brown in the best way.

I let myself imagine Connor stringing lights on our tree—would we get real or fake? The smell of a real tree would be hard to beat...

"I'm losing it," I said out loud to the empty room. Through the window, the lights of the briefly quiet city seemed to agree.

Connor was only in Albany a few hours upstate, and I was acting as though he were on the other side of the world. How did I miss him this much? We'd talked, we'd texted, we'd talked more. But I ached to be with him.

I didn't know what his mom had looked like, but I was haunted by images of Connor finding her. My dad's death had been sudden—a heart attack likely brought on by drinking and smoking—and it had been unbearable at first. But I couldn't begin to fathom the trauma Connor had experienced.

All I wanted was to hold him and make sure he was never, ever hurt again.

"What is wrong with me?" I muttered. I couldn't be in love already. I'd never been in love before, so I couldn't compare these feelings to anything else, but...

If this wasn't love, I had to have acquired a tropical disease. And there was a distinct dearth of mosquitoes in New York City in December. It wasn't malaria, no matter how feverish and restless I was.

From the kitchen, my phone pinged with a reminder, and I groaned. I had obligations to fulfill. Reports to finish at the office, another charity lunch, blah, blah, *blah*. Had I ever enjoyed these things? Had I ever enjoyed *anything* before Connor?

"That's absurd," I told myself sternly. "Get a grip."

The problem was that I didn't want to. I wanted to recklessly plunge forward the way I had on Thanksgiving. Asking Connor to pretend to be my boyfriend had been wild and ridiculous—and potentially the greatest decision I'd ever made.

I needed to step back and assess the risk. Take this time away from Connor to breathe and figure out if this was only infatuation or if we could really have a future together.

My phone rang, and I crossed to the kitchen island in what

might have been called a run. Bordering on flying. It was only as I swiped to answer that I realized it was Grandmother's assistant, Sonia.

"Hi, Reid. Sorry to call so early. You need to clear your schedule for lunch."

"Brett couldn't share my calendar?" Typically, my assistant would handle this sort of thing. I'd always been informal with Sonia and Brett and insisted they call me by my first name—much to Grandmother's distaste.

"He said lunch was blocked off, but he didn't know why. This is urgent, so I decided to call myself. I apologize for the inconvenience."

"It's fine. Let me just…" My brain was so full of Connor that I'd barely been thinking of anything else. I put her on speaker and tapped my phone, skimming my calendar. "Oh. I can't." I had a follow-up call with Angela Barker, who was being incredibly generous with her time and energy. "I have…" I tried to think of anything that could plausibly pre-empt a demand from Grandmother and came up blank. "I can't."

Sonia paused before saying quietly, "I don't believe Mrs. Cabot will accept any response except for meeting her and the other parties at Le Gabriel at noon. Sharp."

"Fine." I softened my tone. "Thank you, Sonia. I hope you and your family have a wonderful holiday if I don't see you before then."

"Thank you. You'll be at Mrs. Cabot's breakfast event on Christmas Day, I presume? I hope you have something else fun planned as well."

"Yes, definitely. Thanks."

If missing Connor and questioning all my life choices except for him was "fun," then sure. Christmas would be a *blast*.

AFTER TIPPING THE driver and closing the ride app, I checked my messages again. Still no reply from Grandmother to my call and two texts asking for more details about lunch. I was in front of the restaurant, so at least I'd find out soon.

Angela had been gracious and understanding of the last-minute cancellation, and we'd rescheduled the call for after the holidays since she was "going dark" for family time in Texas. Connor had mentioned Olivia was flying home.

Beside the restaurant, I stepped into the doorway of a bar that was currently dark to get out of the miserably cold drizzle. The snow had melted, the city was dreary and wet. With Connor, it had felt like Christmas magic was in the air, and now it had vanished.

I'd tried to choke down the disappointment at not speaking with Angela today, but I needed a minute before I put on my happy Utopia business face. I could have had Angela's suggestions to work on over Christmas since I'd only be killing time until Connor was back. Now, the days stretched out even more dismally.

How could I miss someone so much when we'd only been dating for a few weeks? And half the time we'd been pretending?

Sighing glumly—and admittedly feeling extremely sorry for myself, which I had to shake off—I stepped back into the drizzle and ducked into Le Gabriel with its crisp white linens, hushed piano carols, and appropriately measured murmur of conversations muffled by the spotless cream fabric wall coverings. Everything at Le Gabriel was exquisitely curated from the wine cellar to the foie gras to the clientele.

Clientele that included Cecilia Weston, her golden hair settling in soft curls around her shoulders, complimenting her cranberry dress perfectly.

I froze as I handed my coat to the hostess, my gaze locking on Cecilia across the dining room in a plush corner booth. She looked as lovely and polished as ever, smiling at something her companions said. They sat in padded chairs with their backs to me, but I would know Grandmother's perfect posture, pink skirt suit, and sleek silver hair anywhere.

"Mr. Cabot? This way, please."

I blinked at the hostess. I could ask for my coat back and make a run for it. I'd text Grandmother with an excuse, and she'd have to deal with it. Or I—

Cecilia waved, her smile widening. Grandmother and the man beside her—Stephen Weston, Cecilia's plastic-surgeon father—turned in their chairs, and there was no escape now. Marshalling my strength and patience, I joined them, sliding in beside Cecilia on the banquette since that was the only option. I didn't stop first to kiss Grandmother's cheeks, which was a petty rebellion.

After a round of pleasantries and champagne cocktails, we ordered lunch, and I said, "What brings us here today?" with gritted teeth I couldn't quite hide. Cecilia's smile faltered, and she glanced at her father. I added, "Though I appreciate the opportunity to catch up."

Cecilia said, "It's been years, hasn't it? I think we were in college the last time we actually spoke."

Grandmother's expression was placid enough to fool most people, but I detected the twitch of tension in her eye as she said, "Did you know Cecilia is working with her father now? Expanding his business."

That didn't answer my question, but I made interested noises, and Cecilia said, "I opened a spa hotel in the Hamptons focused on medical tourism."

"Medical tourism," I echoed. "Plastic surgery?"

"Yes, but only simple, low-risk procedures."

"Ah. Face lifts and liposuction for the rich and famous?"

Cecilia lifted her glass in a mock toast. "Precisely. It's a lucrative business, and we think there are certain other world markets where we could combine a luxury hotel experience with wellness and appropriate procedures."

Servers arrived with our lunches, and I poked at my duck and pork cassoulet, dread building in me. This was why Grandmother had been so eager to set up me and Cecilia? So Utopia could open new properties for plastic surgery tourism? Cecilia and I didn't need to be a couple to go into business together. Perhaps Grandmother had simply decided Cecilia was the most eligible young woman in town.

Emphasis on *woman*.

My tie felt like it was choking me. I loosened it, garnering pursed lips from Grandmother. I was tempted to order another drink as Stephen detailed a new procedure involving neck fat. I wondered what Connor would think. Had Dr. Weston gone into medicine as an idealistic youth hoping to help people, or had he always preyed on people's insecurities?

I ate a bite of rich duck and white beans with dill. I was probably being unfair. I asked Stephen, "Do you ever treat patients with disfigurements or people who've been in accidents?"

"Occasionally, but my focus is on cosmetics. Don't worry, we won't be bringing desperate cases to your hotel."

There it was. I smiled thinly, swirling my glass of Bordeaux. "My hotel?"

"That's what we need to discuss," Grandmother said smoothly.

"You know, I'd actually like to discuss affordable housing," I blurted. Three sets of eyes stared blankly. I gulped my wine and ordered myself to stop talking.

Cecilia asked, "Affordable housing? Yes, I imagine there's a need for it." Her sculpted brows met. "But you don't need to worry about that."

"No, I don't need to. None of us do." I motioned around the table. "We should, though. We should worry about a lot of things we ignore."

"Darling, I appreciate your passion, but let's stay on topic," Grandmother said.

"You don't, though." What was I doing? Why wasn't I nodding and smiling like usual? "My passion doesn't lie in luxury hotels. You know that, but you ignore it."

Grandmother's nostrils flared. She'd spilled a drop of coq au vin on her crisp white blouse. "We're here to celebrate the season and discuss an excellent business opportunity with the Westons. You and I can speak later about…other topics."

As Grandmother and I stared daggers at each other, Cecilia said, "Er, uh, what are your plans for Christmas? My parents are leaving tomorrow for a South American cruise that looks incredible. Doesn't it, Daddy?"

"Oh yes, we'll be hitting all the highlights. Machu Picchu, that huge waterfall in Argentina. I think it's Argentina?"

"You'll soon find out," Grandmother said.

"I suppose you'll both be at Elizabeth's annual Christmas breakfast," Stephen said.

"Yes," I replied. "I'd much rather be with my boyfriend, but I don't get a choice." I cringed as soon as the childish words were out. I didn't regret mentioning Connor at all—to hell with what Grandmother thought—but petulance wasn't a good look.

Grandmother's face had flushed pink and her mouth pressed into a grim line. In the silence, Cecilia said, "It… Well, it is a good cause."

Shame rushed through me. "Yes, of course. A wonderful cause." I shook my head. "Forgive me. I'm just missing Connor." That probably wouldn't improve my grandmother's mood, but it was the truth.

Cecilia's face brightened. "Understandable. You two looked very much in love when I spotted you last week." She leaned closer and whispered conspiratorially, "He's very cute. I hear he's in med school?"

So, it seemed Cecilia had no interest in me, which was a relief. I answered, "Yes, at Columbia. He's going to be a wonderful doctor."

"If he decides to get into plastics, let me know," Stephen said through a bite of his steak.

"Will do," I said, belatedly tapping my reserves of politeness. "Thank you."

Grandmother delicately cleared her throat. "Yes, well. Cecilia, dear, why haven't you been snapped up?"

Cecilia waved a dismissive hand. "Oh, I'm not looking to settle down anytime soon."

For a moment, Grandmother was stunned into silence.

I said, "Your parents haven't tried to fix you up?"

"Oh, they've tried." She winked at her father, who shrugged nonchalantly. "They even suggested one of the Masterson boys."

I grimanced—*grinced*. "Veto."

"Indeed," Cecilia agreed. "Why isn't Connor coming with you to the breakfast on Christmas?"

"He's visiting his family in Albany." What was he doing now? God, I wished I was there.

She asked, "How did you two meet?"

Before I could answer, Grandmother coughed and pretended to nearly choke, which was an excellent distraction. Honestly, I wanted to sit back with my arms crossed until she was done, but I managed to make the required sympathetic noises.

"Goodness, what a fuss," Grandmother said after drinking water. "I'm quite all right. Cecilia, we'd love to hear more about your wellness venture. I think Utopia could be an excellent fit for your vision."

"I think so too, Mrs. Cabot." Cecilia glanced at me with an apologetic smile before launching into her spiel.

I listened and nodded and said all the right things. Grandmother relaxed by degrees, and by the time she paid the huge bill, you'd never have known I'd upset her.

When I walked her out to the waiting town car, holding her umbrella aloft, she gripped my arm with surprising strength, her tone ice cold. "Darling, I simply can't imagine what got into you."

"We need to talk." I opened the car door for her. It was time to say everything on my mind. Show her my proposal—everything. What was I waiting for? "If you're free now—"

Without meeting my gaze, she simply said, "Veto," and slid into the back seat. "I'll see you Christmas morning, bright and early."

Chapter Seventeen

Connor

EIGHT DAYS. *EIGHT days.* As much as I loved Christmas, how could I be expected to be apart from Reid for *eight* more days?

Tomorrow was Christmas Eve, and even in my room at midnight, the house smelled like the gingerbread cookies Seth had baked hours before. It was comforting and cozy, and I was tucked in my bed with snow falling beyond my window, the sky glowing white.

And I was horny as fuck.

I'd gone years without sex, but now that the seal was broken—so to speak—I was ravenous. How was I supposed to go *eight* more days?

It wasn't only sex. I wanted to hug Reid and smell his pepper-lilac-or-maybe-lily cologne. Hold him and feel his arms around me and the rumble of his laughter against my chest. Talk to him for hours about anything. About everything.

And, yes, I wanted to fuck him every way known to man. If the aliens had any ideas, I was all ears.

I flipped from one side to the other, sighing so loudly I half-expected Logan and Seth to shout for me to pipe down. I hadn't heard from him in the afternoon, but then he'd texted that he was out for dinner with Addison and some friends, which was great. Great! This was the part when I was supposed to go to sleep and talk to him in the morning.

I kicked at the blankets and flopped onto my stomach. My boxers were bunched, and I felt hot. I restlessly stripped off my T-shirt. Then goosebumps spread over my chest and I pulled it back on.

Obviously, I could jack off. I'd done it a million times, and I could get the release I needed. But it would be hollow without Reid. I wanted *him*. I wasn't just normal horny. This was next-level horny. I'd thought I'd known just how horny a person could get, but nope.

NOPE.

My phone buzzed with a video call, and I flicked on the lamp, eagerly swiping to reveal Reid's gorgeous face. He said, "Hey, baby," and I could have melted into a puddle of goo. He was *beaming* at me, and god, I wanted to lick his whole face. That couldn't be normal.

I sat up against the Ricky Tortuga poster. "Hey, yourself."

Reid asked, "Were you sleeping?" His brow furrowed, and I imagined tracing the creases with my tongue. "You have bed head."

"Oh!" I squinted at my image in the corner of the screen and tamped down my hair.

"It's adorable. Don't change a thing. I just don't want to keep you up if you're tired."

"I wasn't sleeping," I said honestly. "How was dinner? How was your day?"

"Dinner was great. Addison says hi."

"Cool. Did you talk to Angela earlier? I think that was today?"

His expression tightened. "I had to reschedule. It'll be after the holidays since she's busy with her family."

"Shit. I'm sorry. Waiting sucks. Did something come up at work?"

Reid did this shrug-nod that was definitely tense. He still wore a suit, so he must have just gotten in. "Yeah, there was a thing. No big deal."

"Are you sure? It kind of looks like it was a big deal."

He smiled, but he was clearly upset. Along with the frustration I'd seen in him before was tiredness. More than that—sadness.

Reid said, "Don't worry about it. What's happening in Albany? Did you get snow? That weather system stayed north of the city. Don't think we're getting a white Christmas here."

"I want to worry about it. What's wrong?"

He rubbed his face, and the camera jostled, the camera sweeping over Reid's living room before he propped his tablet on the coffee table and slumped on the couch. His charcoal suit jacket was undone, and he loosened the knot on his purple tie before slipping it free and dropping it to the cushion beside him. The camera looked up at him—and his crotch, but I focused on his weary, beautiful face.

"I think I'm having a midlife crisis. At twenty-nine." He snorted. "I'm almost thirty, and what have I accomplished? I could leave Utopia tomorrow, and it wouldn't make even a tiny bit of difference. The company and Grandmother would keep going without missing a beat."

"Then what's keeping you there? Other than guilt?"

"Great question." He shook his head. "Do I have to answer that right now?"

"Nope. You don't have to do anything right now. We can hang. Relax."

His smile was undeniably fond this time. "That sounds good." He shrugged out of his jacket and popped open the top three buttons on his white dress shirt. I could see a smattering of dark hair below his throat. Predictably, I wanted to lick that triangle of tender flesh.

Memories of grinding in his lap resurfaced. I swallowed hard. "There's a way we could relieve stress."

"Mm?" He yawned. "Night time yoga? What do you prescribe?"

"I was thinking orgasms."

That perked him up, but his grin was quickly replaced by a frown. "You vetoed phone sex."

"I can change my mind, right?"

"Yes, as long as it's not to cheer me up. You have to want it too."

"Trust me, I want it. I'm inspired by the view. Jesus, do you know how good you look in that suit? So hot."

He grinned. "I try. You look hot too."

I snorted. "In my Harvard crew T-shirt with Ricky Tortuga behind me?"

"Take it off if you don't like it."

Lust zapped me like a lightning strike. "Right. I could do that." I shifted, holding up my phone and tugging at my tee collar with my free hand. Did I have a fever? Blood rushed in my ears.

"You don't have to. I'm very capable of jerking off and thinking about you. My spank bank has had recent deposits."

I burst out laughing. "You're such a nerd. I never would have dreamed in a million years I'd hear Reid Cabot say 'spank bank.'"

"I'm all class. How could you possibly resist me?"

"I can't. The thing is, I need you." I glanced at my door. I hadn't heard a peep from my dads since they'd gone to bed around ten. "Like, *that*."

Reid licked his lips, and boy, was that a smirk and a half. "Tell me what you need."

I sighed noisily. "I'm horny as hell, okay?"

"Me too." He spread his legs wide and palmed the bulge of his cock through the smooth, tailored pants. "You wanna do this?" he asked, his low voice sending shivers down my spine.

"Hell, yeah."

"Yeah?" He watched me intently, pausing to give me another

out.

"Yes."

"Take it off."

I glanced at the door. "Hold on." I leapt up and turned on the pedestal fan in the corner for the noise, pointing it away from the bed before locking the door. I stripped off the tee and my boxers before clambering back on the bed and grabbing my phone. I reached for the lamp.

"I want to see you," Reid said. "Unless you want to switch to audio only?"

"But then I can't see you. Fuck it. Let's do it." Holy shit, was I actually having phone sex? On camera? *Here?*

"Are you naked yet? I can't tell from this angle." Reid had unbuttoned his own shirt completely and left it hanging open. He toyed with his nipples.

"Yeah," I whispered. "I'm naked. We have to be quiet."

He rubbed his dick. "Mmm. I'll try."

I turned down the volume on my phone, Reid's breathing still sounding loud even with the fan. I leaned back against Ricky's feet, checking my image in the bottom corner to make sure it was okay and I wasn't showing Reid up my nose or something.

With my fingers hooked around the pop socket on the back of my phone, I propped my left wrist on my bent knee.

Reid whispered, "Doctor, I have a painful condition. I've tried everything."

My heart *boomed*. Phone sex *and* role play? Teenage me really would never fucking believe this, though I also wanted to tell Reid not to jinx it. I wasn't a doctor yet. What if I'd bombed my exams? They might take away my scholarship. Then I'd be working at CVS every night...

"Veto?" Reid asked in his normal voice.

"No!" I croaked out, "What seems to be the problem? This is your, uh, doctor here." I reached blindly for the lube in my beside table drawer, my eyes locked on my phone.

With the low angle of Reid's camera, his cock looked *huge* as he pulled it out. "I'm so hard." His eyes twinkled, and I couldn't bite back a laugh.

I put on a serious doctor voice. "We'll have to run some tests. I've never seen anything quite so large and…tumescent."

Reid snorted, and we both giggled. Like, actually *giggled*. Reid put on a serious face, and I did too. "Doctor, it hurts. I can't stop myself from touching it."

"Take off your pants and stroke it. Let me see."

He did, stripping off his trousers and briefs, leaving only the open dress shirt. A flush spread up his chest as he worked himself. I breathed quickly, shallow little gasps as I jerked off. In the bottom of my screen, I could see my face was pink, my lips parted.

"Do you like watching me, Doctor?" Reid whispered.

I could only nod. Not being able to smell him or feel him or taste the salt of his sweat or lingering coffee on his tongue made watching him even more intense than usual.

I'd looked at him a million times and admired his hotness, but watching now, I zeroed in on the hair around his left nipple, the cords of muscle in his neck as he stroked himself, the flex of his wide thighs.

"It's helping. I feel better already." He moaned, thumbing the drops of precum from the tip of his shaft. If we'd been in the same room, I would have dropped to my knees to swallow him. I wanted to choke on his dick. Biting my lip, I swallowed a moan.

"Let me see you," Reid murmured.

I held my phone farther away, trying to get the right angle. I probably should have been embarrassed, but it was Reid. I wanted to give him whatever he needed. I wanted to give him everything.

"Doctor, I need to watch you come. It's the only cure."

I gasped, and I would have slapped a hand over my mouth if I'd had one free. Bent legs wide, I dug my heels into the mattress and jerked faster, arching up into my hand, straining, trying to keep the camera on my dick, my arm shaking, balls tightening—

I sprayed my load on my stomach while Reid moaned and encouraged me. "Baby, that's so good. Fuck, you're beautiful."

Bringing my phone screen back up, I focused on him. I was still breathing hard, slumping back against Ricky. Reid's arm worked, his back arched. His balls were flushed and heavy, and I wanted to suck them and feel his wiry hair on my tongue.

"That's it," I whispered. "You're such a good patient. Show me your hole." I had no clue where these words were coming from, but I didn't try to stop them from spilling out.

Reid eagerly spread his hairy legs even more, putting his feet on the coffee table and shifting his ass to the edge of the couch. It was hard to actually see, but then Reid pushed his middle finger inside, his gaze locked on me. I shook through an aftershock as I teased my spent dick.

"You're going to make me hard again." I moaned softly.

That sent Reid over the edge, and I couldn't have looked away for a million dollars as he came all over his stomach and chest while he finger fucked himself.

"Jesus," I whispered.

Panting, Reid nodded. "I'm cured."

"Same."

"What's that old saying? 'Physician, cure thyself?' Achievement unlocked."

We laughed, and Reid swiped at the mess on his skin with his fingers. He was boneless against the couch, clearly in no rush to go clean up.

"Oh my god," I mumbled. "How are you this hot?" *And how do you want me?* "I would have shit twice and died if I'd seen you do this when I was in high school."

"Glad to be of service now. And thank you," Reid murmured. He'd dragged a velvet throw blanket over him and yawned widely.

Soon, I'd have to creep out to the bathroom to scrub the drying jizz off me, but in the meantime, I pulled the covers up.

"It was my pleasure. As you saw." Another thrill shivered through me. Being with Reid was better than my wildest dreams, and I'd had some…inventive fantasies. "Hey, did we get to everything on your New Yorker list?"

"Not quite. I keep expanding it. We can tackle more in the new year."

My heart leapt. "Cool. Any hints?"

"Hmm. Maybe. Pick a number."

"Twelve."

Reid curled on his side, his head pillowed on the arm of the couch. "Why twelve?"

"It was my mom's favorite number."

"Favorite? Not lucky?"

"No. It was just the number she always picked."

"Example?"

I held up my phone and shimmied down so my head was on my pillow. "If we were trying a new Chinese place for takeout, she'd go with entree number twelve, no matter what it was. When she bought lottery tickets, twelve was always her first number. Stuff like that. I guess she hoped it would be good luck." It certainly hadn't worked.

Reid dug his phone out of his pants pocket and tapped the screen. "Well, number twelve is possibly the most authentic New York experience there is: step on a rat."

Laughing, I cried, "Veto!" before remembering my dads were sleeping close by. I put my finger to my lips and shushed as if Reid was the one who'd shouted.

"I don't make the rules. New York does." His shoulders shook with laughter under the blanket.

"You're a weirdo."

"I love that I can be a weirdo with you."

My breath caught. *Love.* We stared at each other, both of us falling silent.

I whispered, "I can imagine Bitsy doesn't enjoy weird."

"Not in the slightest." He reached for something on the floor, picking up the discarded purple tie. "I feel like I've been wearing a disguise for as long as I can remember."

"You came out, though. You've been peeling it away."

He seemed to ponder this, stroking the smooth, shiny material. "I suppose so." His gaze locked on me. "But you're the first person to really see me. To listen to me. To *hear* me."

"I…" My mouth was bone dry. "I'm glad." It wasn't enough of a response, but it was all I could come up with. I'd undoubtedly think of a million eloquent thoughts tomorrow.

"We should sleep. Thank you again. For trusting me with that."

"Of course. It's the next best thing until I see you again."

"Eight more days," Reid said.

That he was counting too was the greatest Christmas present ever.

Chapter Eighteen

Reid

ASHER GROANED AS he mumbled, "Hello?"

"Hey, it's me." Fiddling with the belt of my robe, I paced the length of my apartment, the hardwood creaking in places under my bare feet. It was still dark and also foggy, a low haze hanging over the city and dampening the familiar lights. "Did I wake you?"

"Dude, it's seven in the morning on Christmas Eve. *Duh.*"

"Sorry. Look, I need a—" I was about to say "favor," but I stopped myself. "I need you to do something for me. For our family."

"Huh? What's going on? Are you okay?"

I bit back my usual answer, which would be that I was fine. Peering out at the shrouded buildings, I said, "No, actually."

Asher's voice sharpened, the sleepy slur disappearing. "What happened? Did you get in an accident?"

"No, nothing like that. I'm not injured. But I need you to go to Grandmother's breakfast event tomorrow."

After a beat of silence, Asher said, "Wait, what? Dude, why are you being so dramatic? And no way—I'm going skiing at Stowe."

"I really need you to step in for me." To step *up*.

"That's always been your deal. You're Gamma's golden grand-child."

I sputtered. "As if you aren't her favorite?"

"Me? Are you on drugs? Gamma loves me, sure, but you two have your whole Utopia thing."

"Yeah, well, I don't want it." I jammed the phone against my ear.

"What? Since when?"

"I don't know. A few years now."

Asher was silent a moment. "But...*what*? Hold up. Are you talking about tomorrow specifically, or in general?"

"In general."

"But it's always been your thing. Even when Dad was alive, we all knew you were going to take over the company one day."

"It's all yours."

"No, no, no. I don't want it. I'm going to be a broker. I know it's not very original, but I like it, and I'm good at it. The family business is all you and Gamma."

"I don't want to spend my life servicing the one percent when I could be helping people."

"You do a ton of charity stuff."

"Yeah, and that's great, but it's not my *job*. It could be, though. Why not? Why should I be Grandmother's golden boy? I'm already not the straight, perfect grandson she wanted. Why stop there?"

"I mean... Yeah. If you're not happy, you should do something about it."

I inhaled and exhaled deeply, excitement zipping through my veins. "I should. I *need* to do something about it. Starting with Christmas."

"Okay, why can't you do Gamma's event tomorrow?"

"I want to spend Christmas with Connor. I've spent every Christmas for a decade in public representing Utopia and our family. The breakfast and toys go to deserving people, which is great. But I want a Christmas that's for me for once. Maybe that's awful and selfish, but I miss Connor. I'm tired of following

Grandmother's orders."

Asher sighed heavily. "I get it. Also, it is seriously weird that you're, what—falling for my best friend?"

"Maybe. I don't know. Actually, yes. Yes. I've fallen for Connor. Hard."

"That was quite a journey." He groaned. "*Fine.* I'll drive up to Stowe tomorrow afternoon instead of today."

Relief *whooshed* through me. "Thanks, man. I owe you. Actually, no. I don't. You need to pull your weight with Grandmother."

"Took me on another journey there. Yeah, okay. That's fair."

"It is? I mean, yes. It is." I felt light enough to float away. Instead of pacing, I spun in a silly little dance move. What was that saying? Dance like no one was watching? I could have done a cartwheel if I hadn't been holding my phone.

"It means that much to you not to have to do this breakfast tomorrow? Since when do you give a shit about Christmas?"

"It's not just one event. It's symbolic. And yeah, I've never really cared about Christmas. There are so many social obligations. But this is the first season when I've actually had fun. I want to decorate. I want to buy presents and roast chestnuts. I keep humming Mariah Carey Christmas songs."

"Holy shit, you *are* in love."

I waited for a bolt of fear or denial.

Nothing.

All I wanted to do was that cartwheel. I laughed—a fizzy bubble of joy. "I am."

"Huh. You sound…happy. I didn't realize how tense you normally are. Wow."

"I'm in love. I need to call Connor. I need to tell him."

"On the phone? No. Veto. If you're going to tell my boy you love him, you are doing that in person. Go buy him gifts as soon as the stores open, then dust off your Audi from the underground parking lot and surprise him in Albany."

My pulse galloped. Was I actually doing this? "I can't surprise him on Christmas Eve! He's with his family."

"They're cool, trust me. This will be the greatest Christmas present ever."

"But they have plans. They aren't expecting me. Connor might not want me to come."

Asher laughed. Loudly. "Bro, he wants you to come. Trust. Hold on. Let me just…"

After the silence stretched out, I asked, "Let you what?"

"There. I just texted Con and asked if I can visit for Christmas."

"And I'm supposed to tag along and impose? No way!"

He sighed heavily. "*I'm* not going. *You're* going. But this way, they know someone's crashing and it won't be a surprise."

"This is a terrible idea. They might say no."

"Logan and Seth love me. They won't say no. They're going to say, 'the more the merrier.' Like, those exact words will come out of Seth's mouth, I guarantee it."

"But they don't even know me."

"What better time to meet the man who's railing their baby boy?"

I groaned. "This is not helping."

"A-ha! Conner just replied: *Of course. Is everything okay?* There. It's done. They're officially expecting a guest, and you can climb down Connor's chimney. God bless us, everyone."

My head spun, and despite my persistent doubts, the urge to cartwheel returned. "Make sure you tell him you're okay. Don't make him worry."

"Yes, *Mom*. Oh, speaking of whom, did she send you pics from that sailboat? Maybe we should spend Christmas with her next year."

After we hung up, I started searching for gift ideas online. I needed something perfect for Connor, and what about his dads? And his extended family gathered on Christmas Eve, I thought he'd said. I needed to get organized.

Before I did, I put down my phone and performed a wobbly cartwheel that culminated in me sprawled on my back by the couch laughing at the ceiling.

All I wanted for Christmas was Connor—and I was going to get my man.

"YOU HAVEN'T SHAVED."

Grandmother stared at me in the foyer of her two-story apartment. She must have heard me speaking to the housekeeper who'd let me in—and who now quickly disappeared down a hallway past framed prints of Utopia ads from decades past. One headline beckoned:

Escape to a world where the sea meets the sky.

What did that even mean? The sea met the sky everywhere there was an ocean on the planet.

"Darling? What's wrong?"

It was Christmas Eve and she wasn't in the office, but Grandmother looked like she was. Navy pantsuit and Hermès scarf knotted at her throat, pearl earrings and matching bracelet on her wrist. The only indication that she wasn't expecting company was that her reading glasses hung from a gold chain around her neck. She never wore them in public.

In stark contrast, I'd tugged on jeans and a sweater. I'd unbuttoned my coat in the sweltering cab on the way over, and no—I hadn't shaved for the first day in…possibly forever?

"Are you ill?" she asked, her sharp gaze intense.

"No," I croaked. I cleared my throat and thrust out the binder I'd been gripping in my sweaty hands. "Please read this. I've been working on it for months. I want to diversify our business. Invest in affordable, sustainable housing. We can easily fund a pilot project while maintaining our current hotels and resorts if we pause any further hotel expansion temporarily."

She peered at the simple black binder uncomprehendingly. "Is this what you were talking about at lunch with the Westons?"

"Yes." I still held out the binder, willing my hand not to shake. She might not have been actual royalty, but in my world, she may as well have been. I felt like I should curtsey. "Will you please read it?"

Lips pursed, she took the binder, then leveled me with a piercing gaze. "Is that all? You'll shave tomorrow morning before the event."

"Actually, I won't be there."

Eyes wide, her mouth gaped. I couldn't remember if I'd ever seen Grandmother look so discombobulated—not even when I announced Connor was my boyfriend on Thanksgiving.

I plowed on since she was apparently stunned silent. "Asher's going to be there, though. Don't worry—the family will be represented."

Grandmother's nostrils flared. "Asher isn't the future president of Utopia. That's wonderful that he's volunteered, but you know how important this event is to our brand. You're always there to give generously to those in need. You are required to be there."

I shrugged. I actually shrugged, which felt as huge as if I'd given her the finger. "The brand will have to survive without me."

"What does that mean?" she asked sharply.

"I'm not sure. For now, it means I won't be at the event tomorrow, and that you and Utopia will be just fine."

She clutched the binder. "Where exactly will you be?"

"In Albany with Connor for Christmas."

The *crack* of the binder spine hitting the marble floor could have been a gunshot. From the corner of my eye, I spotted the housekeeper hurrying toward us—then just as quickly backing away.

Grandmother clenched her fists. "Enough with this nonsense! That boy is not suitable."

"He's not a boy. And why not?"

"You know precisely why."

"His gender or that he was on scholarship at Rencliffe?"

"Enough." She turned on her heel, the binder still flung open and abandoned on the floor.

"No! Tell me why Connor isn't good enough. Because he has two dads?"

Her nose wrinkled as she faced me. "Good god. They've clearly corrupted that boy."

"Jesus Christ, don't be ridiculous."

"I will not stand here in my own home and be spoken to in this manner. What has gotten into you? What would your father say?"

"I have no idea. I barely remember him. He's like a shadow."

"I remember every minute."

Guilt and grief punched. *Hard.* "I'm sorry. I wish I did remember him more."

"You were twelve when he passed. You must remember."

"Not much. He was always working, and I was away at Rencliffe. I've been alive longer without him."

Her brow furrowed, and she was silent as if counting the years and thinking it couldn't possibly be true.

"He's been more present in his absence and the pressure that put on me than he was when he was alive." At her flinch, I added, "I wish that wasn't the case. And I know you don't want me to be bisexual—"

"Enough." She raised her palm, schooling her expression back into stone. "This ridiculous rebellion needs to end. You and Cecilia aren't a match, that much is clear. But—"

"This isn't rebellion. This is who. I. Am. I'm bisexual, and I'm in love with a man." I motioned to the binder. "And I want to help make the world a better place. I want to use my privilege to make a practical, sustainable difference. At least try to. Not open new hotels for facelifts and collagen injections."

Grandmother pinched the bridge of her nose. "I might have expected this idealistic claptrap when you were in college. I suppose I have *Connor* to thank."

"This has been building for a long time. And yes, Connor helped me see more clearly. I'm spending Christmas with him. If you'll read my proposal over the holidays, we can discuss it in January. Angela Barker's very interested in it."

Grandmother exhaled in disgust. "That tacky woman."

I gritted my teeth. "She's gone out of her way to help me."

"How wonderful." Sarcasm dripped from Grandmother's tongue.

I couldn't leave my proposal abandoned on the floor, so I placed it on the small round console table beside a wing-backed chair no one ever sat in.

"I have to get on the road. They're calling for a major snowstorm upstate. Merry Christmas."

Striding to the private elevator, I jabbed the button. I didn't let myself look back in the silence as the old door slid open slowly, though I sensed she was still there.

"Darling."

My heart clenched. I shouldn't care what she thought of me or my relationship with Connor, but I did. I wanted her to love me in all my bisexual glory. I wanted to still be her darling. I turned, extending my arm behind me to keep the elevator open.

"Drive carefully."

With that, she gracefully walked out of the foyer, head high, her heels tapping the marble. My proposal still sat on the table, but at least it wasn't on the floor.

Two hours later on the highway as snow fell more and more thickly and traffic slowed in a sea of red taillights, I paused the podcast I hadn't heard a word of and tapped the navigation screen to see if Connor had replied to my texts and the system somehow hadn't notified me. No red dot on his name. I dialed his number with a tap. It rang out, and I didn't leave another message.

I'd decided once I was on the road that surprising him—and his parents—was a terrible idea no matter what my little brother thought. Did the silence in response to my messages mean that I wasn't welcome? Surely if it was a problem, Connor would have simply told me that.

It was still early afternoon, but it could have been sunset. Visibility was decreasing, and we crawled past a car that had spun into the ditch, the flashing lights of a state trooper casting an eerie glow in the gloom. Every mile farther from the city had me questioning if it was time to turn around.

"Where is he?" I said out loud.

Had he been in an accident? Was he breaking up with me— he'd lived up to his fake boyfriend obligations, and perhaps he'd rethought continuing our relationship? Had I done something or said something? I replayed the last conversation we'd had—the incredibly hot phone sex and afterglow.

Naturally, remembering that made my cock swell, and I shifted restlessly. The windshield wipers thumped back and forth, the thick, wet snow sticky. I deeply regretted not buying winter tires for my car, but I drove it so infrequently and usually only in the city. At least I could stay slow and steady in the right-hand lane while more daring drivers passed on the left.

"Where is Connor?"

Chapter Nineteen

Connor

"RESOURCE CARD, PLEASE," I said, extending my hand to Seth.

He grumbled and passed one over. He wasn't very competitive generally speaking, but Catan brought it out in him.

"I can build a road now," I said. "Sweet."

Across from me at the dining table, Logan rolled the dice. He leaned back to read the number, and I finally asked, "When was the last time you had your eyes checked?"

Logan practically growled, but there was no heat to it. "My eyes are fine."

"You need reading glasses," Seth and I said in unison.

"I was a goddamn Marine," Logan muttered as he played a Year of Plenty card.

"I'm afraid that doesn't exempt you from the ravages of aging, my dear." Seth squeezed Logan's arm and kissed his cheek.

The ornamental clock ticked on the wall below green garland boughs decorated with white berries and red ribbons. I squinted out the window. "I hope the roads are okay. I should check if Asher's texted."

"Nice try," Logan said. "No phones during game time."

"What if he gets in an accident?"

Logan and Seth shared a glance, and as usual, they had a whole conversation in a blink. Seth said, "Yes, I think this is an exception."

I practically ran to where our phones sat on the kitchen island, hoping there'd be messages from Reid too. God, I missed him so much. But when I looked at the screen, there were no messages from anyone. No notifications.

"Shit!" No Wi-Fi signal, and the cell coverage was terrible out where we lived, the one bar not giving me anything. "Wi-Fi's out!" I called to Logan and Seth.

Seth joined me in the kitchen. "I'll reboot it and see if that makes a difference. Hope we don't lose power."

I peered out the window. The snow was piling up, but at least it wasn't too windy. Visibility would hopefully be okay. "I hope Asher gets here soon. I hate not having a way to contact him." Or Reid.

"Ahem," Seth said pointedly, followed by a low buzzing sound.

I turned and found him holding out the old land line phone that sat in the corner of the counter in all its beige, plastic glory.

"Oh, right."

"This is exactly why we still have it," Seth said with an arched eyebrow.

"Okay, okay." I'd teased them about it and how it wasn't even a cordless. Apparently, cordless phones didn't work without power, but the ancient ones just plugged into the wall did. It was strange to hear a dial tone as I punched in Asher's numbers on the buttons. A number I had to look up in my contacts since I knew zero phone numbers off by heart except my own.

"No answer," I said after getting Asher's voicemail. I left a quick message and considered calling Reid, but Seth was still in the kitchen checking on a recipe for later. I'd barely put the phone back in its holder when it rang again.

I picked it up. "Where are you, jackass?"

"I'm at home freaking out over the weather report," Aunt

Jenna said. "Though I'd appreciate not being called a jackass."

Laughing, I clapped a hand over my mouth. "My bad. I thought you were Asher. This phone doesn't even have call display."

"At least it's working. I've been texting and calling Seth and Logan, but I assume they aren't going through."

"Yeah, sorry. Here you go."

I handed the phone to Seth and opened the fridge, poking around and idly peeling the wrapper off a cheese slice. My dads always had processed cheese in the fridge when I visited since I loved grilled cheese. Actual cheese was good too, but there was something weirdly comforting about the processed slices.

"Mm," Seth was saying. "I agree. You don't want to take the risk. You only see Jun's parents a couple of times a year. It's best to get on the road now. Let me get Logan."

I ate another cheese slice and leaned against the island while Logan talked to Jenna and Seth waited with slumped shoulders.

Logan said, "You sure you want to take Pop with you? He can stay with us. I know he can't do the stairs, but we could bring down a mattress or something." After a silence, he said, "Okay."

When Logan hung up after telling her to drive safely and call when they arrived, I asked, "They're not coming tonight?"

Logan sighed heavily. "The snow we're getting now is moving west overnight and gaining momentum. They're going to get hit with a huge storm tomorrow. The highways might close."

"Shit," I said. "Yeah, I guess it's better if they go now." It had become tradition to celebrate together on Christmas Eve with turkey and all the fixings before having a more chill Christmas Day. Usually, Aunt Jenna and Uncle Jun went to his family or had them visit for Christmas Day. "Even if that means we don't get Aunt Jenna's turkey," I added in a tone dangerously close to a whine.

Seth was already looking in the freezer. "We have steaks. We can shovel off the back porch and fire up the grill."

"Sure," Logan said distantly, staring at his feet, arms crossed and leaning against the counter.

"It sucks that we can't all have Christmas Eve together like usual," I said.

"Yeah," Logan agreed, still clearly preoccupied.

Seth left the meat on the counter and joined Logan. He didn't say anything—just waited until Logan spit out whatever it was on his mind.

After a minute, Logan said, "This medicine Pop has to take for the swelling in his legs—Jenna has to keep nagging him to take it." He looked at me. "Is there something else he can take instead? He hates it."

"I'm not sure, but from what I know, I doubt it. Is the reason he doesn't want to take it because he has to urinate too frequently? Which means getting up more often? It's likely a mobility issue."

"Right." Logan seemed to think about it. "That's probably it. He just wants to sit in that chair even more than he used to."

Seth asked, "Why does the congestive heart failure cause the swelling? I'm not clear on the reason."

He was asking me, and Logan looked to me as well. I explained the correlation between his heart condition and the edema as they nodded, answering a few more questions that came up.

"Talking like a doc already," Logan said with a big smile, and I flushed with pride.

"I still have a ton to learn," I insisted.

"And you'll learn it," Logan said firmly. "You were always so good at learning. Do you remember the first time I met you? Most kids would be playing video games, but you were memorizing the periodic table with those cards. There's a name for them…"

I fiddled with Seth's recipe for butternut squash casserole sitting on the island counter, spinning the paper under my finger. "Flash cards."

"Right, right." Logan had that distant look again. "Veronica was so damn proud of you."

My throat was too thick to speak. I shrugged and opened the fridge, thinking of the night she died and how I *had* been playing video games. I knew I shouldn't let myself spiral down this hole, but my asshole brain was off and running.

If I hadn't been wearing headphones, would I have heard her call for help? Even if she hadn't been able to call out, I might have heard her hit the bedroom floor...

Instead, she'd lain there all night. Alone. Until I'd finally gone looking for her in the morning, annoyed that she wasn't making me breakfast because I was a selfish little—

"You okay?" Logan asked. I could sense he and Seth close behind me. I stared into the fridge, blinking back tears.

"Yeah," I rasped, grabbing the water pitcher and closing the fridge too hard. I poured a glass, splashing water all over the counter and over Seth's recipe. "Shit! Sorry."

"It's okay," Seth murmured, squeezing my shoulder and shaking the paper.

Sometimes, the memory of finding her there that morning punched so hard that it eclipsed everything else in the world. I breathed through it, knowing it would pass, and I would go on. I'd be happy again, and that was allowed.

God, I wished Reid was with me. As much as I loved my dads, I ached for Reid's comfort. It was probably only infatuation, I knew that. Everything was shiny and new, and I couldn't let myself get too invested.

I laughed harshly. Too fucking late for that.

"Hey." Logan nudged my arm. "What's up?"

"Sorry. I'm in my head. I'm fine."

Maybe keeping Reid to myself was a mistake. As much as I wanted to keep this amazing new thing to myself until I knew for sure it was real and not going to disappear tomorrow, the urge to let it all spill out in an excited rush was strong.

Asher would be here soon, and I could talk to him. I managed a genuine smile for my dads, pulling the door on my mom memories ajar. I'd never close that door entirely, but I'd learned over time how to function with it in the background.

I said, "Really. I guess we should defrost the steaks and stuff."

Seth chuckled. "Who's 'we'? Since when do you help out in the kitchen?"

"I help!"

"Please provide evidence of past 'helping,'" Seth said.

"I grated the Parmesan when we had that walnut pesto pasta."

"That was last year!"

The phone rang again, and Logan picked it up while I tried to think of a more recent example. I said, "Um… Oh! I totally made sangria this summer for the barbecue on Uncle Jun's birthday."

Seth submerged the bagged steaks in water in the sink. "I'll give you that one. Barely."

Logan growled, "No. Connor doesn't live here anymore. No idea where he is," and hung up the phone with a bang.

Seth frowned. "Who was that?"

Grim-faced, Logan turned to me. My stomach clenched. "What?"

Seth raised his hands. "All right. Whatever's going on, let's all take a deep breath and talk about it calmly."

"That was a fucking collection agency," Logan gritted out

No. No, no, *no*. I shook his head and sputtered, "I—I paid it! Last month."

Fuck me. *Fuck.* This wasn't supposed to happen. I borrowed that money from Reid, and I paid the whole stupid debt. It was done, and my dads were never supposed to know. It was Christmas Eve, and this wasn't right.

"If you've gotten into trouble with money, tell us what happened," Seth said steadily.

"No!" I protested—not sure what I was actually saying and cringing at how childish I sounded. "I mean, I'm not. It's fine!"

Logan's mouth was a thin line, and he paced on the other side of the island. "Why would they call?"

"I don't know," I heard myself say. "You hung up on them, or I could have asked."

He scoffed. "You never answer a collections call or tell them they have the right number. Trust me." His nostrils flared. "Just tell us."

The doorbell rang, and relief rushed through me. Asher was here, and hopefully he could be the distraction we needed to at least table this conversation—more like a confrontation—until after Christmas. I needed time to figure out how to explain.

Logan stalked out of the kitchen and into the front room, disappearing into the little foyer as Hercules scampered off upstairs. I was about to follow Logan to the door when his terse question rang out.

"Who the hell are you?"

Chapter Twenty

Reid

B RUSHING FLUFFY SNOW from my hair in the falling darkness, I waited on the doorstep of the lovely little house and tried to calm my racing heart. Connor still hadn't been answering his phone, and now I was showing up announced—which wasn't how I wanted to meet his dads. I checked my screen one more time, but I didn't have a signal anymore.

They'd surely notice the car in the driveway eventually, and I couldn't stand on their stoop all night. I rang the doorbell, which chimed pleasantly. My suitcase and bag of gifts were still in the trunk since I already felt uncomfortable appearing on the doorstep.

"This was a terrible idea," I muttered under my breath, cursing my brother. I glanced around. I'd parked on the left side of the long driveway, and the car was already almost covered in snow. Connor's dads lived outside Albany, and though I could see the blue and gold and red holiday lights of neighbors beyond stands of bare trees, it was private and felt very much like being in the country. To me at least.

I was so used to the noise of Manhattan, and it was almost eerie in the complete stillness, my breath clouding on every exhale. What a perfect place to celebrate Christmas. Footsteps approached, and I squared my shoulders. The house was lit with rainbow bulbs, warm golden light shining from inside. I could imagine how cozy and peaceful—

The merry wreath made of bright ornaments jingled violently as the door was wrenched open and a thunderous man glared. "Who the hell are you?"

"Uh…" Okay, Connor definitely hadn't gotten my messages. "I'm Reid Cabot."

The muscled man—Logan, based on Connor's descriptions—blinked at me in obvious confusion before barking, "What do you want? Asher's not here yet."

"I know. He's actually not coming."

Logan's scowl softened. "Is he okay?"

"Oh, yes! He's fine. Nothing to worry about. Is, uh, Connor home?" Good lord, I sounded and felt sixteen years old.

Relief flooded me as Connor's voice neared, saying, "Since when do you ring the bell?" As he appeared behind Logan, his jaw dropped and eyes widened.

And wow. I was in love with Connor.

Any doubt evaporated. I'd missed him more than I'd thought it was possible to miss another human. It was actually *painful* not to leap into his arms. I needed to touch him and taste him and breathe him into every cell in my body.

First, I needed to speak. "Hey. I know I'm here unannounced—uninvited, actually. I had to see you."

Connor reached for me immediately. "Are you okay? Did something happen?" He had hold of my hand, and I realized I'd left my gloves in the car.

"Yes. No. I'm fine, and so is Asher. You didn't get my messages? Clearly you didn't. I'm so sorry to show up like this. I can get a hotel."

"What?" Connor tugged me inside, elbowing Logan out of the way. "Don't be ridiculous."

I stepped into the warmth, stamping my boots on the mat. I smiled tentatively at the other man who appeared. "Hi. I'm Reid."

"Hi. I'm Seth, and this is my husband, Logan." Seth's gaze dropped to where—oops, Connor and I were holding hands. "It seems we have something to chat about."

"First things first," Logan muttered, closing the door.

Connor squirmed, letting go of my hand and crossing his arms. "I told you, it's nothing."

I stooped to take off my leather ankle boots and tried to make sense of the tension that seemed to only partially involve me. Seth took a hanger from the hall closet and was clearly waiting to hang up my coat. I smiled awkwardly as I passed it over.

I thanked him and said, "I'm interrupting. Do you want me to...?" I wasn't sure what to offer.

"No," Connor said, rubbing his face. "You need to hear it too." He took my hand again, then seemed to realize what he was doing. He glanced at his dads, shrugged, and led me through the neat house past pale gray walls and a stainless-steel kitchen with pale blue subway tile backsplash, gray quartz countertops, and white cabinets.

We stepped down into a lovely den at the back of the house with a vaulted white beam ceiling. I inhaled pine from the fresh Christmas tree with multicolored lights and a mishmash of ornaments with no discernable theme as opposed to the orderly trees my family had up even when I was little.

There was a sectional leather couch and well-padded recliner across from a wall-mounted TV. A gas fireplace stove flickered in the corner by sliding glass doors. Beyond, snow blanketed a patio.

Connor motioned for me to sit on the couch, perching beside me, his foot tapping the hardwood floor. He let go of my hand, fidgeting. Logan prowled back and forth, Seth sitting on the other end of the couch.

Not how I imagined this going.

Seth asked Connor, "How did you get into debt?"

Oh. Not what I'd expected either. I couldn't pretend I wasn't eager to find out.

Connor cracked his knuckles rhythmically and said, "It doesn't matter. It's paid off now."

Presumably, that was the ten grand. Was there more? I murmured, "If you need more money—"

"*No.*" Connor didn't look at me. "I paid off the rest with the money you loaned me. I don't want more. That's not why—" He motioned between us. "It's not for your money."

I honestly hadn't considered that for a moment, and the idea was like a slap in the face. "I know," I said evenly. "It was a loan, and it has nothing to do with us. With the us we've become."

Connor squeezed his eyes shut. "I know. I'm sorry." He looked at me beseechingly. "I don't know why I said that."

He was clearly on the defensive. "I get it." I took his hand gently, giving him a chance to pull away. My breath caught when he gripped my fingers.

"Why did you feed us some bullshit about being fake boyfriends?" Logan asked sharply. "I don't get it."

"It wasn't bullshit when I told you," Connor snapped back.

Seth held up his hands, his expression pinched in concern. "Time out. We're upset because we're worried. Remember that we're all on the same team." He looked to me. "Including Reid, it seems."

"Definitely," I agreed.

After rubbing his face, his stubble scratching, Logan nodded, pacing again. "Okay. Let's leave this Reid thing for later. Collections agency first. Spill it. Why didn't you tell us you were in debt?"

When Connor didn't answer after a few moments, Seth said, "I imagine it's because he knew we'd be upset and concerned. So, we're all going to breathe, and *sit down*, and talk about it. Without yelling. Right?" He gave Logan a pointed look.

Logan nodded as he sat on the edge of the recliner. "I—" He

took another deep breath, rubbing his chest with his knuckles.

"Okay?" Seth stood and perched on the arm of Logan's chair. As Logan leaned slightly forward, Seth ran his palm over Logan's back in slow circles.

"I'm sorry," Connor whispered miserably, his shoulders hunched. He still gripped my hand, and I squeezed back.

Seth leaned over Logan, and they murmured to each other. Logan squeezed Seth's knee, and I watched with a swell of longing. Their years of loving were apparent not only in the big moments, but in the smallest.

Logan exhaled noisily, and when he spoke, his voice was much calmer. "I know what it's like to have those fuckers hunting you. I never wanted that for you. I don't understand what happened. You have a full ride for tuition, you've worked summers, and we help with your rent and food. You saved up for years for that goddamn motorcycle. How do you have collections on your ass?"

"Mike," Connor whispered.

"That motherfucking piece of—" Logan's nostrils flared, his face red. If he was a cartoon character, steam would be coming out of his ears. But he didn't say anything else.

"Okay," Seth said, still on the arm of Logan's chair, his hand on Logan's shoulder. "Did he get you to lend him money?"

"No." Connor sighed. "He texted to see how I was doing. He asked for my address, and I thought…" He *grinced*. "It's pathetic, I know. I thought maybe he wanted to send me a birthday card or something. That maybe he wanted to keep in touch better. I've never even visited him in Florida once despite all his promises. But what he wanted was to take out credit cards in my name."

The awful betrayal of that punched my gut. As absent as my parents were, they'd never have hurt me like that. "It's not your fault," I said softly.

Connor's smile was brittle. "It is. I should have known better. I didn't get bills in the mail since it was all digital. But eventually a collections notice came. Connor Lisowski had accounts in arrears."

I asked, "Did you tell them what happened?"

"Yeah. They told me they were putting out an alert or whatever. That he wouldn't be able to open any more accounts in my name. I guess that didn't work."

"We'll call and get some answers after Christmas," Seth assured. "Maybe he'd opened it before and it slipped through."

"This shouldn't be on you," Logan said. "We should be able to clear your name. It's not your debt."

I'd never seen Connor so dejected, and I ached to hold him. He said, "They told me I had to file a police report. I just…" He shrugged, an almost violent motion. "I couldn't do it. I know I'm supposed to hate him, but…"

"No, sweetheart," Seth said, coming to Connor's other side.

"It's my job to hate that selfish piece of shit," Logan snarled. "Not yours."

Connor nodded. "You must hate him more than anyone. If he'd been a half—*quarter*—decent father, you wouldn't have been stuck with me."

"*Stuck*," Logan repeated like he'd swallowed something rancid. "Is that what you think after all these years? After, after…" He motioned with his arm. "All this?" He blinked, jerking as though he'd been slapped.

I wished I could take the words back for Connor, but all I could do was watch as his eyes widened in horror and he shook his head. "No," he rasped. "No! I don't. I'm sorry. I know that's not true. I just—"

Connor dropped his face into his hands, releasing mine. "You've both done so much for me, and you didn't have to, and I want to make you proud. I'm supposed to be a grown-up. A doctor soon! I didn't want you to know how stupid I'd been."

"We *are* proud," Seth said, his Adam's apple bobbing and

voice thick.

Logan stood. "We couldn't be prouder."

"I know," Connor mumbled. He lifted his head, blinking back tears. "I thought being an adult would be easier."

His dads shared a glance and laughed. Logan said, "Welcome to adulthood, where everyone's just trying to get and keep their shit together."

Connor shook his head. "I paid off five grand with the rest of my savings from summer jobs, and then I borrowed ten from Reid to end it. I *thought* I had my shit together."

I snorted. "Join the club."

He peered at me. "What about Bitsy's event tomorrow? You're bailing?"

"Asher's taking my place. Grandmother and I had it out, and I wanted to be with you for Christmas." I laughed nervously. "It was Asher's idea to say he was coming and for me to surprise you instead. A truly terrible idea, and for the record, I've been calling and texting to warn you I was coming. I can still go to a hotel."

Connor's face transformed, that perfect dimple appearing. "It's the best surprise. I missed you so much this week."

"Me too." I couldn't wait to be alone so I could kiss him senseless.

"Anyone who puts that smile on our kid's face can stay for Christmas," Logan said. He extended his hand. "Logan Derwood. We didn't meet the right way."

I jumped up and shook his hand. "It's wonderful to meet you." I shook Seth's hand as well. "Both of you."

Seth said, "And you loaned Connor money for this debt?"

I nodded. Connor stood too and said, "I'm paying him back the ten grand. I got a job at CVS starting in January."

Seth and Logan exclaimed in unison, talking over each other about how school had to come first, and they'd give him the money. Connor held up his hands with a smile.

"Thank you. We can talk about it later, right? It's Christmas Eve. Can we just open some wine and make dinner and open a few presents?" His eyes widened on me. "I don't have anything for you."

"You've given me more than enough." I brushed back his hair, needing to touch him.

"All right, all right, keep it PG," Logan said without heat.

Connor playfully huffed. "I'm not thirteen anymore."

"Good thing," Logan said. "You were a real pain the ass back then."

I automatically opened my mouth to defend him, but Connor laughed. "I really was."

Seth said, "You were both pains in the rear end. Luckily, you met me." He kissed Logan lightly. "Now, let's open that wine and hear how our son and his new boyfriend got together—and why we're just hearing about it now."

Around the kitchen island, we drank and talked, Seth preparing a steak marinade while Connor and Logan chopped vegetables. I was given the job of peeling potatoes in the sink, and I didn't admit I'd never done it before in my life. I rolled up my sleeves and got to work.

Connor told his dads our story, and I interjected here and there. Christmas carols played in the background while outside the windows, snow nestled the world in a beautiful, peaceful blanket. Holiday lights shone in the darkness.

My face was flushed from wine and laughter, and as "Silent Night" played, the lyrics "all is calm, all is bright" had never felt more true.

I turned to Connor as he explained about the New Yorker activities and blurted, "The lights are brighter with you."

Three sets of eyes stared. Connor asked, "Which lights?"

"All of them. Like in the city—I've been sleepwalking. Not paying attention to how amazing the world around me is. When I look out my window now, I see it through your eyes. Everything's brighter." I forced a laugh. "I'm not saying this properly. It's the wine."

Connor watched me, biting his lip. "You're saying it just right."

We smiled at each other, and he was so beautiful and sweet and kind and smart and—

Logan coughed loudly and nodded to Seth. "Let's shovel off the barbecue."

Maybe it should have been strange that Connor's dads were leaving us alone to kiss, but the only thing that mattered was Connor back in my arms and his sigh against my lips.

Chapter Twenty-One

Connor

"IT SUCKS THAT we couldn't see everyone and have Aunt Jenna's turkey, but these steaks are awesome," I said.

"Mm." Across the dining table, Reid swallowed his bite. "Compliments to the chef."

At the end of the reclaimed wood table with a fresh pine and ribbon wreath on the wall behind him, Seth smiled. "Steak may not be traditional holiday fare, but I admit it's delicious."

"I haven't had a Christmas celebration at home since I was a little boy," Reid said. "Whether it's turkey or steak or tofurkey, I'm happy."

To my left at the other end of the table, Logan shuddered. "No tofu for Christmas."

"You know we need to start trying more plant-based protein," Seth said, spearing a roasted potato. "Though perhaps not on Christmas Eve." He frowned at Reid. "Your family doesn't celebrate?"

"Not like this. My grandmother has a charity breakfast event Christmas morning. It's a wonderful cause, but..." He glanced at me. "It's refreshing to have a quiet Christmas."

I couldn't believe Reid was actually here across the table from me. I was still shellshocked from having to admit what had happened with my father—and I had a phone call to make that was long overdue. First, I could have dinner with my dads and my for-real actual boyfriend.

"Thank you again for including me," Reid said. "Not that I gave you much choice."

I watched Logan and Seth's smiles, looking for cracks under the surface. But they seemed to like Reid—or they were faking it really well, and Logan was the worst at pretending he liked someone when he didn't.

Please let them like Reid. Maybe even love him one day.

I shouldn't have been thinking about love, but it filled me like a helium balloon trying to rise, bouncing around inside me. I loved Reid. I loved my dads. I loved Christmas, and wine, and grilled meat.

Did I mention I loved Reid?

There was only that one black shadow looming in the corner. As Reid told Logan and Seth about his housing project ideas, I psyched myself up the way I would for an exam. Maybe I'd been studying for this one my whole life.

When we were stuffed, I helped bring the plates to the kitchen before telling Reid I'd be back. Upstairs in my room, I shut the door. I had just enough of a signal now. The phone rang. And rang, my nervous energy faltering.

Don't tell me he's not going to answer.

I wanted to get this over with. Done. I *needed* to get this *done.*

"Hey, kiddo," Mike drawled in his raspy smoker's voice. "Calling to say merry Christmas to your old man? Can't remember the last time."

I gripped the phone, ordering myself to stay calm and keep focused. "No," I said.

"No?" He laughed awkwardly. "Well, okay. Actually, I could use you. I've got this pain in my stomach."

"Where?" I asked, cursing myself.

"On the left side. Comes and goes, but it hurts like a son of a bitch."

"Lower left quadrant? Or upper?" Why wasn't I just telling him to go to hell?

"Lower." He described a few more symptoms.

"Go to the doctor. I bet you need a colonoscopy. It sounds like diverticulitis, which is when you have diverticulosis in your colon and it's inflamed."

"Colonoscopy? Is that where they stick a camera up your butt? No fuckin' way."

I gritted my teeth. "It's a medical procedure." *It doesn't make you queer, you homophobic idiot.* I knew what he was thinking. I could read his small, pathetic mind.

I was so *done*.

"I know what you did. I know about the credit cards you took out in my name."

There wasn't even a pause before he launched into a strident defense. "What're you talking about? I didn't do that!"

"You did. I know it, and you know it."

"I didn't do anything. Why are you accusing me? What about those two—"

"Don't! Don't you dare say that word."

I could practically hear him roll his eyes. "So sensitive. I always said they'd be a bad influence, didn't I?"

He had. My father had been saying that for years. From the time he'd learned Logan and Seth were in a relationship, he'd sneered and spouted insults. More than that—*hate*.

He seized on the opportunity to deflect attention away from what he'd done. Listening to him now launch into a familiar rant about how Logan and Seth had made me soft, and that they shouldn't be allowed to have children, I couldn't breathe.

My pulse thundered in my ears, and I shook all over. My chest was so tight I couldn't move from the pain.

But I didn't need to assess myself for signs of a heart attack. After years of trying to ignore him without alienating him because

I'd still somehow wanted my father's approval, this was over.

It wasn't only his approval I'd longed for, but signs that he cared about me even a tiny bit. Maybe I'd put up with his hatred because if he was angry about Logan and Seth that meant he had to care about me.

He didn't.

My father didn't care about anyone but himself. I didn't owe him anything, and I never wanted a single thing from him again.

"Shut. Up." I gritted out the words. "Shut your hateful fucking mouth."

Silence.

Then, "What did you just say to me?"

"You heard me." It was the first time in my whole life that I'd stood up to him. Even if I was shaking, I wasn't backing down. Not now. Not ever again.

"Boy, you don't talk to me like that. I'm your father—"

"No!" I screamed. My throat was raw from the force of that single word. I had to pull in a few shuddering breaths before I could go on.

"*No.* You were nothing more than a sperm donor. You've never been a real father. My mom raised me on her own, and then Logan and Seth took over. They've done everything for me. So much more than I deserved. Even when I was an ungrateful little asshole, they were so good to me. They're my dads. The only fathers that have ever mattered. You're *nothing.*"

I could imagine his lip curling in disgust. "Those queers—"

"Yeah, they are! You think it's an insult, but it's not. Fuck you. And you know what? I'm queer too. And it's not because of Logan and Seth. They didn't brainwash me, or 'groom' me or any that other ignorant, hateful bullshit you've been spouting at me for years. I'm proud of who I am and who they are."

I pressed the phone to my ear so hard it hurt. As Mike swore and shouted, I took a deep, cleansing breath and exhaled slowly. I wasn't afraid anymore.

Over his tirade, I calmly said, "I'm telling the police what you did. Never talk to me again. You're the one who needs to be ashamed."

I hung up.

My knees trembled on the way downstairs. Reid, Logan, and Seth stood near the foot of the stairs, waiting with worried expressions that filled my soul with even more love, the helium back. I could have floated.

I managed a smile. "So, that went well. But I'm okay. I am. Is it time for dessert?" I was babbling, but I really *was* okay. "I was afraid of proving him right. I knew it was irrational, but every time I came close to telling you guys or Asher or anyone that I'm gay, I got too scared. I could hear him in my head saying terrible things."

Before any of them could reply, I added, "Not you, Reid. I wasn't going to tell you. Mostly because I had such a giant crush on you and we didn't really *talk*." A laugh bubbled up on that awesome helium. "I promise I'm not having a breakdown."

The three of them exchanged worried looks, and I hugged them in turn, letting myself linger for a few extra seconds to inhale Reid's now-familiar scent. I couldn't wait to get him alone and—

Wait. I stepped away. "So, we don't have a guest room." I looked to my dads. "It's cool if Reid sleeps with me, right?" *Awkwarrrd.*

Seth said, "You're both adults. And we trust you to be respectful."

"Of course." Reid nodded seriously. "I should get my things from the car."

"Oh, let me show you my bike!" I practically bounced. "It's in the garage."

"All right. Even though I think it's far too risky."

Logan exclaimed, "Thank you! Glad your boyfriend has a

good head on his shoulders."

"Yeah, yeah," I muttered, not able to hide my grin. *My boyfriend.*

I shrugged into my leather jacket and clomped outside, not bothering to lace my boots or grab a hat and gloves. Snow fell thickly around us as we hurried to Reid's car and then into the cold, concrete garage. He left his suitcase and a large Nordstrom's bag by the entrance.

Reid followed me deeper into the garage, slipping between Seth's SUV and Logan's pickup. The lightbulb overhead didn't do much in the shadows, but I still made a flourish with my hands.

"Here she is. My pride and joy." I rubbed my palm over the leather seat.

"Very nice. Looks sturdy."

I swung my leg over the cold seat. "Extremely sturdy." I motioned to my helmet, which sat on the cluttered workbench nearby. "And safety is a priority, I promise."

"Uh-huh." Reid watched me, licking his lips.

With a wicked grin, I leaned forward, showing off my ass. "You're rethinking your veto, aren't you? Imagine wrapping yourself around me from behind. The powerful engine between our legs, the wind on our faces, the road unfurling before us. Did I mention how close you'll be pressed against me?"

"I admit it has…appeal."

"Promise you'll think about a ride? No pressure."

"Oh, I'll think about it. Especially the way your ass looks when you're sitting on that bike."

"C'mere." I crooked my finger.

It was going to be too weird getting off in my room later with my dads right down the hall. I stumbled off the bike and tugged at Reid's fly as he devoured my mouth.

We had our dicks out in record time, Reid's big hand wrapped around both as we kissed and panted. I licked Reid's cheek and chin. "Love the stubble."

"Mmm. Maybe I'll keep it. By the way, I have a present for you."

"I know," I moaned, thrusting my hips into his grasp, our shafts rubbing roughly.

We laughed at how cheesy I was, and then all we could do was gasp into each other's mouths as we came.

Good thing Reid had an extra pair of socks in his suitcase that we used to clean up. I eyed the Nordstrom's bag. "Is my present in there?"

"No peeking. Although I will tell you I bought your dads a Le Creuset casserole dish. Do you think they'll like that? There are some chocolate truffles as well, and—"

I kissed him soundly. "It's all perfect. Thank you."

"You're okay? After that talk with your…Mike?"

"I am. I really am. And before you say it, I'm paying you back. I can do a couple of shifts a week at CVS. Whether you or my dads like it or not."

"*Or*—and hear me out—we defer the loan until you're a working doctor."

My jaw tightened. "Reid. We agreed."

"Yes, but it's insane for you to work nights for minimum wage at CVS when you should be resting and studying."

"I need to get used to sleep deprivation."

He sighed. "Aren't there summer jobs at hospitals or clinics or research labs med students can get that will pay better?"

"Well, yeah. And I will! But that's not for months."

"Baby, that's fine. You know I don't need the money. And I know that you'll pay me back. Please don't burn out working a crappy night job." He cupped my face, stroking gently with his thumb. "I'll worry about you. Wouldn't you if our positions were reversed?"

I wanted to argue, but he had me there. "But I don't know

what other debt there might be. Although I am going to report him to the police, so maybe I'll be off the hook for it. Clear my record."

"Yes! See? Let's get that ball rolling right after Christmas. And in the meantime, you can focus on studying. Not to mention spending time with me. I'm selfish. I want you all to myself at night. CVS can butt out."

I had to admit I wasn't looking forward to stocking shelves and getting no sleep, and relief flowed through me, mingling with the euphoria from finally telling Mike where to go.

"Okay," I said. "It's settled. Thank you. Now will you kiss me again even though it's freezing out here?"

Reid grinned. "Damn right I will."

Later, we sprawled on the sectional with my dads watching *Die Hard* because it never got old. Reid and I held hands, and so did Logan and Seth. It was really honestly so fucking sweet I could barely stand it.

As Hans Gruber ordered his henchman to *Shoot. The. Glass*, I said, "I don't want his name. Lisowski. It's the only thing I'm stuck with from him, and I don't want it."

Logan and Seth shared a glance before nodding. Seth said, "How can we help?"

Reid stroked my knuckles as I swallowed a lump of emotion. "You already have. So much. I know when you got married, Seth changed his name to Derwood."

Seth nodded. "Marston is the name of a family who want nothing to do with me. I don't miss it at all."

"Would it be cool if I changed my name to Derwood too?"

Logan was beside me, and he exhaled forcefully. "Are you kidding? Of course. I'd love it. We'd all love it."

It was the answer I'd expected, but it was still a relief. "My mom wouldn't mind, right? She'd had Mike's name, and then changed it to yours. She always said that being a foster kid, she'd never been attached to her old name."

Logan nodded. "I think Veronica would like for you to have our name."

"She would, right?" My eyes burned.

Logan was the only one who'd known her. As disastrous as their short marriage had turned out, he'd loved her once. And I was so, so lucky that he loved me.

"Damn right," Logan croaked, his eyes glittering. He swiped at them. "Connor Derwood. Has a nice ring to it."

"That'll be *Dr.* Connor Derwood," Seth said thickly. "And it's music to my ears."

"Yeah." Joy bubbled up, and I laughed as I swiped my eyes. "Me too." Beside me, still holding my hand, Reid grinned.

"Come on, enough of this sappy stuff," Logan said. "Let's open a few presents. It's Christmas."

He and Seth loved the blue casserole dish from Reid, and I was pleased that they'd wrapped a box of Lindt chocolates for him while we'd been outside. I ripped the shiny paper off the slim box Reid gave me and lifted the lid.

"Whoa." I gingerly lifted one of the buttery black leather gloves and pulled it over my hand.

"The clerk said they're perfect for motorcycle riding. Should be flexible and form-fitting," Reid said. "But with reinforced material that will protect your hands."

"They're perfect. Thank you." I put on the other and flexed my fingers. I drew Reid close for a kiss before remembering my dads were sitting right there.

They only smiled and passed me another gift.

Chapter Twenty-Two

Reid

GRANDMOTHER'S POISED PROFILE picture appeared on my phone screen the next morning, and I bolted up in Connor's bed, going from a drowse to wide awake. Not her assistant, but her. I straightened the collar of my T-shirt even though she couldn't see me.

Sitting up in bed beside me in sweats, Connor put down his tablet and watched me as I put the phone to my ear and answered.

"Reid, it's your grandmother."

"Yes. Hello. Uh, how did the breakfast go?"

Asher had texted that everything was good, but Grandmother might have a different perspective. He'd also said that he'd "had a little talk" with her, though wouldn't go into details.

She said, "It went smoothly as always. We didn't even miss you."

Beside me, Connor could clearly hear her because his eyes bugged. I wasn't sure whether to be offended or relieved. "I'm glad it went smoothly."

"I misspoke. What I mean to say is that Asher stepped in without a hitch. You were right. You don't have to be there every Christmas. I'm glad you can take some time off with your…friend."

Even as relief flowed, I had to say, "Boyfriend. Connor's my boyfriend."

"Yes." She cleared her throat delicately. "I...acknowledge that."

Wow. Apparently, Asher's "little talk" was bearing fruit? Part of me wanted to roll my eyes at her acknowledgment and say, "*Big whoop*," but I found myself grinning. "Thank you."

"I took a look at your proposal this morning. It's well reasoned and intriguing."

My pulse thudded, and Connor rubbed my thigh. "It is? What I mean to say is, yes. Thank you. I really think it's an opportunity to grow our business and do good in the world."

"Mm. Prepare to present it to the board at the next meeting in January. I'll postpone my trip south so I can be there in person."

"So you can veto?" I asked before stopping myself.

Her voice stayed clipped, all business. "No, darling."

Darling. That word of approval meant more to me than I wanted to admit. "Thank you. I'll see you in the new year. I'm taking these days off work."

"Evidently," she said, and I could picture her back in the office behind that old desk. Before I could say anything else, the line went dead.

"I guess that went well?" Connor asked.

"Amazingly."

"That's dark."

I had to laugh. "It's a low bar."

"I guess Asher's come-to-Jesus with her worked."

"Hold on. You know details? Spill. What did he say?" I wasn't sure whether to laugh in delight or cry that my little brother had stood up for me.

Connor raised his hands. "You'll have to ask him. But I'm glad she's coming around." He nuzzled my face, rubbing against my stubble.

We kissed, and I chased the rich coffee flavor in Connor's mouth. I'd woken earlier to find him gone, the murmur of voices coming from downstairs along with the scent of fresh brewing dark roast. It had been so comforting that I'd fallen back asleep.

"You're sure your dads are gone?" I asked.

Connor nodded. "They're hiking the trail to the river. Won't be back for hours."

"How about a shower?"

"Sure. It's just next door, remember? Do you need a fresh towel?" He got up.

I caught his wrist. "I mean together."

"Oh!" Connor's face flushed that adorable pink. "Right." An adorable smile lifted his lips. "Sounds good."

The shower was a standard bathtub with shower curtain setup. The water pressure was nice and strong, and we took turns shampooing and shuffling around to get under the nozzle.

I had to laugh. "I confess I'm used to a roomier shower."

Connor grinned. "Is showering together one of those things that looks sexy in the movies but is awkward and annoying in real life?"

"Well, yes. But all is not lost."

I lathered my hand with shower gel and slipped my fingers between Connor's ass cheeks, urging him close for a kiss. Our semi-hard cocks rubbed together. I circled the rim of his hole.

"Mmm." Connor gave me a lazy smile. "It's getting better already."

I whispered in his ear, "Just wait," and sank to my knees.

He jumped at the first touch of my tongue to his hole, but I steadied him with my hands firm on his hips. The next swipe of the flat of my tongue was long and slow, up and down his crack, my thumbs spreading his cheeks.

"Jesus, Reid!" Connor's knees trembled already.

"Are you cold?" I huffed a hot breath on his hole.

"What?" He leaned against the wall at the end of the tub, his arms folded on the tile. "I'm shaking because you're licking my ass and it feels incredible."

"I meant is the tile cold." The hot water fell on my back where I kneeled.

"Oh. Yeah, but who could give a shit about that when *you're licking my ass?*"

Laughing, I stood and turned off the water. "You said hours, right? Think we can risk going back to your room?"

Connor didn't bother answering—he practically tripped out of the tub, tossed me a towel, and raced back to his room, rubbing a towel over himself as he went.

With the door firmly locked, we fell onto his bed, still wet and not caring even a little. "You want to come on my tongue, baby?" I asked, grinding down against him.

"Oh my god," he moaned. "Yes. But actually—" He nudged a hand against my chest, and I sat up, straddling his thighs.

"Hmm?" I asked, caressing his slim pecs and sliding my thumbs along his collar bones.

"You said you've been fucked before. Penetrated, I mean."

"Definitely. Is that what you want?" The lust that had already scorched my veins burned even hotter. "You want your cock inside me?"

Lips parted, Connor nodded. "You don't mind?"

I barked out a laugh as I crawled off him. "Not even a little. Get the condom and lube from my suitcase. How do you want me?"

"Um..." Connor stared with blown pupils. "That was easy." He practically vaulted across the room to my suitcase. "How do you like it?"

I got onto all fours. "Will you fuck me from behind?"

I didn't have to ask twice.

As he pushed into me tentatively, I bore down. "You won't break me," I promised. His cock was a good size, and the burn was absolutely delicious.

"*Fuck*," he mumbled as he thrust harder. His right hand was slick with lube where he clutched my hip. "I'm going to start talking like a porno again."

I laughed. "Do I feel nice and tight, baby?"

"*Yes*. It's so good."

His pubes tickled my ass, and I squeezed around his shaft. He probably wasn't going to last long, but I didn't care. This was about Connor. Another first time I'd been lucky enough to claim.

I wanted them all. I wanted *everything*.

We strained and swore, and I dropped onto my elbows, pushing back against Connor's clumsy thrusts. My cock bobbed, throbbing and leaking even though I wasn't touching it.

"Feels so good," I moaned, loving the sound of our damp skin slapping and Connor's ragged gasps. "Come in my ass, baby. I want you so much. Never wanted anyone like this."

He jerked and shook, his fingers digging into my hips as he came. I twisted my neck to watch his silent, open-mouthed shouts of climax. His skin was red, his wet hair flopping over his forehead. I wanted to keep him inside me, but as I squeezed, he hissed and withdrew, clearly oversensitive already.

Before I could say anything, he tossed the condom at the little garbage can under his desk and flopped onto his back. "Fuck my mouth?"

Kneeling over him, I fed my cock between his lips, and we both moaned. The give and take between us felt like a perfect circle. I came in his hot, wet, generous mouth.

In the end, we hopped back in the shower, kissing and smiling and touching gently. I told him about the circle, and Connor beamed.

"Like an ouroboros," he said. "A snake eating its own tail. But, um, in a sexy way?"

"Very, very sexy," I agreed, kissing him again. "We'd better get out. Get dressed. Being caught by your dads would be very, very, unsexy. And I have a weird request."

He frowned. "Weird how? After what we just did…"

"It's not sex-related. It's weird in that it's probably extraordinarily dorky and will shatter any remaining mystique I might have."

"If you think I haven't figured out that you're a massive dork, you're sadly mistaken."

I couldn't argue with that, and soon, we were out front of the house in our winter gear amid fat, steadily falling snow. Connor bent and made a snowball in his gloved hands.

"It's your lucky day. Perfect packing snow." He tossed the ball up and caught it. "If I weren't so mature, I'd throw this at you."

"Lucky for me Dr. Lis—" I stopped and corrected myself. "Dr. Derwood would never do such a thing when he's supposed to be teaching me a vital task."

Connor grinned. "Lucky indeed. And I like the sound of that." He bit his lip. "Dr. Derwood."

"Me too."

He tossed the snowball over his shoulder. "You've seriously never built a snowman?"

"Never."

"Well, it's the perfect day to start. Nothing says Christmas like building snow people. Get on your knees and roll."

I arched a dubious brow.

Connor rolled his eyes. "Mind out of the gutter! I mean, for the moment. It can go back in the gutter later."

"If my grandmother were here, she'd say I'd lost all dignity."

Connor's expression grew serious, and he kissed me softly. "If she doesn't accept you the way you are, it's her loss."

I took a deep breath and nodded. "Dignity's overrated."

Connor dropped to his knees and scooped snow towards him, and I joined in. When we had a sizeable ball, we rolled it forward, not caring that we were soaking our jeans, our laughter just for us, muffled by the falling snow.

Epilogue

Connor

Five Years Later

JOYOUS SHRIEKS ECHOED around the community center as children chased each other and played with their new toys. I wasn't sure how they weren't puking given their full stomachs, but those were kids for you.

I'd been stationed on the waffles, putting them on plates with tongs before pouring maple syrup imported from Quebec over them. Only the best for Reid's grandmother.

Hundreds of people had filed through the breakfast line and met Santa, who lingered and chatted with Reid and Bitsy and a few of her society ladies. Calling her "Bitsy" to her face had been weird as hell at first, but I was used to it now.

I took another bite of the breakfast sandwich I'd made from leftovers of waffles, bacon, and scrambled eggs. My phone buzzed in the pocket of my leather jacket that I'd slung over a folding chair.

Asher was supposed to call from Greece, where he was visiting with his and Reid's mom, but it was Olivia's face that filled the screen. I swiped to answer the video call as I swallowed and put my paper plate on the chair.

"Hey, Liv!"

"Merry Christmas!" She turned her camera to pan over her parents and younger sister having breakfast on a terrace with palm trees and the perfectly blue ocean and sky in the sunshine. "Hello from Aruba, a.k.a. paradise that we're never leaving."

"I bet." I turned my phone. "Hello from the new Utopia Vision Community Hub."

Angela clapped delightedly. She wore reindeer antlers with bells in her poufy blonde hair. "Love all that natural light! Can't wait to see it for myself in March. Did Reid tell you I'll be there for the groundbreaking on the new rental units?"

"Yep. It'll be great to see you."

"How are the solar panels working at the center?"

"Perfectly even though it's been nothing but gray skies. Proving wrong the naysayers who don't understand how solar panels work."

"Are you having a white Christmas?" asked Makayla, Olivia's younger sister, who attended my old alma mater in Boston.

"Not in the city. It's supposed to snow overnight tonight in Albany, though. Reid and I are driving up soon."

"Say hi to Will and Michael for me if you see them," Makayla said.

"They're coming for dinner tonight, so definitely."

"Hi from all of us!" Angela grinned. "I just love those boys. And you tell Reid's grandmama that I'm looking forward to seeing her in March," she added with a mischievous wink.

Angela had been an integral partner in the new branch of Utopia's business: Utopia Vision, a separately incorporated company of which Reid was president and CEO.

"And Reid, too, of course. How's your pumpkin pie of a man? Tell him merry Christmas from the Barkers."

"He's great, and I will."

Olivia shook her head, grinning. "The way your exhausted face lights up just hearing his name."

I rolled my eyes, but I couldn't hide my smile, glancing over at Reid in his slacks and form-fitting red cashmere sweater. His dark, trimmed beard somehow made his bright smile even sexier.

The Barkers whistled and laughed, and I knew I was blushing. Angela said, "You do look tired though, sugar."

"Yeah, it was a busy night. A long week of night shifts, but that's how it goes in residency. Especially since I'm on an ER rotation."

I yawned. I'd decided on neurology, and treating acute cases was more stressful than being on the ward. It was a rush, though. I'd identified subtle stroke symptoms in a young woman the night before, and we'd been able to start immediate treatment.

That rush had definitely faded now. I yawned again. "Sorry. Long night. Wait, I said that already."

The Barkers laughed, but then Angela frowned. "I hope you're eating right."

I didn't tell her dinner last night had been a Twix from the hospital vending machine at midnight. "Yep. Don't worry."

"Well, I know your daddies will make sure. We just talked to them, and they are hard at work in the kitchen already."

"I can't wait."

The thought of being home warmed my chest. I'd moved into Reid's place a few years ago, and it was very much home now too. Reid owned it, but we split the bills equally, and since I'd ended up being refunded the ten grand of debt after a long legal process, we'd been able to make a fresh, even start together.

But there'd always be something special about *home*-home in Albany. I'd worked Thanksgiving, and I'd have to go in New Year's Eve, but at least Christmas Day was mine.

We said our goodbyes, and I slumped on the chair to finish my makeshift sandwich. My lower back was a little sore from all the standing at the hospital and then while dishing out waffles. When I finished eating, I caught Reid's eye, and he nodded without me needing to say a word.

After zipping up my jacket, I lingered near the door while

Reid said his goodbyes. He'd just taken my hand when a man called, "Sorry, can I get one more shot of the Cabots and Santa?"

Reid returned to where his grandmother stood by the massive tree decorated in rainbow lights and handmade ornaments from the kids in the neighborhood. Bitsy wore one of her elegant pantsuits, this one in festive green and paired with glittering ruby jewelry. Her version of a Christmas sweater.

"You too," Bitsy said.

She was looking at me for some reason, and it took me a few seconds to understand that, yes, she was talking to me. I pointed at my chest, and she nodded.

Reid *beamed*—I still wanted to lick his entire face when he did that—and held out his arm to tuck me by his side. I put my arm around his waist, leaning into his warmth and smiling for the camera.

The photographer took about twenty-five shots, and my face hurt from smiling by the time he asked, "Name?"

Bitsy said, "This is Dr. Connor Derwood. My grandson's partner."

Now that my name had officially been changed, a process I knew Reid had called in favors to expedite, I loved hearing it. And coming from Bitsy—with the addition of "partner" no less!—it was an unexpected hit of adrenaline.

"Got it." The photographer gave us a thumbs-up. "Are you from the city?"

"Albany," I said.

"Although he is an official New Yorker now," Reid said with a grin. "Got his certificate and everything."

It had been rolled in my stocking one Christmas with an official-looking custom seal. We still made lists of activities to try and both of us had full veto power. There was a checklist on our fridge now, and we'd finally be ticking off skating at Wollman Rink on New Year's Day with Addison and her new girlfriend.

The photographer seemed puzzled, but said, "Uh, great. Merry Christmas, folks."

Reid hugged his grandmother and pressed a kiss to her cheek. I nodded to her. "Merry Christmas."

"And to you." She nodded with a ghost of a smile. "Give my best to your parents."

I fell asleep almost as soon as my ass hit the heated leather seats of Reid's Audi. When Reid placed his palm on my thigh, his fingertips tracing the inseam on my jeans, I jerked awake and swiped the drool from the corner of my mouth. Blinking, I realized we were home.

The old ornament wreath still hung on the front door, and multicolored lights brightened the gray afternoon from the eaves and bushes. It would look beautiful when it snowed later.

"Sorry to wake you," Reid murmured, still caressing my inner thigh.

"S'okay." I rubbed my face. "I wasn't very good company."

"You needed the rest. I listened to that new kidnapping podcast Will and Michael recommended. Three hours flew by." He leaned close and kissed my cheek.

"We didn't talk about this morning, though. That was cool with your grandmother including me in the picture."

Reid smiled, although it was sad. "Honestly the best Christmas present she could ever give me. I know I shouldn't care what she thinks, but…"

I kissed him lightly. "Of course you care. Family can be…challenging, but you still love them. And she's come around. The plans for development sound amazing. Angela's excited."

Now he grinned. "Me too. Did I tell you we lined up our first pick for plumbing?"

"No! That's awesome." I rubbed my face. "Sorry I haven't been around this week to talk about it."

He scoffed. "You're working your ass off saving lives. Don't apologize."

"Your work is important too."

"I know. But I'm not pulling night shifts on hardly any sleep with overtime because of staff shortages. I'm so glad you have a few days off finally."

"Me too," I mumbled through another yawn before slapping my own face. "Okay, time to wake up. Oh!" I straightened with a bolt of adrenaline. "I know just the thing."

We carried in our bags as Logan and Seth greeted us, the house smelling of ginger and pine and roasting meat. I inhaled deeply, a wonderful calm flowing through me as I hugged my dads. *Christmas.* I wished I could bottle it for those long shifts when I needed a break.

I rooted around in the drawer in the hall. "I'm just going for a quick ride while the roads are clear."

"Be careful," Logan said with his usual hint of concerned grumbling. These days, he said it in perfect unison with Reid.

Seth chuckled. "I know you're always careful."

In the garage, I strapped on my helmet securely, jumping when Reid spoke from the open door. "You have another one of those?"

"Helmet? Yeah." My heart skipped. "Wait. Are you serious? You're un-vetoing?"

He tucked his scarf into his pea coat. "I performed another risk analysis, and I'm ready to give it a try."

I squeezed past Logan's truck and eagerly pulled the extra helmet out of the storage cabinet in the corner. Reid waited patiently while I buckled it on him, triple-checking the fit. "Are you sure? You don't have to."

"I know, but I want to."

"Why?"

"Because you love it," he said simply.

I tugged on my riding gloves he'd given me our first Christmas, now well worn like a second skin. "I love you. I'm going to kiss the shit out of you as soon as these helmets are off."

"I love you too, baby."

With Reid's thighs hugging my hips and my bike's engine purring, I drove us around the quiet neighborhood. There were still lots of trees, even though more housing lots were being built.

We should have both been wearing leathers, but there was little to no traffic, and I decided it was an acceptable risk. Reid clung to me tightly, his arms locked around my waist.

"Okay?" I yelled back.

"So far, so good!"

"Faster?"

"Faster," Reid agreed. I turned onto a long, straight, empty road and increased the throttle. The wind was icy, but the freedom and power of riding kept hot adrenaline pumping.

"Faster!" Reid shouted with a joyful laugh, and my heart soared.

But I said, "This is fast enough!"

I could imagine my mom telling me about her dream motorcycle and how important safety was. I wasn't sure if her voice in my head was even what she'd sounded like.

I'd never watched the few ancient videos I had of her on an external drive, old files that had been on her phone when she'd died. Logan had kept them for me, but it had hurt too much. Maybe we could watch them later.

Fat flakes of snow began drifting down, and I turned toward home. Back in the garage, Reid *whooped* as he stepped off the bike and removed his helmet. "Okay, I see the appeal. Consider occasionally riding on the back of your motorcycle officially un-vetoed."

I kicked down the stand and took off my own helmet, not caring that my hair was sticking up. "You want to learn to drive one sometime? I'm getting you full leathers too." I waggled my brows. "You'll look so hot."

Alarm tensed Reid's face. "Drive it myself? No, no, no. I mean, I'll wear the leather, but I'll stay on the back, baby. Also, I believe I was promised a kiss."

He swept me into his arms and almost off my feet, and we kissed deeply until Reid groaned and pulled away, his lips shiny. "To be continued." He nuzzled me, and I rubbed against the scratch of his beard, not caring how red my face was.

I nodded. "Tonight in my room. We'll have to be so, so quiet."

He arched a brow. "Are you sure?"

We'd never had sex in my room when my dads were home, but the adrenaline from the ride had me nodding eagerly before I turned to put away our helmets.

Reid caught me from behind, his arm around my waist and lips at my ear. "We will *really* have to be quiet. Do you think you can control yourself?" He pressed his half-hard cock against my ass. Then, he yanked off his glove and covered my mouth with his bare hand. "You won't be able to make a sound."

I moaned in his grasp, nodding. Merry Christmas to *me*.

We had dinner early around five. Will and Michael brought a tray of creamy scalloped potatoes, and the six of us toasted with red wine at the dining table.

Tomorrow, we'd be playing a marathon game of *Catan*, but tonight, Seth had set the table with the new green holiday place mats and napkins Logan had given him.

The stuffing was always my favorite, and even though Aunt Jenna's was the best, she'd given my dads the recipe before leaving on a cruise with Uncle Jun's family. It tasted almost as good.

I swallowed another bite and said, "You crushed the stuffing."

"And the bird," Will said in that delightful Scottish accent. "This is delicious."

Michael said, "It really is. By the way, I love your tie, Logan."

He wore a dress shirt and this year's tie, an annual gift from Seth. Back in the day, Logan had needed the formal wear for job interviews. He hardly ever had cause to wear a tie now, but he did every Christmas. The ties had become more and more jokey as the years went by, and this one was holiday-themed with Rudolf driving a convertible.

Michael added, "It reminds me of our first Christmas ornament together," giving Will a tender smile.

"Ah yes." Will smiled. "Kevin the surfing koala. We're finally heading back down under for our honeymoon next year. We'll have to see if we can pick up a friend for Kevin."

Beside me, Reid asked, "Do they have Christmas stores all year round in Australia the way we do here in tourist towns?"

Michael grinned. "Only one way to find out."

"Who won the bet this year?" I asked Seth.

He passed over the roasted vegetables without me having to ask, and I scooped more perfectly charred squash onto my plate.

Seth said, "Logan didn't guess Rudolph or a convertible." He pushed back his chair at the end of the table and lifted his foot, pulling up his pant leg enough so we could see his sock. "However, I successfully predicted stripes."

"Only so many patterns," Logan said. "Especially since you won't wear 'em if they're too bright."

"Now, don't be sour just because I'm winning." Seth winked.

After dinner, Will and Michael left before the roads got too bad. I washed, and Reid dried the dishes that wouldn't fit in the dishwasher before flopping on the sectional with very full bellies.

Logan put on his glasses to look at a cruise photo Aunt Jenna had sent to Seth and me, knowing one of us would show him since he'd become even grumpier about not always having his phone with him. Then he turned on the TV while Seth yawned widely. Outside, snow piled up on the back deck.

The worn recliner Pop had always used was still in the corner by the tree even though he'd been gone more than a year now. I missed him with a pang, closing my eyes and replaying the last time I'd seen him sitting there.

It had been just like almost every other time he'd been over—Pop drinking a beer from the bottle, watching TV, and saying little. Hercules had often sat on his lap, thought he was gone now too. It was comforting in a weird way that the last time I'd seen Pop it had been so normal.

I fell asleep halfway through *Scrooged*, and I woke curled into Reid's side. Only the colored Christmas tree lights were on, the muted TV casting flickering blue light.

"Hey," Reid whispered.

"Hey. Shit, sorry. Are my dads in bed?"

"Yes. Don't be sorry. It's ridiculous how much residents have to work. You need the sleep."

I arched my back and stretched my arms. "I know."

"You must be tired," I said, stifling another yawn. "We should go to bed." I remembered what we'd said in the garage earlier, excitement sparking to life. "And be very, very quiet." I cupped Reid's dick through his pants. "Silent night."

His breath tickled my ear. "That can wait. Sleep now."

Now I was wide awake. "The hell it can wait. I need you to fuck my brains out. Quietly. *Then* I'll be able to sleep."

"We'll see." Reid kissed me and ran a palm over my head.

"Are you trying to tell me you're going to veto for my own good?"

"I probably should. Doctors are notorious for not taking care of themselves."

"We're also notorious for getting our way."

A slow grin spread over his face. "Doctor, I have a problem. My partner works too hard. How can I encourage him to relax?"

"Hmm." I tapped my chin. "I think I have just the prescription. You might be reluctant at first, but this treatment will work wonders for you both."

Unsurprisingly, I got my way.

We woke late the day after Christmas to several feet of fresh, perfect snow. Tomorrow, Reid and I would have to get back to the city so I could work another shift.

Today, we were warm inside with leftovers, boxes of the kind of chocolates I only ate at the holidays, board games to play, and my dads.

Christmas didn't get better than this. Hell, neither did life. When I was an angry, grieving kid, I'd never have been able to even imagine this kind of peace.

Reid brought me a hot mug of coffee in bed with a kiss, and I could picture even more happiness in the years ahead. In the days and hours and little moments we'd share.

I could imagine *everything*.

THE END

About the Author

Keira aims for the perfect mix of character, plot, and heat in her M/M romances. She writes everything from swashbuckling pirates to heartwarming holiday escapism. Her fave tropes are enemies to lovers, age gaps, forced proximity, and passionate virgins. Although she loves delicious angst along the way, Keira guarantees happy endings!

Discover more at:

keiraandrews.com

Printed in Great Britain
by Amazon

32126391R00151